I0764535

RIVERSIDE REMEMBERED

Wallace Neal Briggs

Illustrations
by Barbara Minton

THE UNIVERSITY PRESS OF KENTUCKY

I extend my sincere thanks to Philip Refbord and Robert Good for typing and correcting the manuscript, to Professor David Dick who kept insisting that my book should be published, and to my dear wife, Olive Terrill Briggs, who kept encouraging me to finish.

Scholarly publisher for the Commonwealth, serving Bellarmine College, Berea College, Centre College of Kentucky, Eastern Kentucky University, The Filson Club, Georgetown College, Kentucky Historical Society, Kentucky State University, Morehead State University, Murray State University, Northern Kentucky University, Transylvania University, University of Kentucky, University of Louisville, and Western Kentucky University.

Editorial and Sales Offices: Lexington, Kentucky 40508-4008

Library of Congress Cataloging-in-Publication Data

Briggs, Wallace Neal, 1915–
Riverside remembered / Wallace Neal Briggs.
p. cm.
ISBN 0-8131-1807-7 (alk. paper)
1. Briggs, Wallace Neal, 1915– —Childhood and youth.
2. Mississippi—Biography. 3. Vacations, Mississippi.
4. Mississippi—Social life and customs. 5. Country life —Mississippi. I. Title.
CT275.B68A3 1992
976.2'062'092—dc20
[B] 92-16397

This book is printed on recycled acid-free paper meeting the requirements of the American National Standard for Permanence of Paper for Printed Library Materials.

♾

For Olive—who did not know all of them—

but loved all of them she knew.

RIVERSIDE REMEMBERED

SUMMER—1920

Daddy was walking directly in front of us carrying two heavy suitcases. Mother was holding my hand and clutching a suitbox under her arm. She shifted it carefully at times, and each time she did I looked up to be sure it was safe. That box was much more important to a six-year-old than either of the heavy valises that my dad carried, for it held the supper that we would eat on the train that evening. We would eat breakfast in the diner the next morning, which was always one of the highlights of the long trip home to Riverside. But Mother's suitbox lunch was packed with most of my favorite food: fried chicken, deviled eggs (which would have to be eaten that evening because they wouldn't keep overnight), thick slices of bread and butter slapped together like sandwiches, homemade cupcakes and chocolate-covered fondant drops that our landlady Mrs. Patton had made the day before for our trip. So the safety of the suitbox was all-important to me.

Daddy stopped at the corner of Sycamore and Chestnut streets and set the suitcases down to rest his arms. Mother took the time to adjust her hat and smooth back her hair, and I danced around excitedly while waiting to cross the street. Mr. Carmichael's Oakland roadster rounded the corner, and he waved to us as he passed. The iceman's wagon was stopped in front of a house closeby. "I want to get a piece of ice," I said and started for the back of the wagon. "Not now, Buster," and I knew by the tone of her voice that Mother meant it. "You'll dribble all over your clean shirt. And remember it hasn't been rinsed off!" I knew she meant the ice, for the shirt was spanking clean.

Daddy had picked up the bags. "Come on, Polly—watch those holes in the street."

I grabbed Mother's waiting hand, and we crossed Chestnut Street and headed for the railroad station three blocks down.

It wasn't the first trip home to Mississippi for me. There was the Christmas we had gone back and I had burned my neck with a sparkler on Christmas Eve. There was the summer of 1918—during the last months of the war—when I had complained to my grandmother, "Mammy, I want something good to eat," whining because, with rationing, there was little or no sugar available. And there was that awful summer barely remembered when Kiddo had cut his knee open on a Coca-Cola bottle, crippling him for the rest of his life. But this was the first trip back home that I could remember with any clarity.

The station was big and full of people I'd never seen before even though we'd lived in Terre Haute for three years. And as mother always said, it was "grimy dirty" with cinders and smoke and soot. I had only been there twice before as far as I could remember—both times to get on the train to ride as far as Effingham, Illinois. My rich uncle from New York and his wife Josie would be on their way to St. Louis to visit her folks. They'd always be in a drawing room, and Uncle Will would have the porter bring us a ginger ale or Coca-Cola, and the three of them would talk and talk while I looked out the window and watched the telegraph poles go flying by. Mother and I would get off at Effingham, eat supper in the depot restaurant, and catch the train back to Terre Haute. So I felt that railroad stations and trains weren't new to me—I'd done this before—but it was hard to control my excitement once we got to the station.

Daddy deposited the suitcases on a long wooden bench and left to check on our tickets and find out if our train would be on time. We sat down to wait—and the waiting was always the hardest part for me.

I guess we were lucky to be making the trip this time. I had been very sick that spring and was just beginning to feel good again. I had been in bed for several weeks, my mouth and lips so swollen that I could eat only liquids—broth, milk, and water. The doctor said my stomach probably looked just like my mouth, and I wondered how he could know that. Mother nursed me slowly back to health almost alone. Daddy traveled for the U.S. government—he was a post office inspector—and was usually gone from home all week long, sometimes longer. So when Auntee wrote asking Mother to come home for a long visit "to get Buster back on his feet," both Mother and Daddy decided it was the thing to do.

Daddy came back from the ticket window. "She's thirty-five minutes late out of Chicago," he announced, consulting his pocket watch, "so she won't be in until about 4:15." He sat down next to me.

Sandwiched between the two, I slyly nudged Mother. "If the train is gonna be late, let's have some of our lunch right now." Daddy grinned and Mother sighed. "Now you know it's all tied up carefully, and I don't want you to have it all mixed up before we get on the train. Besides, you know the doctor said you should eat at regular hours and eat slowly." She looked at me and smiled. "Anyway, you're so excited right now you couldn't keep anything down. We'll unpack the lunch just as soon as we leave the station."

I turned to Daddy.

"What time is it now?"

"Two minutes later than it was before."

"Aw, Daddy, sure enough what time?"

He pulled his watch out again and looked at it for a long time. "It's exactly five minutes of four. She should be pullin' in in about twenty minutes."

I sighed and fidgeted and swung my legs back and forth. Watching me out of the corner of his eye, Daddy suddenly said: "Want something to think about before the train comes? Something you've never done before? A sort of last-minute surprise?"

I looked up at him. There was a teasing look in his face—as if he knew something no one else did. He took a deep important breath before he spoke again.

"We're going to ride Pullman this trip!"

I kept looking at him for a time before his words made any sense.

"On a Pullman—all the way?"

"Yep. All the way!"

I turned to Mother and whispered: "Can we afford to?" They both laughed out loud, and I was suddenly laughing with them out of sheer happiness, I guess. We would leave Indiana in about fifteen minutes and ride all the way to Mississippi in a Pullman. All the way—first class!

The atmosphere of the station began to change before I was aware of it. Daddy picked up the bags and, turning to Mother, said, "We board from gate three. We'd better get there ahead of the crowd."

Mother seemed a little flustered and began smoothing her dress, inspecting the lunch box for some unknown reason, and adjusting her hat again for no reason at all as far as I could tell.

People were beginning to move toward the high iron gate that separated the waiting room from the train tracks. Daddy handed his tickets to the gateman for inspection, and after that I was oblivious to everything else. There was a loud, melodic whistle from someplace I couldn't see, a frightening rumble that increased by the second and even shook the station floor; then there was the engine pulling in on its special track followed by endless baggage cars, mail cars, day coaches, and several Pullmans. The engine came to a stop beyond my vision, and the whole train quivered for a moment before it let off its steam and seemed to say, "Let's rest a while before we take off for Evansville."

We were through the iron gate now, and Daddy was walking rapidly toward the rear of the train. We passed two or three day coaches where I could see people looking out the windows. Mother was looking straight ahead, following Daddy at a breathtaking pace and pulling me along with a viselike grip on my hand.

"Don't dally, Buster. This train won't wait for you or anybody else."

Suddenly there was a Negro man in a white coat who took Daddy's bags, said "Lower and upper 8, yes sir," and with a broad grin helped Mother and me up the steps and into the vestibule of the Pullman car. It was called Red Desert.

I don't remember anything much until the train pulled out of the station. We were settled in green plush seats facing each other, and I remember Mother saying, "Oh, I'm glad we're not on the sunny side." Our bags had been stored under the seats, and then slowly we were moving. We crossed Chestnut Street with red lights flashing while a few automobiles and wagons waited at the crossing. I thought I saw Jack Spinder on his bicycle pumping up the street. Main Street passed in a blur, and suddenly we were in open country. I watched a few remaining houses as they passed quickly by the window—houses and barns I'd never seen before—then I turned to Mother.

"Can we eat our lunch now?"

"Well, I don't know why not. We're on our way at last."

The chicken and the buttered bread were good, but the deviled eggs were best of all. I ate five or six halves before I'd filled up on them. The porter had brought a table, which he fastened between the seats, and Daddy had brought coffee for him and Mother and a ginger ale for me from the car vendor. It tasted good, but I couldn't concentrate on the food. The wires strung between the telegraph poles seemed to be jerked up and down by a giant hand. We were going fast now. The Pullman car swayed rhythmically from side to side; we passed a little town that was gone before I could see it. The sun was making long shadows in the car, and I yawned a big one. Mother looked at me and winked.

"We'll have the porter make up the berth as soon as it's good dark. Won't be long now."

We stopped at some little town—Princeton, I think it was—and the lights were on in the station before we left. As we pulled out, the porter came to make up our berth, and I sat in the seat across the aisle to watch. He unlocked the curved top above the seats and pulled it down; like a magician, he slid the lower seats together and covered them with a mattress; he fastened green curtains around lower and upper berths so that I couldn't see what other miracles he was working. But he was quick, for in a few minutes Daddy took me to the lower berth and helped me undress. He folded my shirt and pants and put them in a little hammock swung between the windows; I took off my socks and shoes and tossed them in with my clothes. I climbed under the snow-white sheets in my underwear and lay very still listening to the constant rumble and bending of the train.

"Mother and I are going to sit up for a while. We'll be right across the aisle if you want us for anything."

He sat down on the edge of the bed and took my hand. "I'll be in the upper berth tonight, and Mother will crawl in with you when we go to bed—so you won't be frightened when you wake up. We'll be in Nashville in the morning for breakfast, and then on to Riverside!"

His hands brushed my cheek, and he said, "Good night, Bus—sleep good, son," and closed the curtain.

I couldn't hear their talking, but I knew they were there. I turned off the little light above my pillow and raised the shade. Dimly racing shadows flew across the bed, but I couldn't see much outside. The train began to slow down and finally came to a stop. Everything seemed too quiet: I could hear Daddy talking, but I couldn't hear the words. I looked out the window; there seemed to be hundreds of lightning bugs in a meadow across the tracks—I had never seen that many at one time before. I watched them almost without breathing. They looked like Christmas tree candles blinking off and on, and there was nothing else I could see. There were two short sudden whistles from the engine, and the train started moving slowly and quietly—cutting off my view of those lightning bugs. I lay down on my pillow to wonder about it, but before I could, I fell asleep.

I woke up choking and coughing. Mother whispered in my ear, "It's all right. We've just passed through a tunnel, and the smoke and cinders blew in the window. Put your head under the covers and breathe." I did as she said and fell asleep again.

The next morning at breakfast I felt at home again in the diner: this was not new to me; I had done this before. The hot cakes were brown and buttery with maple syrup oozing down the sides. As I ate them I half listened to Mother talking. She was saying something about the rough roadbed and those endless tunnels through the mountains.

"Really, Wallace," Mother said. "I don't think I closed my eyes all night long. I just can't sleep on a train."

I couldn't understand that. I had planned to stay awake all night long and look out the window. But the rhythm of the train was soothing to me, and my eyes just wouldn't stay open.

After breakfast we walked back to our berth. The porter had

made it up into seats again while we were eating breakfast. We all sat down, and Mother checked to see if our bags were all safe under the seats. Then she began moving around frantically as if she were searching for something.

"Oh, Wallace," she cried. "I can't find my purse anywhere." She really looked like she was about to cry. "I had a five-dollar bill in there, and the key to the front door and the keys to the trunk. Oh, my stars, I must have left it in the diner!"

"Take it easy, Polly," said Daddy as he stood up. "I'll go and look for it. Now just take it easy. We'll find it."

I said, "I'll go with you Daddy," and followed him down the aisle. We went through two Pullman cars and back to the diner again. Daddy had just pulled open the door to the diner when the Negro waiter, who had served our breakfast, looked up and saw us coming back to our table. He grinned and came forward to meet us, holding up Mother's purse.

"I think the lady left this on the window sill," he said.

Daddy took the purse, opened it up, and saw that everything that Mother had mentioned was inside.

"Thanks, George. My wife will be glad to know you found it," and he reached in his pocket and gave him a quarter.

We started back to our car, and I asked Daddy, "How did you know that waiter's name?"

"Oh, I don't know his real name. But when you travel on a Pullman you always call the porters and waiters 'George.'"

"Why?" I asked.

"I really don't know, son; it's just a habit, I guess." I kept wondering about that for the rest of the morning, but I couldn't figure it out at all.

We had just finished the last of our chicken and the cupcakes for lunch when the train slowed down, began winding through a tangle of tracks, and finally stopped on the outskirts of some big city. I could see tall buildings from the window.

"What place is this, Daddy?"

"Birmingham, Alabama. Just about 150 miles to go."

Mother heaved a big sigh. "And this is where the hot part of the trip begins!"

We backed into the station, and when the train had finally stopped, Daddy turned to Mother.

"Do you want to stretch your legs, Polly?"

Mother seemed a little bit uneasy. "No, I think I'll just stay here and try to keep cool. It's probably hotter out there on the platform than it is in here."

"Bus?"

"Are you going, too?"

"I sure am."

"Me, too."

And we walked together down the length of the car and out onto the station platform.

There were a good many people getting on and off the train, but some of them were just walking up and down stretching their legs like us. We walked past the window of our car, and I waved to Mother; she waved back nervously. I noticed a man in overalls with an oil can doing something above the wheels of our car.

"What's that man doing?"

Daddy turned to look, and when he saw who I was pointing to he said, "Oh, he's putting oil in that cup above the wheels, so we won't have a hot box."

"What's a hot box?"

Daddy pointed at the big steel wheels under our end of the car. "See that big rod the wheels are hung on? Well, that train man fills that little cup with oil so the wheels will roll easier and won't get too hot."

"But what happens if—"

"Board!" The upswinging call came from our porter, who was standing at the other end of our car. Daddy grabbed my hand and yelled, "Come on, Bus, let's go," and we ran to the steps of our car just as the train jerked into movement.

Mother was in the vestibule frantically looking for us. When she saw us racing up the steps, her mouth tightened and she turned into the Pullman without a word. We followed her down the aisle and sat down in our seats, breathless with laughter. Daddy and I were facing her, and although she didn't say a word, I could tell from her face that she was going to have one of her explosions.

The train was picking up some speed now; I tried to watch what was left of Birmingham go by and keep an eye on Mother, too. I squirmed in my seat by the window and finally blurted out, "We saw a man fixin' a hot box, Mother. That's why we didn't—"

"Really, Wallace." I could tell the explosion was starting, and I wished I had kept still. "What in the world were you thinking of? You almost missed the train! What in—"

"Why, we didn't—"

"What in heaven's name would I have done! All the bags to take care of and no ticket to show who I am or where I'm going, and you and Buster looking at some overheated box."

"Hot box," I corrected.

"And you, young man, you just keep quiet and speak when you are spoken to! You hear me now!"

I heard, and I dried up.

"I, God, Polly! I just wanted a breath of fresh air, and so did Bus. No need to get on your high horse! I, God!" And Daddy jumped up angrily and disappeared down the aisle.

We sat without speaking, Mother and I—she tight-lipped and regretful, smoothing her hair and straightening her dress. I put my nose against the window screen and felt the hot, moist air against my face. The red clay gullies and low hills of West Alabama were beginning to appear, and before long we were on a long high trestle leading up to a river.

Mother suddenly leaned over toward the window. "This must be the Tombigbee we're coming to. Pappy used to play on these bluffs when he was a boy. He saw a Civil War battle being fought from here when he was about twelve years old." And she leaned back, remembering.

"Did Pappy ever fight in the war?" Before she could answer, Daddy came striding up the aisle, sat down next to me, and beamed at Mother and the world as he announced, "Well, sir, only about sixty miles and we'll be home! Yes, sir."

He seemed very happy about something, and his breath had

that funny medicine-like smell I had noticed before when he came home from long trips and swung me up and kissed me. I didn't know what it was, but I knew that Mother didn't like it. I watched her now, and, sure enough, her mouth had that cramped tight look again. Daddy didn't seem to notice her mouth, so I curled up beside him and fell into a hot, heavy sleep.

I woke up with movement all around me. Mother wasn't there, and the porter was getting our bags from under the seats. Daddy was sitting across from me and asked, "Have a good nap, Bus?" I yawned and tried to nod a yes. "We've just passed Basic City—only about ten miles and we'll be in Enterprise."

I looked around for Mother, and Daddy said, "Polly's gone to the ladies' restroom to fix herself up. She'll be back in a minute."

And there she was, coming down the aisle, hair silky-smooth, face beaming, hat in place, everything in order. My, she did look pretty! She sat down, crossed her legs carefully, and fussed with her collar.

"Well, we are almost there," she said, and I couldn't remember her ever looking so young or happy. She edged over to the window to look out. "Just after we cross the Chunky River bridge look carefully and maybe you'll see Mammy waving. She can see the train, and if she didn't go with Allie to the station to meet us, she'll wave a towel or an apron or something when we pass Riverside." Her words got all thick and jumbled, and I looked up. There was a tear rolling down her cheek. But before I could speak she scooted over to the window and pressed her face against the screen. She looked about as old as me. And she was almost shouting. I'd never heard my mother shout before.

"Look, Wallace, look! There's Mammy. She's waving a towel—or is it a sheet? Look, look, Buster, look! That's your Mammy—she's waving a sheet to welcome us home!"

I looked quickly and started to wave, but big oak trees were now covering the view of the house. The train was slowing down for the flag stop ahead, and as I continued to watch from the window, I saw him, a little Negro boy, standing on the top of a stile, waving wildly at each car as it rushed past him. I waved

back, but I don't think that he saw me, for he kept jumping up and down, still waving, until he had disappeared from view.

"Do you think he saw me?" I asked.

"Who, honey?" Mother was adjusting her hat. She looked out the window quickly again. "Was somebody standing on the back stoop with Mammy? I didn't see—"

"No, I mean that little boy that was sitting on the stile."

"I didn't see anybody, Bus." She had gathered up her purse and was now holding it clasped tightly in her hands.

"Well, we're almost there!" I heard Daddy say as he stood up in the aisle.

I was still looking out the window. "I wonder who he was?" I said.

It was Allie and Bubba and Sissy who met us at the station. There was a flurry of kissing and hugging and getting our bags, and Dad disappeared into the baggage room to see if our trunk had arrived on the same train. Sissy and I hugged and then looked at each other to see if we had changed in two years. I guess we had, for we were suddenly shy with each other. Bubba, who was driving the horse and wagon, smiled in his slow quiet way, jumped down from the wagon, and said to me "Hello, little Yankee boy. How you doing?"

"I'm not a Yankee! I just live up North." Allie laughed in that deep warm way that I remembered, and everything began to seem all right again. Allie was mother's only sister—four years older and four children wiser. She and her husband, Cally Gunn, and her mother and father lived at the place we called Riverside. Her four children, my first cousins, lived there too, and I guess they were the only brothers and sister I ever knew. Kiddo—Kenneth really—was the oldest; tall and lean, he walked with a limp because of that knee injury as a young boy. Bubba—really Carlton—was next. He was big and stocky, almost fat, except that he never moved or walked fat. Sissy—Mary Evelyn for real—was the only girl and just fifteen months older than me. Whatever she did I always wanted to do; and if she decided she didn't want to, then it wasn't important. And there was a new baby back at the house that I had never seen. This must be the Billy that I remembered Mother looking up from a letter more than a year ago and speaking of to Daddy: "Well, Allie's had another baby. She says they're going to name this one William—William Neal after Billy." I couldn't tell whether Mother was pleased or not.

Daddy came out of the little station with a long look as if expecting another explosion from Mother. "Well, Polly, looks as if our trunk didn't arrive, at least not on this train." And as if that were a cue, the engine shrilled shortly and the train began to move, leaving us huddled on the platform. Our Pullman—the Red Desert—passed by us, and for a moment I felt like crying. I had slept on that car last night, and it had brought us to Riverside safely—without a single hot box. It was a good ole Pullman car.

"Cally will pick it up tomorrow when he comes in to the mill," Allie said. "It'll probably be on the afternoon train tomorrow. Make haste, now, and let's get the bags and you children in the wagon. Mammy and Pappy will be frettin' if we don't get back soon." She turned to Bubba. "Son, help your Aunt Polly up to the seat. Mary Evelyn, you and Bussie Boy get in back of the wagon, and Bus, you hold on tight—you're not used to ridin' in a wagon bed, so you take care. Make haste, now!"

Sissy and I climbed onto the tailgate and hung our legs over the back. She turned and laughed at me, and I felt happy all over. Mother and Daddy turned to see if we were all settled.

Bubba whipped the reins over the horse's back and called out, "Giddap, Polly!" Daddy gave a startled look at Allie and snickered. "You mean you've named the horse Polly?" She nodded a yes. Then Daddy roared with laughter and said, "I'll be damn! The same old Pug!" He was the only one who ever called Allie Pug—it was his special name for her—and she seemed to like it. Just before the wagon jolted to a start I heard Mother laugh, too. It was more like a giggle. Then we were moving slowly down the red clay road to Riverside.

It wasn't a very big farm, the place we called Riverside. I never knew its exact size, probably close to a hundred acres, but its boundaries always seemed endless to me. Down in one corner of the big front lawn was the artesian well, where icy cold water flowed endlessly from an iron pipe into a concrete water trough. The water trough was our summer icebox; sealed containers of fresh milk were stored there, and ripe watermelons were cooled there, weighted down with brickbats until time for them to be sliced open into juicy pink curves the color of Allie's crepe myrtle bushes. To the east of the house, sloping down a ways, was the big barn and a cow lot, shaded by an old sweet gum tree whose prickly balls, which fell to the barnyard in later summer and fall, we were always very careful to avoid in our bare feet. Just below the barn and facing the front lawn were row after row of lacy pecan trees, over a hundred in all, running almost down to the railroad tracks. Pappy proudly called them his paper shells.

"Why does he call them that?" I asked Sissy once. "I never did ever see any paper on 'em."

"Course not, you silly!" she giggled. "It's 'cause their shells are so thin. Don't you know nothin'?"

The southern edge of the farm ended at the foot of the front lawn just beyond the lane. A barbed wire fence separated the Jennings' cow pasture from the lane. We called it the lane since it was the only road leading up to the house; it passed Riverside and came to a dead end at the railroad tracks. And it was the only way to get to Enterprise for weekly supplies. "Turn south at the end of the lane," Mammy would always say if anyone asked for directions to Enterprise. Or if we were going shopping in Meridian for big, important things, "Turn north at the end of the lane!"

The house itself stood on a slight rise at the top of the front lawn, an old two-story house that had been standing there before the Civil War—not a big house but sprawling and comfortable for its time. It always seemed to be in need of a coat of paint, except for the two tall columns on either side of the wide front porch, and I never could understand this. The rest of the house paint might be peeling or have weathered a dull milky gray, but those two columns were always white—clean white and straight and strong. A covered front porch—Mammy called it the veranda—ran the entire length of the house, and on hot humid days or rainy days, this was always our special play area, unless one of the violent electrical storms came up suddenly. Then we would hear an urgent voice call from the front hall: "You children come on in the house now; get on a featherbed until this blows over!" If it rained long and hard enough, the roof would always leak, and then pans and milk pails and even cooking pots were hastily placed under dripping rainwater. After such a storm, Mother or Allie would often sigh and say, "Well, now, the rain barrel's full and the buckets are full, too. I guess I'll just have to wash my hair tomorrow."

In the front hallway there was a long winding stairway that

led to the bedrooms on the second floor, and the curving banister rail made a wonderful slide for Sissy and me, unless we were caught doing it, which happened more often than we liked. Then Mammy would stand at the foot of the stairs and call up to us. "Now, Mary Evelyn, Buster, you all know that banister rail isn't too stout, and I don't want you children getting hurt. Just stop it right now, you hear me?" But if Allie saw us doing it, which she frequently did, she would giggle like a girl and shake her head but never say a word about it to Mammy. I always felt that she would secretly love to be sliding down with us. And I always wished that one day she would.

I don't know who first named the place Riverside—little Chunky River was almost a mile from the house—but no one in the little town of Enterprise ever referred to it as the Neal place as they did the Carpenter place or the Jennings place. It was always Riverside.

A part of General Grant's Union forces camped at the house for several days just before their march on Vicksburg, and we were always told that the owners of the house had buried their silver, money, and other valuables in various places around the grounds. Bubba and Sissy and I spent many hours digging around the big oak trees in the front yard, in the peach orchard back of the house, even in Allie's prized flower beds, looking for money or treasures. Kiddo would watch us, then laugh and shrug, "When are you kids gonna learn you're wastin' your time?"

Bubba was closer to Kiddo's age, and sometimes he'd quit digging and go off fishing or hunting with Kiddo. But Sissy and I would just keep digging for treasure.

Mammy and Pappy bought Riverside in 1912 to work as a farm. Their oldest daughter, Allie Ava, had married several years before to Mr. L.C. Gunn (Cally), who worked in a department store in Meridian, Mississippi. After Kiddo and Bubba were born, Cally became ill and was told by a local doctor that he had tuberculosis and must have a long period of complete bed rest. So Allie and Cally and the two boys moved to Enterprise to live with Mammy and Pappy, where they hoped Cally would regain his health. Sissy was born the next year, and the Billy I had never seen came along in 1919.

Every time we returned to Riverside I always waited breathlessly for my first glimpse of the sturdy white columns and the tall east and west chimneys. As we turned into the shady lane leading to the house, I breathed a sigh of relief; they were still there.

All of them—Mammy, Pappy, Kiddo—were waiting for us under the big columns as we drove up into the front yard. There was a big wicker baby buggy on the front porch, and Kiddo was smiling shyly and pushing it back and forth.

Mother jumped down from the high wagon seat. No one helped her. She rushed up the steps and grabbed Mammy around the waist. They didn't say anything; they just stayed there hugging each other, rocking back and forth. Then things got sort of blurry; everybody moving and talking at once, Pappy kissing Mother and repeating over and over, "Daughter, Daughter," Cally slapping Daddy on the back, Mother making baby talk to the baby carriage and saying "Oh, Allie, he's just beautiful, simply beautiful." Sissy had hopped down and was helping Bubba with the suitcases, and I sat very still on the tailgate of the wagon feeling a little left out. Kiddo's head popped up from the side of the wagon, and he stuck his tongue out and chanted,

"Yankee doodle, Buster Boy,
He's a little Yankee
He's a little Yankee—"

I jumped off the wagon and stood facing him. I was getting mad now, and I knew I wasn't going to behave myself. "I am not a Yankee. I am not, and you know it, too. You and Bubba quit teasing me, you hear?"

"Then why do you talk like a Yankee? You sure do sound funny to me. Just like a Yankee."

I knew I didn't talk the way they did. Sometimes I couldn't quite understand what they said in their soft slurring way. It made me feel mean—I wanted to get even. "Well, maybe I do sound funny to you, but I don't walk as funny as you—so there!"

I was sorry right away, because his face sort of drooped for a minute. Then he smiled weakly and put his arm around my neck. "Of course I was teasin' you. I guess I was so anxious for you all to get here that I forgot to tell you how glad I am. We'll have us a time this summer, you bet!"

I felt almost sick for a minute. His arm was around my shoulder now, and I was afraid I might cry. I wanted to tell him that I was sorry, but I didn't know how to tell him. I stopped and looked up at him. "You really and truly don't walk any funnier than I do, Kiddo. Really and truly."

He backed away from me and looked me up and down. "Well, I don't know about that now. Mama told me about all those treatments you been havin' to help your infantile paralysis. Maybe you are gettin' better. Maybe that Yankee air's been good for you." He laughed when he said it, then quickly added, "Come on now, lemme see you walk over here."

I knew he meant it—he wasn't fooling. I stood as tall as I could and walked over to the steps where he waited. He watched me very carefully. When I got in front of him he didn't say a word. Then he slapped me on the back like Cally did to Daddy.

"Yep, I think you're comin' along. You're doin' better, Bus." He put his arm around me again, and I did the same. I could feel his bony shoulder blades through his shirt. "Come on, let's go in the house. Mama's fixed a real good supper." And the two of us limped slowly up the steps and into the house.

I ate some more fried chicken with cornbread and buttermilk, but I didn't like Pappy's home-cured ham. It was too salty. Everybody kept eating and talking long after they had finished supper, but Allie pushed back her chair suddenly. "Good gracious! I've been so excited I even forgot to feed the baby." She left the dining room as the others laughed. When she didn't come back right away I turned to Sissy who was sitting next to me. "When is Auntee coming back to feed the baby?"

"Oh, I guess she'll feed him in the parlor or the front bedroom."

"Why doesn't she bring him back here to do it?"

"Oh, I guess she doesn't want to expose herself to everybody at the supper table."

I didn't know what she meant by that, and I guess she saw that I didn't. "Don't you know how babies are fed, Bus?" I shook my head. "Come on then." She got up and pulled me by the hand. "You all excuse us, hear? We're goin' to watch Mother feed the baby."

Mother looked a little uneasy and opened her mouth to say something, but then she didn't, because Cally had asked her a question and she hadn't heard what he said. "What did you say, Cally?" she asked.

Sissy led me into the front bedroom. Allie was sitting in the big hickory-bottom rocking chair with the little baby snuggled in her arms. He was making funny little noises with his mouth. The top of Allie's dress was open, and she was pushing a big fat nipple into Billy's mouth. The nipple was sort of pink and dripping milk, and it seemed to be part of her.

"Here you are, you little pig." The baby started sucking on the nipple. He got very quiet, and I stood there hardly breathing. The nipple slipped out of his mouth once, and his hands started moving in every direction. Allie quickly slipped the nipple back in his mouth.

"Isn't he a fine baby boy, Bus?" Allie was smiling at me and rocking slowly back and forth. I guess I must have nodded yes; I was so surprised I couldn't speak. I kept watching the baby sucking the nipple, and finally I just had to know. "Auntee"—I kept looking at it. "Auntee, does that thing belong to you?"

"What thing, Bus?"

Sissy started laughing as if she couldn't stop. "He means your dinner bag, Mother." And she kept on laughing. Allie stopped rocking, and with a kind of tender look on her face she said, "Come here, son."

I walked over to the chair, and, without disturbing the baby, she put her arm around me. "Yes, Bussie boy, this thing is mine. It belongs to me because my babies all belong to me. It's called a mother's breast, and it's one of the best things God ever invented."

She took her arm away from me for a minute to make the baby more comfortable. Then she took my hand and pulled me to her again. "You see, Buster," she spoke very softly, looking right at me, "when little babies come into the world, they can't eat anything at first because they don't have any teeth, and their little stomachs are very tender. So they can't eat the things you and Sissy eat. They have to have milk—lots of it—many times a day. So when I have a new little baby my breast fills up with milk, and that's the way Billy Boy here gets his dinner."

I was looking at her very hard. She patted my hand. "Someday if Polly has another little boy or girl you'll see what I mean."

"I think I see what you mean now." I looked down at the baby. He was almost asleep, but every now and then he'd make a few more sucking noises. "It makes him happy and sleepy, doesn't it?"

"It surely does." And she slowly took the nipple out of Billy's mouth, put it back inside her dress, leaned over, and kissed me. "I bet I know another little boy who's getting sleepy, too. You all go tell Polly it's past your bedtime. They've had enough talking for one day." She lifted the baby carefully to her shoulder. "Mary Evelyn, honey, go light me a lamp and bring it in here before I put the baby to bed. Make haste, now."

Sissy and I tiptoed toward the door. She went on into the hall to light the lamp, and I stood in the doorway looking back into the bedroom. Allie was holding the baby over her shoulder, rocking back and forth and softly singing,

> "Go tell Aunt Rhodie
> Go tell Aunt Rhodie
> Go tell Aunt Rhodie
> The old gray goose is dead."

The baby Billy was sound asleep.

"Wake up, sleepyhead! You gonna spend the whole day in bed?" Allie was standing by the side of the bed in the little back bedroom. She had her hands folded under her apron, her head cocked to one side, grinning at me. She nodded toward the dining room.

"Your mother's in there havin' a late breakfast. So you might as well go in and keep her company." She pulled the sheet back, gave me a playful slap. "Make haste, now, I've got work to do around here." She turned to go but stopped at the door to the dining room.

"Oh, I forgot. Kiddo and Bubba are waiting for you to get up. They're out on the front porch. They want to take you and Sissy down to the branch this morning."

"To go swimming?" I asked.

"I don't know, Bus. I didn't ask them." And then she was gone.

I didn't remember going to sleep the night before. After all the lamps were lit, Pappy called us into the front parlor for family prayer. He prayed something about being thankful for our safe trip and watching over us in the days to come and to keep us safe through the night. Then he started on the Lord's Prayer, and I fell asleep.

After I'd eaten some hot biscuits with butter and ribbon cane molasses, I went through the front hall to the porch. Bubba and Kiddo were sitting on the steps. Sissy came running up from the flower bed where she'd been watering Allie's verbena. She was excited.

"Bus—Bubba and Kiddo were down to the branch this morning seining for minnows, and they saw something down there, and they want us to see it too. And I've asked 'em and asked 'em, and they won't tell me what it is—the mean things. They say we've got to see it for ourselves."

"I'd better get my bathing suit." I turned to go in the house.

"Won't need it!" Bubba was getting up from the steps. "You'll be too excited to think about goin' swimmin'."

"Excited about what?"

Kiddo was getting a little put out. "You gonna stand here talkin' till sundown, little Yankee Boy, or you wanna go see what it is?"

"Come on, Bus, they're gonna tell us anyway." Sissy grabbed my hand, and we raced ahead down the big front lawn.

The branch was one of my favorite places. It was a little creek that ran through the Jennings' pasture, and it was where most of us had learned to swim—with one foot on the bottom. All of us—grown-ups and children, too—also used the branch as our bathtub. The water was always cold and amber clear unless a sudden summer storm sent it rushing out of its banks.

The water flowed over a series of smooth flat stones, and there was a big white sandbar on one side. Allie called it Mother Nature's own sandpile. It was a good place to be in the sun and get warm after paddling around in the cold water.

Sissy held the barbed wire fence up for me to climb under, then I held it up for her, and we ran on, down past the big cedar trees, and finally reached the branch.

I didn't see anything and neither did Sissy at first. The water looked clean and cool, and I wished I'd brought my bathing suit. "Well," I thought, "maybe I'll go on in with my coveralls since I'm already here."

Then Sissy was pointing to the sandbar and saying in a funny kind of voice. "Buster, look a-yonder!"

Then I saw it too. It was like something in a dream or maybe like one of those big pictures in a Sears, Roebuck catalog that hung on a nail in the outdoor privy back of the orchard. Sissy and I walked slowly down to the sandbar, and when I saw it was real and wouldn't disappear, I dropped to my knees in front of it.

It was a castle—a real fairy-tale castle, just like the ones I'd seen in storybooks Mother read to me. It had a drawbridge. It had towers—four of 'em with little matchstick flags on top of each one. It had high walls and low walls protecting the castle, and two little tin soldiers were standing on the high wall looking out over the branch. It was the prettiest thing I had ever seen in my life.

I looked up at Sissy, who was kneeling on the other side of the castle. "Where did it come from?" I was whispering—and wondered why. "Who made it?"

"I guess the fairies did!" I looked up. Kiddo and Bubba had

followed us and were watching us closely. Kiddo sat down beside of me.

Sissy kept looking at the castle and then at Kiddo. "You all were down here this morning—you said you were—and I'll bet you made it. You made it for a surprise." She turned to Bubba. "That's when you did it, wasn't it? This morning when you were down here?"

"You don't believe in anything, do you?" Bubba got up and kicked some sand with his foot. "We came down here to seine for minnows this morning. We wasn't studyin' about building no castle. Didn't have enough time to catch minnows and build a castle anyway. Anybody with any sense would know that!"

"I don't care who built it," I said. "I think it's the prettiest castle I ever saw. Better than Cinderella's castle."

Kiddo laughed. "Cinderella didn't have a castle. That belonged to the prince."

"It belonged to her after she married the prince."

"Well, I guess you're right about that, Bus." Kiddo laughed again.

I didn't know whether they had built it or not, and I didn't care. The castle was there—to look at, to play with, to enjoy. It would be there every time we came down to go swimming. Then I had a sudden thought.

"Kiddo, do you s'pose we could find something to cover it with—you know—in case it rains or something?"

"It's not gonna rain today—not likely. So just have fun with it now."

Sissy and I started moving the tin soldiers to different places on the high walls, so they could see out over the countryside. I looked very closely at the drawbridge half buried in the sand, and it looked very much to me like an old pancake turner. Sissy edged up close to me with one of the tin soldiers in her hand. She whispered, "This is one of Kiddo's tin soldiers that Daddy got for him one Christmas. I'm sure they must have built it this morning. Don't let on we know."

Bubba had been skipping flat stones across the branch and saw us whispering. He came up to Kiddo, and I heard them talking but paid no attention to them until I heard Bubba say, "Kiddo, let's be the Doughboys chargin' the Huns at the fort." He was making a big ball out of red clay from the bank.

"Who are the Huns?" I asked Kiddo.

"Don't you know nothin', Yankee Boy?" He was forming a ball of red clay at the same time. "They're the German Army that we whipped in Europe on Armistice's Day in 1918!"

Both of them were moving toward the castle, scooping up more clay from the creek banks as they edged closer. I didn't know what was going on until Bubba suddenly yelled, "Fire!" and then both he and Kiddo started throwing clay balls at the castle as fast as they could make them.

The first one they threw missed completely; but the second one hit a tower, and the little flag fell down. Bubba hit one of the high walls, and it crumbled up, part of it falling into the moat.

"Stop it! Stop it!" I was almost screaming. "What are you doing that for? Stop it now. You hear me?"

Both of them were still throwing at the castle, laughing and crouching as if somebody were throwing things at them, too. I looked at the castle; one of the towers had fallen completely, the moat was stopped up, branch water was lapping at the walls, and some of the sand was crumbling. One of the tin soldiers had fallen into the moat and lay there drowning. I felt like I was drowning, too.

"You stop it now! Why do you wanna tear it up? Stop it now, you hear?"

The battle went on around the castle. They kept on yelling and throwing the red clay balls, and suddenly I couldn't stand it anymore. If they were going to tear it up and stop my fun, then I'd do something to stop theirs. I didn't know why, but I ran right up to the castle—what was left of it—and jumped on the very middle of it, and stomped and stomped and stomped on it until there was nothing left but a pile of sand and red clay. Then I sat down on it.

Both of them had stopped throwing their mud balls, and they looked at me queerly.

"What'd you do that for?" Bubba looked surprised. "Why'd

you spoil the fun? Just when we were about to beat the Huns?" And he turned and walked up the sandbar in disgust.

I picked up one of the drowned tin soldiers and looked at him. His face was all covered with sand, and I threw him back into the moat. Let him stay drowned. Sissy came and sat down by me.

"Boy, you sure tore it down quicker than they could!" She looked a little surprised.

Kiddo was watching me very quietly. I saw him moving up to where I sat, and he stood there for a while saying nothing. I looked up at him and felt sort of sick.

"Why did you wanna tear it down?" He looked at me. He looked at what was left of the castle and then back at me. "We were just having a play battle—like in the World War." He stopped for a minute and then went on. "We were having a good time, too, Bus. Just like you and Sissy did a little while ago." He looked at me again and was silent.

"But why did you have to tear it down?" I still didn't understand at all.

He didn't say anything, and then he tried again. "You know how you asked us a little while ago could we find something to cover the castle if it rained?" I nodded. "Well it was too big to cover. And if it rained, the water would wash it away. Or if some of the Jennings' cows came down for a drink they'd probably trample all over it. And we couldn't do anything about that, now could we?"

I kept looking at the pile of sand and couldn't look at him at all. He leaned closer and finally said, "You and Sissy had fun with it at first, didn't you? And Bub and I had fun playing war. So we all had fun while it lasted, but, just like Mammy says, nothing ever lasts forever."

I scooped up some of the sand that had been part of the castle; it was getting so dry it wouldn't even hold together anymore and fell through my fingers. I picked up the little tin soldier lying in the moat and cleaned sand off of his face.

"I just wish it could have lasted a little longer," I said, and I wasn't even sure if I meant the castle or the fun.

"I could build you another one just like it tomorrow, Bus, but it would be gone before you leave for home."

I just sat there.

"Come on, Bus." Kiddo got up and pulled me up with him. "Mammy'll be ringin' the dinner bell soon."

Bubba and Sissy were halfway up the Jennings' pasture by now. Kiddo took me by the hand, and we started after them. I turned for one last look at where the sand castle had stood, and then we went on up to the house for dinner.

I had been at Riverside for two weeks before I met the boy who would become one of my best friends. When I got up that morning I didn't feel too good, but I ate as much breakfast as I could so Mammy wouldn't say I was a sickly eater. Sissy wasn't around to play with; she was in the front room in bed dosed up with Calomel. That meant she couldn't be up and around until her bowels had acted. It also meant she couldn't eat any pickles or anything sour until the Calomel had worked through her because if she did Mammy said all her teeth would fall out.

Sissy was in bed because Daddy had given me three dollars the day he left to go back to Terre Haute; his vacation was over. The three dollars had to last me the rest of the time, and he told me to spend just a little every week. Mother said to give the money to her and she would give me a little every so often, but Daddy said no, he thought it was time I learned the value of a dollar. So I had three whole dollar bills in my pocket the day we took Daddy to catch the train.

Cally drove the wagon, and Daddy sat on the high seat with him. Sissy and I rode the tailgate, which we liked better anyway. Mother wouldn't go to the station with us because she said she hated goodbyes, and then right after she said it, she hugged and kissed Daddy a long time, then turned and ran into the house.

When we got to Enterprise, Cally stopped the wagon by the side of the station. Daddy jumped down, got his bags, took them to the station platform, and set them down. Cally joined him there, and Sissy and I went out on the railroad track to walk the crossties. She could do it much faster than I could, but I managed to keep pretty close to her. We hadn't gone very far when Cally called out: "Oh, Sissy—you and Buster come on back now. Number 44 is on time, and I want you off those tracks right now!"

We skipped up to the platform and sat on the one bench for passengers to wait. "Wish I was goin' to Terre Haute," Sissy dangled her legs back and forth, "or just any place at all, just so's I could ride on that train."

All at once I had an idea I'd never thought of before. "Maybe you could come up to visit us next summer."

Sissy looked at me for a minute, and there was an excited expression on her face. Then she shrugged her shoulders and looked away, kicking at some loose gravel. "I don't think so, Bus. Billy'll be walkin' by next summer, and I'll have to be a big help to Mother. He'll be at that stage where he gets into everything."

She was looking away from me at someplace far down the tracks. "Well, maybe sometime you can." And for a minute or two we just sat there very quiet.

Sissy heard it first. She jumped up from the bench. "I heard it. I heard it whistlin'." She ran over to Daddy. "I think the train's comin', Uncle Wallace. I heard it whistlin' down the track!"

By that time we could see the engine puffing smoke. It blew another long blast almost as if it were angry at having to stop. Way down the track a porter was leaning out of the vestibule of a Pullman, and Cally and Daddy were hurrying down there with the bags. Sissy and I trotted along behind them trying to keep up and trying not to get in the way. As we reached the car where the porter was, Daddy handed his bags up to him, grabbed me and swung me up in his arms, kissed me and whispered in my ear, "Now you be a good boy, have lots of fun this summer, and take good care of Polly for me." He set me down and then grabbed Sissy and did the same thing, but I couldn't hear what he said to her. He shook Cally's hand and said, "Thanks for everything, Cally, and you take good care of Pug now." Just then there were two short whistles, and the train started moving. Daddy jumped on the steps, the porter followed him and closed the door, and Daddy started waving. The last thing we saw was Daddy's hand sticking out the side of the car still waving.

We turned and walked back up the platform to the station. "It wasn't the Red Desert!" I mumbled.

"What?"

"I said it wasn't the Red Desert." I started crying a little.

Sissy took my hand and started skipping up to the wagon. "Come on, Bus. Lets go on home and go swimming in the branch."

Cally had been watching us, and as we sat down on the tailgate he came up and put his hands on our knees and said, "I guess you might not have time to go swimming this afternoon. I have to go over to the mill on some business. I don't think it will take me very long. I'm just going across the tracks to the mill office over yonder." He pointed to a little shed across the tracks. "Do you think you children will be all right when I'm gone?"

"Sure we will," Sissy smiled. "We'll wait for you right here." Then she jumped off the wagon and asked, "But can we walk around a little and just look at things, Daddy?"

"All right, but you be careful, and don't get out of sight of the wagon, you hear?"

"We won't!"

Cally stepped across the railroad tracks lifting his feet very high so as not to kick up the gravel roadbed.

"Come on." Sissy had my hand. "Let's go over to Williams' store. They've got lots of things in there to look at, and he won't mind."

We crossed the dusty road from the station and stood in front of the store. A big white sign painted in black letters said R.J. Williams General Store.

"Wanna go inside for a minute and look around?" Sissy asked.

"Sure I do," I answered and stuck my hands importantly in my pants pocket. And then I felt them. I'd forgotten all about them, the three one-dollar bills that Daddy had given me that morning. There they were. I could feel them as my fingers closed around them. And I suddenly didn't have to pretend important; I *was* important!

"And we won't just look around in that ole Williams' store," I announced. "We might even buy out that ole Williams' store!"

"What with, I'd like to know." Sissy looked at me with a smirk on her face.

"Just watch this!" I pulled the three one-dollar bills out of my pocket and stuck them right in her face.

She couldn't see how many there were, but she knew they were dollar bills. "Where'd you get those?" She looked like she thought I'd stolen them from somebody. She almost sounded like my mother.

"Daddy gave 'em to me this morning before we left home. They're my 'lowance for the summer!" I folded them up and put them back in my pocket. I grabbed Sissy's hand. "Come on. We're gonna have us a treat!" And we marched into R.J. Williams Store.

It was cool and dark inside after the glare from the road. At first I couldn't see anything at all, but after a while I could make out two ladies and a little girl standing by a side counter. They were talking, and Sissy went up to the girl and said, "Hi, Erda Mae, how you doin'?" and then, "Good afternoon, Mrs. Jones, Miss Lottie, how are you all?" They spoke to Sissy and then turned back to their talking again. Erda Mae edged over closer to Sissy and asked, "Who's he?" pointing at me, and Sissy said, "He's my first cousin from Terre Haute, and he's spending the summer with us."

The girl moved right over to where I was standing. She looked me up and down with tight, knowing eyes and said, "My name is Erda Mae Jones. What's yours?" I told her Buster Briggs. She kept on staring at me openly and then she asked, "You Miss Polly's boy?" It surprised me so that she knew my mother's name that I couldn't answer yes or no. She just kept looking at me, waiting for me to say something. Finally I managed to blurt out, "How did you know my mother's name?" And then she smiled. It wasn't even any kind of smile I'd ever seen before, and she said, "I know a lot more than you do, or probably ever will."

One of the ladies called to her and said, "Come on back over here now, Erda Mae. We got to get home in a hurry, you hear me now?"

Erda Mae started toward her mother and then came back to stand in front of me again. She was nearly a head taller than me, and her eyes sort of slitted as she looked down at me.

"I live in the gray house across from the Clarks. You know where it is?" I nodded yes. "Well, if you get tired of all your cousins and your aunts and uncles, you can come up to play with me anytime you want to." She crossed over to where her mother stood, and they left the store together, but she kept her eyes on me all the way out.

"Who was that?" I asked as I crossed to the pickle barrel where Sissy was looking inside.

"Oh, she's that silly Erda Mae Jones. She lives up the road from us a piece." Sissy was looking at the big fat pickles in the barrel. "She's in the third grade and thinks she knows it all, but I just think she's sorta silly." She kept looking at the pickles.

"Do you want one?" I asked her.

"Do you?"

"I don't like 'em much, but you take one."

"I just purely love 'em."

So Sissy had a big dill pickle; we had two orange Nehi's apiece, a Black Cow sucker apiece, and a whole package of Lorna Doones, and after I'd paid for it all, I still had two dollars and sixty-five cents left.

We left the Williams' store and got to the wagon just as Cally was crossing the railroad tracks. He seemed pleased that we were sitting there waiting for him, and he called us his "good chillun." He untied the horse, turned the wagon around, and we headed for home.

Sissy got sick during supper. She had taken only a few bites at the supper table when she got up quickly, without even an excuse me, ran out to the back stoop, and vomited all over it. Allie followed her out, and when they came back in Sissy looked sort of white and peaked and she wasn't saying anything. Allie took her into the front bedroom.

Mother said to me, "Did you all have anything to eat in town?"

I had eaten most of my supper, but it didn't taste as good as it usually did. And I was worried. Mother looked upset.

"We just had some Lorna Doones."

"Anything else?"

"We had a Black Cow all-day sucker."

"And what else?"

"An orange Nehi pop."

"Was there anything else, Buster?"

"Well, Sissy ate a big dill pickle."

"Lord have pity. No wonder the child is vomiting. Nobody's stomach can take all that kind of treatment. She'll be bilious for days." Mammy got up from the table. "I'll have to dose her good with Calomel tonight." And she walked out of the dining room sort of tight-lipped.

On the day I first met Leroy, Sissy was sick in bed with Calomel. Bubba and Kiddo were helping Allie in the garden. Pappy and Cally were hoeing cotton in the fields. Mammy and Mother were cooking dinner. And so I had no one to play with. Nothing seemed to be going right that morning as I sat down on the front steps and looked aimlessly across the front lawn. Then I saw a big fat Negro woman that I never remembered seeing before down by the artesian well. As I watched, I could see she was starting a fire under a big black kettle, and she began taking clothes out of several baskets near the well. Then she began to sing, her voice floated up to me strong and clear.

> "Swing low, sweet chariot
> Comin' for to carry me home."

It was a pretty voice, but I could feel a lonesomeness in it, too.

I got up from the front steps and walked halfway down the front lawn toward the well, and then I stopped. The woman had put her hands on her hips and stood there looking at me for the longest time. Then she did something I'd never seen before in my life. She reached into her big apron pocket and pulled out a funny-looking pipe and stuck it in her mouth. Then she picked up a piece of pine kindling, held it into the fire under the kettle, and lit her pipe with it. When the pipe began to smoke, she threw the piece of kindling into the fire and stood there puffing. The smoke curled up around her face and hung in the air above her. Then she shifted the pipe to the corner of her mouth without ever touching it with her hand and spoke for the first time.

"Has you seen that good-for-nothin' Leroy round here this mornin'?"

"No, ma'am."

She threw back her head and let out a big laugh that made her apron shake all over.

"Now will you just listen to this chile yes ma'amin' me all over the place!" She took a couple of steps toward me to look at me closer. "Now I just bet me you must be Miss Polly's boy." She cocked her head knowingly. "Ain't that right?"

"Yes, ma'am," I said again, and she laughed so hard this time she had to sit down by the side of the artesian well. She picked up the bottom of her big apron and wiped her eyes with it.

"Now ain't you somethin'—yes ma'amin' me and bein' a regular li'l gentleman." Then her voice got sort of quiet and gentle, and she stretched out her big arms to me.

"C'mere, chile, and let Mattie Riley see how your li'l ole leg doin' since you had that impetile paralysis."

I didn't ask her how she knew about my infantile paralysis. She seemed to know everything, but she sounded so nice that I ran right over to her. She picked me up and put me right in the middle of her lap. It felt just like sitting on one of Mammy's big featherbeds. She picked up my right leg and looked at it closely, and then she picked up my left leg and looked at it. My right leg was a little smaller and shorter than the other one. She moved the right leg up and down very slowly, then she grabbed my foot and held it firmly in her big hands.

"Lemme see if'n you can wiggle your toes." And it was then I knew she had said exactly the same thing to me before—someplace, sometime. I couldn't remember when it was—maybe it was that Christmas when I had burned my neck with a sparkler. I wasn't sure, but I knew she had said those very same words to me before. And she was saying it again right now.

"Come on, now. Show Mattie Riley how you can wiggle your toes."

I tried to wiggle them, but like always they didn't move very much, but Mattie Riley seemed to think it was pretty good. That's what she said anyway.

"Well now, that's pretty good. Better'n it was the last time you done tried it for me."

I knew it, I knew it! I knew I had tried to wiggle my toes for her before this. I turned around in her lap to look at her. She was smiling at me and patting my leg. She had taken the pipe out of her mouth.

"When was it that I tried it before?" I asked.

"Well, lemme see now." She stuck the pipe back in her mouth and puffed on it a few times trying hard to think when. "It musta been more than two years ago, that time when you and Miss Polly done come down here to Riverside for Christmas."

"And I burned my neck with a sparkler!"

She looked surprised. "Lawd, chile, does you remember that time?"

"I sure does—I mean, sure do. And see, I've still got a scar from it." And I turned my face up so she could see my neck.

She looked at it carefully and ran her finger over the scar. "It's just a little un though. You won't be able to see it when you're growed up."

I jumped down from her lap and walked over to the kettle. The water inside was starting to bubble. "You doin' the washin' today?" I asked.

"As shore as the Lawd made li'l green apples I'm doin' the washin', if'n that fire ever get goin' good." She got up and sort of waddled over to the kettle to see how the fire was doing. Then she began mumbling to herself, and half of what she said I couldn't understand. But after she had put a few more sticks of wood on the fire, she straightened up, put her hands on her hips, and looked all around her.

"Now where in the world has that good-for-nothin' Leroy

done tuck his self off to? He was s'pose to get this here fire started." She walked down past the well to the lane and shaded her eyes looking toward the railroad track in the distance. She cupped her hands around her mouth, and called out in a sing-song way, "Leroy! Oh, Leroy!" Then she listened for a minute. All I could hear was the fire making a crackling noise. "I tells you now, that young-un o' mine gonna be the death o' me before the day's over. He's more'n likely settin' on that stile by the railroad track just waitin' for some old train to come by. That boy got a plum passion for watchin' the trains go by." She put her hands on her hips again and said, "Huh!" and I could tell she was put out with Leroy.

I ran down to where she was standing. "I'll run down there and see if I can find him."

She turned to me. "You ever been down there before? I mean by your own self?"

"Oh, sure," I said, "I've been down there before so I could watch the trains, too." I didn't tell her that Kiddo or Bubba had always been with me.

"Well, bless the good Lawd! I sho' didn't know we had two train lovers in this family." She started up toward the kettle. "Well you go on if'n you got a mind to, but you tell that Leroy to get his self up here to hep me unless he wants his bottom tanned." And she started dropping clothes in the kettle and stirring them with a big stick.

I started down the lane to the railroad track, looking back at the house every now and then. As long as I could see the house I knew I wasn't disobeying Mother, who always said, "You can play anywhere you want to at Riverside as long as you stay in sight of the house, but don't go any further, unless a grown-up or Kiddo or Bubba goes with you."

When I'd gone far enough that I couldn't see the house anymore, I got a little scared and started to turn back, but I kept on going and walked in the middle of the lane. I figured that nothing could grab me from the high weeds and bushes that grew on either side if I stayed in the middle. And it wasn't long before I could see the fence that separated the railroad property from the lane. There was a wooden stile that went up and down over the fence, and on top of it sat a little Negro boy not too much bigger than me.

Then suddenly I was remembering the day we had arrived on the train from Terre Haute, and I had seen a little Negro boy sitting on the stile, waving wildly to the train as it passed, and I wondered if he might be the same one, if he might be Mattie Riley's Leroy.

I stood perfectly still when I saw him and watched him for a long time. I guess he hadn't heard me coming down the lane because he was talking to himself, saying something about "that ole caboose gonna be red this time, gonna be a red un this time for sho'." He still didn't know I was standing there, so I yelled, "Leroy!"

He stopped talking to himself, but he didn't turn around, he just hunched down further on the stile and sat there like a statue. When he didn't answer me or even turn around to look at me I got sort of mad and put my hands on my hips the way his mother did and called again, "Leroy, your mother is looking for you!"

He turned then and looked at me for a long time. His face was so black it glistened in the sun.

"How come you know what my name is?" He wore a scared look on his face. "How come you know my mama?"

"Because she's up at the house washing the clothes, and she told me to come look for you, that's why!" I said. I was a little afraid of him; he looked like he was getting mad.

"Who're you, anyway?" he said after a time. "Somebody who comes down here callin' Leroy, just like he own me? Who are you?"

"I'm Buster Briggs," I answered. "And I'm staying up at the house visiting my Mammy, Mrs. Neal." Then I added, "And your mother said you better get up to the house right now."

He looked at me and then he smiled, a big wide grin. "Where you from, white boy?" He was laughing at me now. "How come you talk so funny? Where you from anyway?"

I didn't like him laughing at me like that, and I told him so. "Well, I sure don't talk as funny as you do!" I was getting mad now. "Everybody down here can understand what I say when I say it. You're the one that talks funny, not me." Then I tried to scare him. "And you sure better get back to the house before Mattie Riley tans your bottom. That's what she said she'd do."

"That don't scare me none," he said. "She done it before, plenty, and if'n I yell loud enough, she quit." And he swung around and looked up the tracks toward Enterprise. I guessed he wasn't going to talk anymore so I just stood there looking at his back, not knowing what to do. I thought he'd forgotten I was there, until he swung around and leaned over the stile. "You like trains?" he asked.

"Sure I do, I come down here on—" I was going to tell him all about riding the Red Desert Pullman car from home, but he didn't wait for me to finish.

"Gonna be big long freight train passin' pretty soon." He scooted over the stile and motioned to me. "You wanna set up here with me and watch it go by?" He turned back toward the railroad track again, but he left room on one side of the stile for me in case I wanted it.

I climbed up the three wooden steps, sat down on the top step, and then swung my legs around so I was facing the tracks. We didn't look at each other for a while; we just sat there not moving or saying anything at all.

I was starting to get tired just sitting there with nothing happening when suddenly Leroy jumped off the stile, ran up to the railroad tracks, fell down on his knees, and put his ear down on one of the steel rails. He crouched there for a time as if he were listening, then he raised his face to me and broke into a wide grin. "Here she come!" he shouted and ran down the bank and climbed back up on the stile by me. He was trembling all over and kept saying over and over almost to himself, "Here she come, here she come!"

And sure enough, it wasn't long before I could see the engine coming down the track, and just before it passed us the engineer blew a long shrill whistle for the Chunky River crossing. Leroy sat there shivering and swaying back and forth. I don't think he even knew I was sitting beside him. He waved to the engineer who didn't even see us; he counted every car until he got to twenty, and then I guess he couldn't count any higher. After that he kept looking down the tracks for the end of the train, and finally he saw what he was looking for. He slapped his legs, laughed out loud, and jumped up on the top step, almost dancing, not even looking at me.

"It's a red un! I knowed it had to be a red un this time. Come on you ole red caboose!" He started waving his arms wildly. I put my arm up to wave at the caboose, too, and as it passed us I saw a man standing on a little platform; he raised his hand and waved back to us.

Leroy's hand stopped in midair and he sat down with a thump like he'd been hit in the stomach with the breath knocked out of him. The caboose of the train disappeared around the curve, but Leroy just sat there looking down the track. He didn't move for the longest time, but finally he took a long, slow breath and let it out. Then he turned to me. "You see that man wavin' to me?"

"Sure I did. He was waving to both of us."

He didn't even hear me. He went right on talking. "Golly Moses. That man on the caboose was wavin' at me!" And he began to make some of the strangest moves I'd ever seen. He jumped off the stile, ran up to the tracks, and began walking the crossties on his hands with his feet in the air. Then he stood up, and even though the sun was awfully hot now, he started walking the rails in his bare feet and kept saying the whole time, "That ole man wavin' to me, wavin' to ole Leroy, just wavin' to me." Then, almost like a circus acrobat I'd seen one time, he did four or five cartwheels down the bank and stretched out on his back right in front of me. He was sweating and breathing hard. He raised himself up on one elbow and grinned at me.

"That ole wavin' man got me so mixed up I about to pee in my pants." He got up, unbuttoned his pants, pulled out his little black peter, and started pee-peeing on everything around; on the sandy red clay, on the yellow bitter weeds, on the big red ants crawling away from it to keep from drowning. He even peed on the stile, close enough to my feet that I had to swing them to the other side. And when I moved my feet out of the way he grinned and started singing:

> "Two li'l niggers laying in the bed
> one raised up to the other one said
> You peed in my warm place."

I had a feeling Mother wouldn't like what he had just done or said, but I started laughing so hard I nearly fell off the stile, and Leroy was laughing just as hard watching me laugh. My sides began to hurt, and I climbed off the stile and sat on the ground by Leroy. He was still chuckling and said, "What you say your name is?"

"It's really Wallace Neal, but everybody down here calls me Buster."

"Where you live, Buster?"

"Terre Haute, Indiana."

"Where that?"

"It's way up north, Leroy, on the—" I had to stop and think for a minute. "It's in Indiana on the Wabash River." That didn't seem to mean anything to him. "It takes a whole day and whole night to get here on the train. When Daddy told me that we were—"

He sat up very straight and opened his eyes real wide. "You come here on a train? On this here railroad track?" He pointed up to the track above us.

"Sure, Leroy," I said. "We got on the train in Terre Haute one day, and we slept all night on the train and rode all the next day until we got here."

He hadn't taken his eyes off my face, but finally he asked, "How you sleep on a train?"

I tried to tell him about the porter, how he made down the berth, and pulled the seats together and put the green curtain all around it and how you crawled in to undress. He looked at me for a long time and asked again, "How do it sleep?" I started to tell him about the little berth again, but he stopped me.

"I means, how do it feel to sleep in that li'l ole bed?"

"Oh, it feels real good. I liked it." But I could tell from the look on his face that wasn't a good enough answer. I thought for a minute how I could tell him what it really felt like. Finally I said, "Leroy, have you seen that big baby buggy that Auntee pushes little Billy back and forth in to put him to sleep? You know, when he has to take a nap?"

He nodded and said, "I know. I done watch Mama push him to sleep in it."

"Well, if that baby buggy was big enough for a grown person, and ran real fast on a track, I guess it might feel something like that. Course that's not it exactly, but—yeah, something like that." It was the best I could do.

Leroy looked up at the railroad track a long time, then he looked down where the caboose had disappeared, and when he finally spoke, he sounded like he was half asleep.

"Sleepin' on a train! Sho' enough, all night long."

My stomach was growling, and I thought it must be nearly dinnertime by now. I stood up and said I'd better be getting back to the house. Leroy jumped up and said, "I go back with you," and he hopped over the stile. I followed him slowly down one step at a time. He looked at my leg and then up at me.

"What wrong with your leg, Buster?"

I told him, and he thought about it for a minute.

"Do it hurt bad?"

"Oh no, it doesn't hurt much, except if I turn my weak ankle. I have to be pretty careful where I walk, and I can't run very fast yet. But Mattie Riley says I'm getting better." And I started on up toward the house.

Leroy walked behind me for a little way, and every time I slowed up he would slow up, until I called out, "Come on, Leroy. It's almost dinnertime by now. Hurry up." I walked on by myself and said, "Well, go on and be a slowpoke if you want to." But suddenly he ran on ahead of me and pointed out a big gully in the lane.

"You best be careful of this here rough spot in the road." Then he hurried back to me. "Here, lemme hold your hand till we gets over that ole gully." He slid his warm moist hand into mine and held it tightly, and we walked on up the road together.

After dinner I told Mother about Leroy, but I didn't tell her about him peeing all over the stile or what he said when he did it. "I think he's going to be one of my best friends this summer," I told her.

When I went to sleep that evening I dreamed about Leroy, and when I woke up in the middle of the night, I had wet the bed.

William Lerond Neal was my grandfather, but all of us called him Pappy, including his wife. He was a stern man as far as morals and religion were concerned, but we loved him and were afraid of him at the same time. I only remember once that he ever joined the whole family in celebrating the Fourth of July on the banks of the Chunky River. That was the time Uncle Will and Aunt Jo came from New York City for a few days' visit at Riverside. He even went so far as to join us at the river for the noonday feast, but he didn't approve of us going in swimming together—men and women, girls and boys. He called it mixed bathing and felt it was wrong.

When I was a little older, I loved to sit up in the front parlor and play Rook with Sissy and Kiddo and Bubba; sometimes we'd play the game until nine-thirty or ten o'clock, until one night Pappy came in and caught us at it. Mammy told us that Pappy had gone to bed early in the east bedroom upstairs. So Kiddo lit the Aladdin lamp in the parlor and put it in the middle of the library table, and the four of us started playing cards. I had just bid for the widow and had got it and was about to name trumps when the parlor door was suddenly thrust open. There stood Pappy. He didn't say anything at all; he just stood in the doorway looking at us. Nobody said anything, so finally I called over to him. "Come on in, Pappy, and watch me play." Kiddo muttered under his breath, "Oh, Lord!" as Pappy walked slowly over to the table.

"What are you all playing?" Pappy asked.

"Rook," I said. "Why don't you sit down and watch?"

I remember Pappy saying one time, "Never wear or wave anything red in front of a bull. It'll make him mad!" When I invited him to sit down and watch us play cards I must have been waving a red flag in front of him, but I didn't know it. He leaned over that table and grabbed every single card he could reach and began tearing them into little pieces. We didn't dare stop him even though we felt miserable as we sat there and watched him. When he had torn every card he could find, he looked at us, still breathing hard, and said, "These things are the instrument of the devil!" Then almost smiling he added, "Now you won't be tempted any more." And he turned and left the room. That was the last time we ever played Rook at Riverside.

Pappy had been born in Alabama before the Civil War. He and his family had moved to Mississippi when he was a young boy, and he had lived there ever since. Mammy always said he should have been a minister in the Methodist Church because he was so religious. He had several brothers and sisters: Uncle Kaze Neal, who lived in Waynesboro and loved sad cake (Mammy said it was the only kind he would eat); Aunt Fannie Hunt, who was deaf as a post and always carried a big black ear trumpet you had to scream into (and even then she would look at you and ask, "What say? What say?"); Uncle Henry Neal lived over in Texas. I'd never seen him, but I'd heard Mammy talk about him before. "I've never known anyone who loves a practical joke better than Brother Henry," she would say. Or, if she was really put out with Pappy over something he had said or done, she would say, "You're a good man, Will—I know it, your children know it, I guess everybody knows it. But sometimes I do wish you could enjoy things a little more like your Brother Henry. You and he are as different as day and night." When she would say that, it always made me wonder if I'd ever see this Brother Henry who was so different from Pappy.

He came for an unexpected visit toward the middle of July that summer, and the way it turned out I was the first one to meet him.

Leroy had come up to the house early that morning to ask me to go fishing with him. "I'm gonna catch me some fish this mornin'," he told me as he stood on the back stoop. "You wanna go with me?"

"I've never been fishing, Leroy," I said, and his eyes got very big. "Never been fishin'?" He sounded as though he didn't believe me. Then he got smart alecky. "What they do up in that Terre Haute town? Just ride around in them sleeping car trains all the time?"

"No, they don't, you smart aleck," I said, but he was laughing by now, and so was I. "I'd really like to go, Leroy, but I can't today. Mother and Mammy and them are going up to the Jennings place to can tomatoes, and Mammy told us not to go off the place till they get back." Then I had an idea. "Why don't you stay here, and we'll have some fun today. We can go fishing some other time. Your Mama's coming over to be with me and Sissy and the baby anyway."

"Mama comin' here?"

I said, "Uh-huh. The folks are gonna leave for the Jennings' just as soon as she gets here."

"Lawdy God, then lemme get my tail outta here. If'n she see me she whup me sho'!" And he was gone out the back gate and down the path to the river just as Mattie Riley plodded up from behind the barn. She closed the gate Leroy had just rushed through and stood there with her hands on her hips and asked me, "Who that I just see runnin' outta here? That no-'count Leroy?"

"I don't know, Mattie," I squirmed. "I guess so."

"You don't know and you guess so." She came on up the steps mumbling to herself but plenty loud enough for me to hear. "I know somebody gonna have to split forty blackjack rails if'n they don't tell me the truth," she said and stomped on into the kitchen.

I went on into the house, careful to avoid Mattie as I passed through the kitchen and went out to sit on the front porch. Sissy was pushing the baby buggy slowly back and forth trying to get Billy to sleep. I asked her, "Are we gonna be here by ourselves all day?"

"I guess so." She pointed to the baby. "Mama's fixed him

some bottles to tide him over till she gets back." Then she added, "But we won't be here by ourselves. Mattie'll be here with us."

"Don't I know it!" I said. Mattie was mad at me.

Sissy looked at me, but she went on pushing the buggy and didn't say anything.

It wasn't long before I heard the wagon coming up from the barn and rumbling into the back yard, so I went out to watch Kiddo and Bubba help load up. They were carrying big baskets of tomatoes and string beans and placing them in the back of the wagon. Cally was sitting in the driver's seat waiting for the ladies to get settled on the tailgate, while Mammy kept giving last-minute instructions.

"Mattie, I don't know when Mr. Neal will come in from the fields, but be sure to have dinner ready no later than twelve-thirty." Mattie kept nodding and saying, "Yes'm" every other word. "And don't let the children out of sight for a minute. They're quick as lightning. Mr. Gunn and the boys will pick us up at the Jennings' when he gets finished at the mill. We should be home by mid-afternoon."

Mother called out from the wagon, "Now Buster, you be sure you mind Mattie Riley. You be a good boy, honey." She bent over and kissed me and sat down on the tailgate of the wagon. Mammy and Allie were on either side of her with two open umbrellas over them.

I laughed at them. They looked funny sitting there with their legs hanging over the back. "You all look pretty silly sittin' there holding umbrellas, and it's not even raining."

Mother laughed too, but Mammy said, "Never you mind, now. At least we won't get too hot and sweaty." She looked up at Cally, who had been waiting for Kiddo and Bubba to climb up on the seat with him. "Make haste, now. I expect Mrs. Jennings is waiting for us right now." And the wagon rolled out of the yard and into the lane.

After they had gone, the house was very still. The only sound I could hear was Mattie Riley, humming softly in the kitchen as she built up the fire in the stove getting ready to cook our dinner. I could hear the baby, too, fretting a little, and Sissy talking to him, trying to quiet him down. The house had never seemed so big and lonesome with none of the folks there to talk to, and there was just nobody to play with. I saw Bessie eating grass down by the well and decided for a minute I'd go tease her with a stick and make her run. But Pappy had seen me doing it once and said, "Don't do that to the cow, son. You'll make her spoil her milk." So I decided just to leave old Bessie alone and let her spoil her own milk; she was eating pretty close to a patch of bitter weeds anyway.

The baby started setting up a loud howl, and Sissy grabbed him up and took him back to the kitchen where Mattie Riley was stirring something on the stove. Sissy looked at her. "I can't get him to take his nap," she said. Mattie looked at the baby and rubbed her finger on the side of his face.

"Hey there, li'l ole Billy Boy," she said, and he yelled louder than ever. Sissy looked a little scared. "What do you think we ought to do, Mattie?"

"Ain't nothin' wrong with this here chile 'ceptin' he missin' his mama's titty." She crossed over to where Sissy was holding the baby. "Miss Allie done leave you a sugar tit?" she asked.

Sissy shook her head. I don't think she knew what it was any more than I did.

"Then I fix him one right now. That'll quieten him down some." She mixed a little sugar in some warm water from the stove and kept stirring it around with a spoon. Then she tore off a clean piece of cloth from a sugar sack and spooned a little of the sugar water on it, twisted the cloth around and around, and tied it up tight with a string. One end of the cloth stuck out all wet and oozy almost like a nipple, and she plopped it into Billy's squalling mouth.

He stopped crying that very minute and started sucking on the twisted end of the cloth. His eyes got all big and excited looking, and then his arms and legs started moving and kicking in every direction. He'd suck for a minute and kick for a minute and then stop to make funny little squeals.

"Ain't never yet seed no young-un that a sugar tit won't

pacify." And she turned back to the stove and started making a pan of cornbread.

Pappy came in from the fields where he'd been hoeing cotton all morning even before Mattie had to ring the dinner bell. He looked all hot and sweaty and said, "Whew! It sure is hot out in that cotton patch this morning. Looks like some of those weeds have grown overnight." He took a big drink of water from the bucket by the kitchen safe, swallowed all of the dipper down, and then mopped his face with a handkerchief as big as a dish rag. "Mattie," he said as he turned to the stove where she stood, "I'm going to lie down and rest a spell before I go back to weed the cornfield this afternoon." He looked at me and Sissy and then said, smiling weakly, "Right after dinner, do you think you could keep these children in the back yard so I could get a catnap?"

"They ain't gonna bother you none, Mr. Neal," she said. "I see to that for sho'." She was dishing up some green beans and cutting the cornbread as she spoke.

Just Sissy, Pappy, and I sat down at the big table for dinner. He prayed over the food for a long time, while Mattie stood above him fanning some flies away from the table. After he'd finished praying ("Oh Lord, how badly we do need rain if you can see fit to send it!"), he began to eat, smiling quietly to himself and saying to Mattie, "You've cooked a fine meal, Mattie. This tastes very good! Thank you." And she grinned at all of us and went into the kitchen.

When Pappy had eaten the late bite, he pushed his chair back from the table and looked at the two of us who were still eating some blackberry cake that Allie had baked yesterday. "Think you two can be sort of quiet while I try to rest a while?"

"Sure, Pappy," Sissy spoke up right away. "We'll take the baby out in the back yard under the oak tree so's he won't bother you." And then she added, "We'll play out there too, and we'll be real quiet."

"That's a good girl," Pappy said. "I'll wait till the sun cools off a little and then head back for the fields." Then he got up, and we heard him going upstairs to the east bedroom.

After Mattie had cleared off the table, Sissy bumped the baby buggy down the back steps, and we sat under the big oak tree. It shaded the whole back yard and half of the house, and it took four grown-ups—Mammy, Allie, Cally, and Mother—to reach around it. I knew because I had seen them do it once. And after they had done it, I remember Mother asking, "How old do you suppose this tree is, Cally?"

"I don't know, Polly. Must be at least a hundred or a hundred and fifty years old. Just look at those branches!"

Those branches seemed to stretch out and over the whole back yard. On the hottest days we would play out there and never once be bothered with the hot summer sun. Sissy had stretched the mosquito netting over Billy's buggy, and he had finally gone sound asleep. Sissy and I were thinking about making some mud pies, except I didn't want to go down to the well to fetch water to mix with the dirt. We were sitting under the tree deciding what to do when Mattie Riley suddenly stuck her head out the back door.

"Somebody comin' up the front lawn!" It couldn't be any of our folks or she would have said so, and anyway her voice sounded too upset. It was somebody she didn't know, and strangers were unusual at Riverside. I ran through the kitchen into the dining room and through the front hall. I stood looking out the front door.

A tall man was walking up the front path. He had on a dark gray suit and carried a small black bag in his hand, and as I watched, he took off his black hat and fanned himself with it. I'd never seen him before and yet I thought I had, but I couldn't remember where. He came on up to the front steps, and I guess he saw me peeping around the door. "Hello there, boy." His voice sounded kind of happy when he spoke. "Is your mamma at home?"

"No, sir," I answered, still looking at him from the doorway. "Just Mattie Riley."

"Who is she?" he wanted to know.

"She's staying with us today while the folks are away." And then I remembered Pappy upstairs asleep. "But Pappy's here. He's taking a nap."

"No, he ain't." It was Mattie, who had come to the door behind me. "Please, sir, can I hep you, sir?" She was looking at him up one side and down the other, and she didn't seem at all sure what to do next.

"Well," the man said, "I'm not sure. I'm looking for Mr. Will Neal. I'm his brother Henry from Texas."

I suddenly came from behind the door, ran right up to him, and said, "Then I know you. I've heard Mammy tell about you. You're as different as day and night!"

When I said that, he laughed and scooped me right into his arms and hugged me real tight and then held me away from him to get a better look at me. He was still laughing when he asked me, "Which one of Allie's boys are you—Bubba?"

"No, sir, I'm Buster. I live in Terre Haute."

"Then you must be one of Polly's boys."

"Yes, sir," I said, but I didn't understand exactly what he meant by one of her boys.

"'Scuse me, sir, Miss Allie and them gone up to Miz Jennings' for some cannin' today, but they be back pretty soon. And I reckon Mr. Neal done gone back to the field. Soon's I heerd you talkin' I went upstairs to call him, but he done gone." Then Mattie Riley started bowing and backing away toward the parlor. "'Scuse me, sir. Come on in to the parlor and set down and rest yourself, and I go call him from the fields," she said and almost ran out to the kitchen.

Brother Henry sat down in the big oak chair by the piano, fanning himself with his hat. Just then Sissy came running up the hill, but she stopped dead still, breathing hard, when she saw the man sitting in her mother's parlor.

I went over and took her hand and led her over to the chair. It was the only time that summer that I felt older than Sissy. "This is Brother Henry, and he's from Texas," I told her. "He's come to see Pappy."

He looked at her for a long time. Then he leaned over and kissed her and said, "Well, you are bound to be Allie's little girl. You look exactly like her."

"Yes, sir, that's what Mammy says." Then she added, "You're Pappy's brother, aren't you?"

"That's right, his oldest brother."

Sissy looked at him for a very long time before she spoke again, as if she weren't sure she should say what she was thinking, but she finally did. "But you don't look oldest. Pappy has a big gray mustache and doesn't wear any teeth."

Brother Henry let out a big laugh and leaned over and whispered to us real loud. "Thank you, missy. That makes me feel real good, but maybe we better not tell him that!"

"'Scuse me, sir." Mattie was standing in the parlor doorway with a big glass in her hand. "I done brung you a cool drink of buttermilk. Might freshen you up after your long trip." She brought it over to him with a big white Sunday napkin on a plate. "I done ring the dinner bell to call Mr. Neal, and I 'speck he be comin' up to the house before long."

"Thank you, Mattie." He took a long drink of buttermilk, smacked his lips, and wiped his mouth. "Ah, that sure does hit the spot." He was taking another drink from the glass when Mattie moved quickly to the front door and looked out.

"Here they come, Mr. Henry. Miss Allie and them, I mean." I ran to the front window and looked out. The wagon was just turning in from the lane, and Mammy and Mother and Allie were still sitting on the tailgate with their legs dangling over. Sissy had run up behind me, and we were jumping up and down with excitement.

"Come on, Sissy, come on. Let's run out to tell 'em about Brother Henry." We were both running to the front door as fast as we could when Brother Henry called to us sharply, "Wait a minute, children!" We stopped and turned to him. He was grinning like a little boy and crooked his finger for us to come closer. When we did he leaned over and put his arms around both of us and sort of whispered to us like it was a secret.

"Tell you what, now! Why don't we just sit here and be talking when they come in. Let's surprise 'em when they come in here. What do you say?"

Sissy and I giggled. It sounded like fun to us. We kept nodding our heads up and down, yes, and then I thought of something Mammy always said.

"You mean like one of your—uh—" I couldn't think of the words she used. "One of your jokes?"

But Brother Henry understood what I meant right away. He laughed and nodded his head.

"Exactly! Just like one of my famous practical jokes." And he seemed to be as excited as we were as we sat there waiting for them to come in.

Cally let Mother and Allie and Mammy out by the front steps, and then we could hear the wagon driving off toward the barn. Sissy and I sat together on the wooden settee, fidgeting and giggling with excitement. Brother Henry shook his head and put his finger up to his lips to quiet us. I heard the front door screen slam to, and Mammy called, "Mattie, we're back," and then she was passing the open parlor door, headed for the kitchen. She saw us out of the side of her eye, changed her mind, and turned toward the parlor. "What in the world are you children doing in here?" Her voice faded away when she saw a man sitting there, and she stood perfectly still.

Brother Henry stood up and smiled. "How are you, Sister Alice? I'm sorry if I frightened you. I've been having a nice talk with the children here."

Mammy still couldn't say anything for a minute. Then she began to try to do everything at once. She smoothed her hair back and straightened her wrinkled dress. "Why, Brother Henry, my, my, what a surprise!" She crossed to him and kissed him on the cheek. "When did you get here and why didn't you let us know you were coming? Did Lottie come with you? Is everything all right at home?"

Brother Henry laughed, "Slow down, Sister Alice, slow down now. I'll tell you all about it while you catch your breath."

Mammy began to fuss with her hair and dress again with a nervous little smile on her face.

"I must look a sight. The girls and I have been up to a neighbor's canning tomatoes all morning till just now." She sat down in a rocker and patted her dress. "I declare, Brother Henry, I've never been so surprised in all my days." She looked up and saw Mother and Auntee standing in the parlor door. "Allie, Polly, will you look who's here. This is your Uncle Henry from Texas."

Mother and Allie came over to kiss him, and then everybody began talking at once. Sissy and I just sat swinging our legs on the settee enjoying all the fuss and excitement. In the middle of it all Mammy stood up and said, "Good gracious, here we sit and talk, and I'll wager Will doesn't even know you're here yet." She turned to us. "One of you children go tell Mattie to ring the dinner bell for him."

"She already has," I said.

"My goodness, won't he be surprised to see you!" And Mammy sat down in the chair again.

Then Brother Henry spoke very slowly and clearly.

"Yes ma'am. I do believe he would be surprised to see me right now!" And a very strange and almost scary thing started to happen right in front of our eyes. Brother Henry slowly and carefully pushed his lower teeth up and out of his mouth with his tongue; he raised his hand and stroked his upper lip like it was a mustache and said, "I declare, I do believe I cut my lip a little when I shaved off my mustache!"

It was so still in the parlor that I could hear Mattie Riley humming softly to herself clear out in the kitchen. No one in the parlor said a word for the longest time, and all I could think of was a magic show I had seen one time in Terre Haute at the Hippodrome where a man named Houdini had changed a pretty girl into an old woman. Then Brother Henry broke the spell and started to snicker; then he began to laugh, harder and harder, until the tears were rolling down his face and he almost choked. He wiped his eyes and said, "Oh, my stars. I'd give anything if you all could see your faces right now," and he started laughing all over again.

Allie leaned over as if she still wasn't sure and asked, "Pappy?" She sounded timid. "Pappy? Pappy, is that really you?" Mother giggled and looked at Mammy. Sissy just sat there stone-still, staring at the teeth in his hand and then staring at his face. I still didn't know whether it was Pappy or not, and I didn't know whether I was about to laugh or cry.

Suddenly Allie began roaring with laughter, and then Mother did, too. They grabbed each other and held on for dear life and kept laughing so hard that it looked like they hurt; they would almost quiet down, then they'd look at Brother Henry—at Pappy—and they'd commence laughing harder than ever. Mother grabbed her sides as if she couldn't get another breath and finally managed to say, "Oh Pappa, I can't believe it. I simply can't believe it. You completely fooled every one of us, even Sissy and Bus, didn't he, Mamma? How in the world—"

"You crazy old fool!" Mammy was standing right in front of him now with her lips pushed so tight together that she could barely talk. Her eyes were snapping like fire, and she was almost shaking she was so mad. "Just because you have to act like a fool is no reason to make all of us look like fools. And scaring the children half to death. And here I sat talking like an idiot, and half worrying about Lottie, that she might be sick or worse."

I heard Mother begin to laugh.

"Hush up right now, Polly! Don't encourage him in this anymore. I've had enough of it, I tell you!"

Pappy had risen from his chair with the most surprised look on his face. "Why, Mamma, I thought you liked practical jokes like Henry is always pulling. I thought you—"

"What Brother Henry does is one thing. What you do is something else again."

"I thought it was pretty good." He smirked at her a little. "Fooled you all right, didn't I?"

"Fools' names in their faces!" she snapped. "Well, I just hope you won't be fool enough to go out in public like this."

"Now Mamma—"

"Be quiet. I mean it!" She turned to go.

"Confound you, woman!" That was strong language for Pappy. He ran over to her and grabbed her arm. "All I did was plan a surprise joke. I thought everybody would enjoy it, 'specially you. You're always talkin' about having more fun and enjoying things. Well, it looks to me like you can't enjoy anything at all, you can't even take a practical joke. That's it, isn't it? You got good and fooled, and you can't even take a joke, and that's pretty sad."

I'd never heard Pappy make such a long speech before. Allie spoke up and said, "Come on now, Mamma, it was all in fun, and we did get fooled all right. Every one of us." And she giggled.

Mammy just stood there looking at all of us. Then she marched to the door and turned to face Allie and Mother.

"I'm going to the kitchen to help Mattie put the canning things away. I've got no time for anymore of this foolishness." Then she stared past Pappy as if he wasn't there. "Oh, and if you should see Mr. Neal, tell him if he wants any supper he'd best get one of you all to fix it for him!" And she went down the hall walking very fast.

Pappy followed her out to the hall. "Confound that woman!" he said. "I thought it would be a good joke and she'd enjoy it. My, but she is as stubborn as they come!"

"Pappa," Mother went up to him. "She'll be all right as soon as she realizes how funny it all was."

"Pappa, when did you plan all this?" Allie was still sitting on the piano bench. "Where did you get that suit, and when did you shave off your mustache? I didn't even know—"

"I don't want to talk about it anymore!" He was standing in the front hall, looking toward the kitchen. "Confounded woman—if she can't take a joke, then let's just forget about it!" And he stomped up the stairs to the east bedroom.

When Cally came in from the barn a little later I heard him ask Allie, "What in the world is the matter with Mammy, do you know?" He looked out the door and lowered his voice. "She's back in the kitchen puttin' some of the canned tomatoes away, and she's broken two jars already. She's even run Mattie out of there, and she won't say a word to anybody. I asked her what was the matter, and all I got out of her was a 'huh.'"

Allie and Mother told him what had happened in the parlor,

and Cally started laughing. "Hush now, Cally, unless you want the roof to blow off again," Allie said.

Later on, I asked mother if that was really Pappy pretending to be Brother Henry, and she said, "Yes, it was, honey, but for heaven sakes, don't say another word about it just now!"

"I thought it was a real good joke, didn't you?"

"It certainly was," she laughed, "but it sure did backfire on poor old Pappy. I guess Allie and I really will have to fix supper this evening." She turned to me quickly. "Now mind you. Don't you and Sissy dare to say anything about this at the supper table tonight!"

Sissy and I went on the front porch to sit on the steps and talk it all over. It was the most exciting thing that had happened at Riverside nearly all summer long and we had been a part of it. Oh, lots of times we did things that were fun and made us laugh, but usually the grown-ups just smiled at us and said something like, "Well that's nice. That must have been fun." But this time they had been a part of it too, along with us, and they had laughed harder than anybody.

"I betcha I know when he did it," Sissy said.

"Did what?" I asked.

"Shaved off his mustache and dressed up like Brother Henry."

"When do you think?"

"When he went upstairs and told us to be quiet that he was gonna take a nap. I'll betcha anything that's when he did it."

"Yeah," I began to think it over. "I bet you're right. 'Cause don't you remember, Sissy, he asked us to be real quiet after dinner, and you said we'd take Billy and play in the back yard, remember?"

"Yeah, that's when he did it." Then she thought about something else. "And most probably Mattie didn't see him come down the stairs and go out because she was cleaning up in the kitchen. I just betcha that's when he did it!"

"Most probably," I agreed.

But something was still bothering Sissy. I could tell from the look on her face. "What is it?" I asked.

"What I can't figure—" She looked uncertain about it. "I can't figure out where he got that suit he was wearing. I've never seen Pappy wearing that suit before."

"Maybe it's his Sunday suit."

"No, it ain't. His Sunday suit is dark blue. I think it's the only real suit he's got."

"Maybe he borrowed it from somebody."

"Who from?"

I didn't know, and we sat there trying hard to figure it out. It sure was a puzzle to us because . . .

"Allie! Polly!" Pappy called. We jumped up and ran to the front screen. He was standing on the stairs, wearing his regular work clothes. And he looked mad. Mother and Allie came out of the front bedroom.

"Have either of you girls seen my lower teeth?" he asked them.

"No, Pappa, I haven't." Allie looked at him, trying to get used to him without his mustache. "Where did you have them last?"

"Right in the parlor when I pulled 'em out of my mouth. And then," he pointed to the kitchen, "your mother got so all-fired mad when she couldn't take a joke, and I followed her out here and stood right here with 'em in my hand," and he banged the newel post with his fist. I looked down at the floor half expecting to see his teeth lying there.

"Have you looked upstairs, Pappa?" Mother asked.

"Yes, I have looked upstairs, Daughter! Mamma may think I'm an old fool, but I'm not blind yet." Pappy never called Mother or Allie "Daughter" unless he was very happy or very mad, and he was very mad. "And if your mother finds 'em she'll more than likely throw 'em in the slop bucket." He turned and went back upstairs.

"We'll look for them down here, Pappa," Allie called after him. "We'll find them down here someplace, I'm sure."

But we didn't. Mother and Allie searched all over the parlor; they sent me and Sissy out to the front porch to look, even though we told them he hadn't been out there all afternoon; they searched the front bedroom, too, with Cally pitching in to help; Mother crept upstairs and looked in both bedrooms, and we could hear Pappy shout, "Polly, I told you they weren't here!" So she ran quickly back downstairs again. Cally even called Mattie into the front hall, whispered something in her ear, and Mattie went out to empty the slop bucket. But before she did, she reached down with her hands and felt all through the slop trying to feel if Pappy's teeth were in there somewhere, but they weren't. We never did find them. When Mattie left in the late afternoon to go home, Mammy finally came out of the kitchen. She walked right into the front parlor, and she didn't look at anyone. She sat down in the big rocker by the fireplace and began rocking back and forth, faster and faster. Sissy saw her from the front bedroom and started skipping over to her. But before she got there, Allie grabbed her arm and swung her back into the hall.

"Mary Evelyn!" When Allie called her Mary Evelyn it meant business. "You just leave Mammy alone, you hear me? Just let her sit there and rock till she's rocked her mad out. You hear me, now!"

So Sissy and I sat together on the front steps, not saying anything at all. It just seemed like a good idea to stay out of the grown-ups' way for the rest of the evening.

Just about sundown we heard Allie going through the house calling, "Come on, everybody. Supper's on the table."

We got up from the steps and went back to the dining room and sat in our side-by-side places. We didn't say a word; neither did anybody else. Someone of the family must have told Kiddo and Bubba about what happened that afternoon because they were sitting across from us, looking down at their plates and not saying a word. Cally was at one end of the table, and Pappy was at his regular place at the head of the table. Mammy was next to him as always. Mother and Allie brought in a pan of hot cornbread and a dish of leftover green beans, and Allie said, "Well, I guess that's it," and they both sat down at their places.

Everything was so quiet that I looked up at all the faces in the lamplight. Pappy sat staring straight in front of him; Mammy's mouth was pushed tight together; Kiddo's eyes were looking at first one and the other, and then he looked down at his plate. Nobody said anything at all. Finally I heard Mammy clear her throat, and I looked up. She was staring hard at Pappy, and then she stretched her neck to be able to see Cally at the far end of the table. "Cally, will you ask Mr. Neal if he is ever going to say the blessing?"

I looked up at Pappy. He hadn't budged, and his eyes didn't look at Mammy one time. He just sat there. And then looking straight at Cally he said, "Well, you tell Mrs. Neal that Mr. Neal isn't here. He's gone to Texas to visit his Brother Henry."

I wanted to laugh, but nobody else seemed to think it was funny, so I didn't.

Very quickly Allie said, "Cally, will you say the blessing, please!"

"Lord forgive us all our sins and save us and bless this food to the nourishment of our bodies we ask in Christ's name. Amen." He said it so low and so fast that I could barely hear. Then Mother and Allie began to pass the food from one of us to the other, but still nobody was talking like they always did at suppertime. Kiddo and Bubba were eating fast with their heads almost down in their plates, and it didn't seem like a good supper at all to me.

Allie finally looked up at Pappy and asked, "Pappy, did you ever find your teeth?" And for the first time Mammy looked up at him, too.

He took a big swallow of his buttermilk, and then very quietly he answered her. "Yes, ma'am, I did."

"Well, I'm glad," Allie said and seemed to be waiting for him to say something more. When he didn't, she finally asked again, "Well, where in the world were they, Pappa?"

We all looked up at him then, but it was a very long time before he ever answered her. But finally he gave a big sigh and said very quietly, "In my mouth."

"In your—" Allie began, but then she stopped right away and put her hand over her mouth.

Everybody sat very still at the table, and it was so quiet all I could hear were the katydids calling to each other from the back yard. Katy-did-she-didn't, katy-did-she-didn't, she-did, she-didn't.

I don't know who it was that giggled first, but before I knew what was happening, everybody at the supper table was laughing, almost as loud or maybe louder than they were that afternoon in the parlor. Kiddo and Bubba looked at each other. Bubba had just taken a drink of buttermilk and spewed it all over his plate. Allie tried so hard not to laugh, but then she just gave in and put her head down on the table by her plate, and her shoulders began to shake like she was crying. But she wasn't. I turned to look at Mammy. Her mouth was all screwed up tight again, but it was different this time, as if it might pop open any minute, and her eyes didn't look mad anymore. She looked right at Pappy and spoke to him like he was really there.

"Well, Pappa, maybe you've finally gotten used to those false teeth after all." And she began laughing too.

Pappy took another sip of buttermilk and wiped his lips as if he still had a mustache, and then he looked at Mammy. "Looks to me like it's all right for you to laugh when the joke's on me, but it's a different story when I play a joke on you." He pushed his chair back from the table and started to get up. Mammy reached over and took his hand.

"Now just wait a minute! You can't blame me for getting mad. You gave me such a shock I couldn't even think straight this afternoon." She got a funny look in her eyes. "How do you think I would feel going up to bed with a perfect stranger tonight?"

"Pshaw, Mamma, what's the matter with you?" Then he looked up and saw me listening to every word. "And don't forget," he leaned over to her, "little pitchers have big ears."

"You talkin' about me?" I asked, and everybody laughed again.

Sissy got up and ran around to Pappy's side. "Pappy, what I want to know is where did you find that suit you had on this afternoon? You know, when you dressed up like—" She looked to see if Mammy was getting mad again. "—when you dressed up like that."

He laughed. "Just shows you how much you all know that goes on around here. Your Uncle Wallace gave me that suit just before he left to go back. Said he had nearly worn it out anyway."

"Well, I never," said Mother, and then she laughed a little, and things seemed to get back to normal all around the table. "I will never forget how he took us all in." She kept shaking her head.

Mammy got up from the table and stood behind Pappy's chair, "Come on, Pappa," she said, "let's go sit on the front porch and cool off a little before we go to—" She looked at me and stopped. "I declare, I'm gonna hafta put some cotton in your big ears, Buster!" She laughed and took Pappy by the arm. "Come on, you old fool," she said, and they went out into the front hall. The last thing we heard was the front screen door slam as they went on out to sit on the porch. Allie and Cally and Mother looked at each other and smiled. Allie let out a big breath. "Well," she said, "I guess the storm is over."

It was getting close to the time for us to go back to Terre Haute. I didn't know it except by the way all the grown-ups were acting. Mammy would sit down on the front porch, fan herself with her apron, and say, "My goodness, I don't know where the summer has gone." I'd look up at her. "But it's still here, isn't it, Mammy?" I'd say, and she'd be looking at me with a kind of sad expression on her face. Or maybe Allie would grab me for no reason at all, hug me real tight, and say, "That's my good Bussie Boy," and go hurrying off to the kitchen. Then one day I came into the little back bedroom, and Mother was packing her trunk.

"Are we going back to Terre Haute today?" I asked.

"No, not today," she said, "but pretty soon."

"When is pretty soon?"

"Well, let me see now." She stopped putting things in the trunk and thought for a minute. "Today is Monday, and Cally got our train tickets for Friday. So we'll catch the afternoon train on Friday."

"This Friday?" She nodded and went back to packing the trunk. "Why can't we stay a little longer?"

She sat down on the bed and folded up some things in little bundles to put in the trunk. "Well, I've got a lot of things to do when we get back. First off, you have to have some warm clothes for winter. You'll be in the first grade this year, and you'll need some new things for school. And Daddy will be home this week, not out on the road. I've already written him when we're leaving, and he'll be at the station to meet us."

"But why can't we stay a little longer?" I wanted to know.

"Now, I just got through telling you, Buster, so don't bother me about it anymore!" She got up from the bed and put the folded things into the trunk. I sat down on the side of the bed and didn't say anything for a while. It got very quiet in the room, until Mother started sniffling as if she had a summer cold.

"I don't want to go back," I said. She turned to look at me and saw that something was the matter. She came over to the bed and put her arm around me and pulled my face up to look at me. "Don't you even want to see your daddy?"

"Sure I do but—"

"Now, honey, listen to me for a minute." She cleared her throat and started again. "Your daddy has been very lonesome for us while we've been down here, so we have to go back to look after him, don't we?" I didn't say anything. "Anyway, we'll come back to Riverside for a visit with all the folks next summer, or the summer after. And that'll be something nice to look forward to, won't it?" I turned my head away. "Won't it?" she asked again.

"I guess so."

"Now then, you run out in the yard and see if you can find Sissy to play with. We've still got four whole days left to do lots of things." Then she smiled. "Maybe we'll go down to the branch tomorrow." She went over to the trunk. "Now you run along and let me finish this. I don't want to be packing this old trunk up to the last minute. Now scoot."

I didn't exactly scoot, but I went on through the house and

out to the front porch. Nobody was in the front yard that I could see, so I went around to the back. Sissy was sitting under the oak tree making some mud pies, and I sat down to watch.

"I'm going to bake some chocolate cakes for the church supper," she said. "Do you want to help me?"

I didn't answer her at all; I just sat there looking at the mud oozing between her fingers. Finally she looked up at me and asked again. "Do you want to help or not?"

"Did you know we're going back home in four days?"

"Uh-huh. Mother told me yesterday."

"Why didn't you tell me then?" I wanted to know. I felt sort of put out that she knew it before I did.

"Well, you know it now anyway, don't you?" And she kept on fiddling with her mud pies. So I got up and started walking around the side of the house. Sissy called to me, "Come on back, Bus, and let's play church supper. Come on. Now."

I kept on going. "I don't want to. I don't feel like it." And that's the way it was that day, and the next day too. I just didn't feel like doing anything. I'd wake up in the morning feeling real good, and then right after breakfast I'd start remembering that we were leaving for Terre Haute in a couple of days, and I wouldn't feel like doing anything. Even the grown-ups began to notice the way I was acting. I heard Mammy say to Mother one afternoon when I was just sitting on the front porch doing nothing at all, "Polly, do you think he might be bilious?" I got up and walked down to the well so she couldn't dose me with Calomel.

The day before we left, Cally and Bubba and Kiddo hauled the trunk out of the house and loaded it into the wagon. Cally was taking the trunk to the station to check it through to Terre Haute so it would arrive there when we did. Mother and Allie were going into town with him. Allie said she was out of vanilla extract for the cake she was going to bake for our train trip, and Mother said she was going along for the ride. After they'd gone, I went in the house to find Sissy. She was in the front bedroom pushing the baby buggy. I stood there and watched her for a while until I got tired; then I said, "I don't see why you have to push that baby buggy all day. This is the very last day I'm gonna be here."

"He'll be asleep in a little while," she whispered, but just then Billy started to cry.

"Oh, shoot," I cried and went out the front door and slammed the screen behind me. Billy let out a squall, and I was glad, but then I was sorry because Sissy would have to push him in the buggy that much longer.

I ran down the front lawn when I saw Mattie Riley standing by the well with some clothes in her hand. "Hi, Mattie," I called as I came up closer. "You washin' the clothes today? Want me to help you get the fire started?"

"Ain't buildin' no fire today," she said, and she smiled down at me. "This here's just a few of Miss Polly's pretty things she gonna wear tomorrow for the train trip. You don't boil clothes like this. You just wash 'em with your hands real easy like."

"Didn't Leroy come over with you today?" I asked. She cocked her eye around to me, but I could tell she wasn't mad.

"Course he come with me," she said, "and then the minute I gets here he done vamoose!"

"I bet I know where he is," I yelled. "You want me to go get him for you?"

"No siree I don't!" I looked up at her very surprised. "Oh, honey, you can go on down to the railroad and set with him if'n you wants to. But I just as soon not have him messin' round up here while I got these clothes to finish. Go on down there if'n you wants to." She smiled at me and turned back to the well trough.

I hurried down the lane toward the stile, but when I got to it there wasn't a sign of Leroy anywhere. I climbed up the steps, stood on the top step, and looked everywhere for him, but Leroy was nowhere in sight. I cupped my hands and yelled "Leroy!" as loud as I could. Everything was very still; I thought I could hear a cowbell from across the railroad tracks, but I wasn't sure.

"Boo!" I jumped so hard that I fell off the stile down onto the red clay bank and skinned my knee on a piece of gravel. It was Leroy all right. He had sneaked up from the bushes behind me and now was sitting on the stile, giggling at me. "Heard you comin' way up the road," he grinned.

"And look what you made me do!" I was holding my knee. He hopped down to look closer.

"Ain't nothin' but a li'l ole scratch." Then he looked up at me with a little worried expression. "It ain't your bad leg, is it?"

He looked so upset I smiled and said, "No, Leroy, it's all right. It's not even bleeding. See?" And I showed him.

"That's good," he said. "'Cause we got to do us a little walkin' today for sho'!"

"Walk where? Where we walking to?"

"I got me some fishin' poles down by the river. I hid 'em down there yestiddy mornin'." He looked at me to see how I was taking his news, and he could see I was getting pretty excited. I stood up, forgetting about my skinned knee. "We going fishing?" I was almost jumping up and down.

Leroy got up very slowly, put his hands on his hips like his mama did, and looked me right in the eye. "You didn't think I'se gonna let you go back to that ole Terre Haute town without catchin' you a single fish, did you? Come on!" He took my hand, and we started off toward the Chunky River bridge.

"It's a good fishin' place right smack under the bridge," he said as we strolled along by the side of the tracks. "There's a ole stump stickin' up outta the water, and that's a good place to fish."

I looked back over my shoulder and couldn't even see the stile or the house, and I wondered for a minute if I'd get a whipping when I got home. But I didn't wonder very long because Leroy had stopped near the river bank and was bending over some willow branches. Then he pulled out two long poles—little tree limbs, they looked like to me—from under the willow trees and strolled on down to the river. I followed as fast as I could, and when I got there, he was busy with a tin can. "These here the worms," he said.

"What are these for?" I asked.

He looked up from his work as if he thought I was joking. When he saw I wasn't, he finished putting a worm on a hook at the end of each string that was tied to the end of the poles. He stuck the ends of the poles into the sand and sat down by me. Very slowly he explained. He sounded like my kindergarten teacher.

"You puts the worm on the hook. Then you throws the hook in the water. If'n the fish see the worm he gonna eat it, and if'n he do, he gonna get caught on the hook. When he pull on the hook to get away, you pull up on the line." He looked at me closely to be certain for sure I was understanding it all. "And there is your fish!" he finished.

Then I asked another silly question. Anyway, Leroy seemed to think it was silly. "What if they don't want the worm?" I asked.

"Then they just ain't bitin'."

He made it sound easy, so I took my pole and threw my line in the river, near the old stump, and stood there waiting. He looked at me and said, "Now just set down on the bank and wait. Sometime there's a lotta waitin' go on when you fishin'."

I looked over at Leroy. He was lying in the warm sand with his legs crossed and using his arms for a pillow. I sat down and did the same thing. I kept looking at my pole to see if anything was pulling on it. Nothing was.

Leroy sat there watching his pole and wiggling his toes in the sand. "You leavin' tomorrow on the train?" I turned to him, but he wasn't even looking at me, just wiggling his toes in the sand. He didn't sound sad, he was just asking a question for himself. He sounded like one of the grown-ups, so I wiggled my toes, too, and said, "Yep."

"You gonna sleep on it again?"

"I guess so. Yep!"

He raised his head to take a quick look at his pole, then he laid down in the sand again. "Sho' do wish I could take me a ride on that train." He looked at the tracks right above our heads. He was still looking up at them when I suddenly saw my pole begin to jerk up and down. "Leroy, Leroy!" I shouted, "What is that movin' my pole? Is that a fish?"

He jumped up, scattering sand all over us, and whispered, "Grab your pole and be quiet. You got a bite for sho'." Then he said, "Take your pole real careful now and give it a good jerk. Hurry up now!"

I took up my pole and raised it up, and there was a fish flopping on the end of the line. "Look, Leroy, look, " I cried, "it's a fish!"

"Jerk your pole back!" he yelled. "Jerk it back or it'll get away!" Leroy was dancing up and down.

I gave the pole a big jerk, and the fish went flying up in the air, flopped over once, hit the water, and disappeared. There was nothing on the end of the line now. I kept looking at it and finally said, "Where'd he go, Leroy? Where'd he go?"

Leroy shook his head in disgust. "He done gone back home to his mammy. He won't be comin' back here today for shore!"

"But I nearly had him, didn't I, Leroy? Didn't I nearly have him?" I was so excited I couldn't hear what Leroy said. "Oh, I wish I'd caught him so I could take it back and show the folks. They'll never believe I really caught a fish."

"Well, you didn't really catch him. He sorta got away."

I wasn't paying much attention to what he said. "But I had him caught, didn't I, Leroy? I had him caught before he got away! What kind of fish do you think it was?"

"Look like a li'l ole perch to me."

"He wasn't so little!" I cried. "He wasn't so little at all. I bet he was nearly 'bout a-a foot long!"

Leroy started laughing so hard that he fell down and began rolling over in the sand. "That's 'bout the best fish story I done ever heard." He kept on laughing and rolling. "'Bout a foot long!"

I stood there watching him with his hands holding his stomach; he was almost squealing, and I was getting madder by the minute. "Well, go on," I said. "Go on! Just keep laughin' all day long. I'm going back to the house and tell the folks. I betcha they won't laugh." And I turned and started up the riverbank.

I hadn't gone very far when I could hear Leroy following along after me, but I didn't even turn around to look at him. I just kept on running toward the stile. I climbed up and over it and went on up the lane as fast as I could. Leroy had caught up with me by then and was trotting by my side. When he saw I wasn't going to slow down to talk to him he said, "It wasn't a foot long." He was breathing hard. "But you can tell 'em it was a pretty good size." He turned his head toward me. "It was. Pretty good size ole fish!"

"I know it," I said and kept on running.

Mattie Riley was walking up the front lawn with a basket of clothes balanced on her head. "I caught a fish, Mattie," I yelled as I ran past her. "I caught a fish!"

"That's good, that's good." Then she said something else, but I had already reached the front steps with Leroy right behind me, and I yanked open the screen door running through the house yelling, "Mother, Mother, Mammy, Auntee, I caught a fish, I caught a fish!" I could hear voices in the kitchen, and I ran out there and bumped into Mother in the doorway and nearly knocked her over.

"Buster, what in the world is the—"

"I caught a fish." I was so breathless by now I could hardly get the words out. "Mother, I caught a fish! I mean, I didn't catch him really, but he was caught on the line and then he—and Leroy said he was a pretty good size, didn't you Leroy?—and then when I pulled him out he—"

I was breathing so hard I couldn't say anything more right then. Mother knelt down by my side and said slowly, "Now just calm down for a minute and then you can tell us all about it." But I didn't want to calm down.

"Leroy said he was most probably a perch, didn't you, Leroy?" Everybody in the kitchen was listening to me now and smiling. Mother and Mammy and Allie, and Bubba, too, who was standing by the stove. I was getting a little tired by now, and I went over to sit on a stool. "And then when I jerked my pole up to catch him, he just sorta flopped over and fell back into the river!" And I sat down, ker-plash!

It wasn't a stool. Mammy had just finished churning, and I was sitting right in the middle of her fresh buttermilk with my legs and head in the air and my bottom stuck in the churn. I was spitting and choking and so surprised that I burst into tears.

I remember that Allie was the first one to reach me. She came over and held my arms while Bubba pulled the churn off of my bottom. I was covered with buttermilk, and some of it was even in my hair and running down my face. As they pulled me out I saw that all of them were laughing, and the harder they laughed the harder I cried. Mammy came over to me, lifted me up in her arms, buttermilk and all, and sat down in a chair with me in her lap.

"There, there, Bussie Boy, you're all right now. You're not hurt. You just got too excited, that's all." And she started wiping my face and hair with a big towel.

By this time, Mother and Allie had found a mop and were cleaning up the buttermilk all over the kitchen floor. Mammy was washing my hands and feet, and I had begun to quiet down a little. Bubba was still laughing as he stood there watching everything that was going on, and then he turned to me with a smirk on his face. "So you caught a pretty good size fish, did you? Well, it's too bad he got away, 'cause if he hadn't—" He was starting to laugh before he finished. "—we could have had fish fried in buttermilk for supper," and then he really let loose. He laughed so hard he had to bend over to keep from falling to the floor.

I was about to tell him to "stop that now!" when he raised up suddenly and got all mad around the mouth. I didn't know what was the matter until he grabbed a handkerchief out of his pocket and said, "Now look what you've done! I bet you've just about ruined 'em, that's what!" I looked down at his feet, and then everyone was staring at them. He had on a pair of brand new shoes that he was wearing around the house that morning to break in, and they were covered with little specks of buttermilk that he was trying to wipe away. I watched him for a minute, and so did the others, trying not to laugh.

Then I looked up at Mother and giggled. "Bubba sorta reminds me of Pappa when his joke backfired on him." They all started laughing again. Bubba stood there looking at all of us and finally said, "Confounded Buster and his damn silly fish," and stalked out of the kitchen.

Mammy finished cleaning me up and put me down, and I ran over to Leroy still standing by the door. Just before we left to go outside, I heard Mammy say, "Like I've always said, Polly, little pitchers have big ears, especially that one. You and Wallace are going to have to watch your p's and q's."

Leroy and I ran out the back door, and when we got to the gate he stopped. "I'm gettin' on home before Mamma catch me. She gonna raise Billy hell if'n she see me!"

He suddenly began sniffing at me—almost like a rabbit—and broke into a wide grin. "You sho' better run down to the branch and wash off your butt 'fore you catch that sleepin' train tomorrow." He began to giggle so hard he could hardly speak. "You startin' to smell like a slop bucket. From now on I guess I better start callin' you Buttermilk Buster!"

He flew out the back gate and started toward home, squealing with laughter. I stood there in a huff with my hands on my hips watching him until he turned suddenly when he reached the pasture gate. He stood there waving and smiling as he called out, "See you next summer." He opened the gate and trotted down the path toward home.

We left for Terre Haute the next day. Mammy wouldn't go to the station with us because she didn't like goodbyes either. When our train passed the stile, there was Leroy—on the top step—waving wildly, almost dancing a jig. I waved back hoping he would see me. And when we passed the Chunky River bridge, there was Mammy, too, standing on the back stoop with a towel in her hands, waving us goodbye.

SUMMER—1924

In July of 1923 Daddy was transferred to Cincinnati, Ohio, and I suppose that was the reason we didn't get back to Riverside that summer. I missed not going, of course, but Mother was busy with packing and moving and then finding a place to live once we got there. It was a busy time for all of us, and we really didn't have a chance to think about going to Riverside. We finally settled in Covington, Kentucky, a city just about the size of Terre Haute. Daddy always called it Cincinnati's bedroom because it was just across the Ohio River from the big city, and many of the people who lived there would go "over the river" to work and come back in the evening to eat and sleep. Mother said she liked living there a little better than Terre Haute because it was closer to home, "not much, but a little." I had been promoted to fourth grade before we moved, and I didn't much like Covington at first; I had to go to a new school, and I didn't know anyone at all, and I kept thinking that everyone in the fourth grade would know a lot more than I did. But Daddy said not to worry; I was probably up with them or maybe even a little ahead of the class.

The first district school started in September, and I could walk to school since we lived only two blocks away. The opening day I was really frightened. It was a big gray brick building with a fenced-in yard for a playground and a big black round thing that looked like a silo attached to the front of it. I didn't know what it was, but I certainly didn't like the looks of it. Later that year I learned that it was a fire escape and it was used only when we had a fire drill. Inside was a circular slide that ran from the third floor to the playground below. The first and second grades were on the first floor and simply walked out the front door during a drill; third- and fourth-grade classes were on the second floor and got a short ride; but the fifth and sixth grades, located on the third floor, always got the longest and best ride of all. They'd whiz around the circular slide three or four times before they'd hit the bottom. Many of the students in my class, right after a fire drill, would say, "I sure hope my teacher passes me to the third floor next year!"

I walked up the front steps into the school on that first morning, found my classroom on the second floor, and went in. It was almost filled with kids about my size, and I had to walk clear to the back of the room to find a seat. Everybody seemed to know each other, but they stared at me and began to whisper when I walked down the aisle between the desks. I sat down and wished the floor would swallow me up.

Then a beautiful young girl came into the room and sat down at the teacher's desk. She shook out her black curly hair, arranged and rearranged some books on her desk, and then she stood up, rapped on the desk with a ruler, and suddenly everything got very quiet. She smiled the nicest smile I could imagine and said: "My name is Miss McArthur. Miss Lucille McArthur. And I will be your teacher this year." She kept right on smiling at us. "But I'm going to need as much help from you this year as I can get." She paused for a minute to get our complete attention. "And do you know why?" Nobody in the class said a thing for a while, and then some little girl near the front door spoke up. "To help you dust the erasers?" she asked.

Miss McArthur laughed and said, "I'm sure I'll need that kind of help as often as I can get it," and she paused, waiting for anyone else to speak. I wanted to ask her if it was because she was a new teacher, but I was afraid to. Then she continued, still smiling, "I'll tell you why I'll need your help. I'm new here. I mean, in Kentucky. I've been teaching for two years, but I've never been in Kentucky before. My home is in Vicksburg, Mississippi, and I feel a little homesick already. So you see, you'll have to help me get used to Kentucky, and my new school, and everything else." I thought she was awfully pretty the minute she came in the room that morning, but when she said that, I fell in love with Miss Lucille McArthur completely. I wasn't afraid of anything anymore, the strange students, the strange building, or anything else about Covington, Kentucky.

When school let out at noon for lunch, I ran all the way home. "Guess what?" I said as soon as Mother opened the door. "Guess where my teacher's from?" Mother looked a little startled. "She's from down home in Mississippi. She lives in Vicks Brothers!"

Then Mother really looked surprised and said, "She lives where?"

"Vicks Brothers," I repeated, "You know, Mother, like the cough drops."

"I'm sure she must have said Vicksburg." She laughed at me. "You're sure she didn't say Vicksburg?"

"I don't know, but I'm sure she said Mississippi."

It was Vicksburg, because one night Mother and Daddy went to a PTA meeting and met Miss McArthur, and when they came home Mother said, "You were right, Bus. She is from Vicksburg, and she's one of the prettiest little things I've ever seen." So in the fourth grade, Miss McArthur made my first year in Covington, Kentucky, one of the happiest times I could remember.

I was a little worried about something on the report card called Composition because I never had that subject in school before. So when the first report came out I was very surprised to see that I had all E's, even in Composition. E was the highest grade you could get, and it stood for Excellent. When I got home that afternoon and showed my report card to Mother, she seemed a little surprised too, but she said, "Oh, Bus, that's just wonderful!" But she kept looking at Composition and would shake her head and smile, "And you were the one that was so worried about your grade in Composition," she said. Then she laughed and added, "Maybe Miss McArthur is just prejudiced in your favor." I didn't exactly know what that meant, but I guess it turned out to be true. Because one time Mother was visiting school when we had something called Parents' Day, and she asked Miss McArthur how I had improved so in Composition. She just smiled at Mother and said, "Oh, Mrs. Briggs, Wallace still makes little mistakes in spelling and grammar, but when he writes about his Mammy and Pappy and his other kinfolk on that farm he calls Riverside, I just get so homesick. I put my head right down on the desk and cry." The next summer when Mother was telling Mammy about the school and what my teacher had said about my compositions, Mammy simply nodded and said, "She sounds like a lovely little lady, and she must be a very fine teacher."

The last day of school that year, I waited after everyone else had left to speak to Miss McArthur. She was cleaning the blackboard, and when she turned and saw me standing in front of her desk, she smiled at me and said, "Well, Wallace, you've certainly made good grades this year, and I've enjoyed having you in my class."

"I have, too," I said.

"I'll be going back home to spend most of the summer with my mother." She lowered her eyes for a minute and then looked up at me, almost as if she were telling me a secret. "I don't think you know that I lost my father at Christmastime." I didn't quite understand what she meant. She hesitated a moment longer. "He—he died two days after Christmas, and Mama is all alone now." She looked at me and smiled quietly. "I haven't told any of the other children, but I thought you might want to know."

"Oh, I do, Miss McArthur. I'm glad to know." Somehow I knew I had used the wrong words, but she smiled and said, "I thought you would be."

"We're going back to Riverside next week!" That was what I had been waiting to tell her, and when I did she dropped the erasers she'd been holding and sat down at one of the desks in the front row. She looked almost as little as one of the girls in her class, and she looked so happy that I was sure that I had said the right thing that time.

"That's wonderful, Wallace," she said. "I know you'll have a grand time this summer. It must be a fine farm. When will you be leaving?"

"Some day next week, I think Mother said," I told her. "I can't remember the very day though."

"Just think, you'll be in Mississippi, and so will I." She laughed a little bit. "At the same time! Who knows? We might even run into each other."

I just stood there beaming because I'd made her happy. She leaned over and patted my arm. "Now you run along home before your Mother starts worrying about you." Just as I got to the door the last thing she said to me was "And if I don't see you in Mississippi this summer I'll see you next fall."

I didn't see her in Mississippi that summer, and I didn't see her the next fall either. She didn't come back to teach the fourth grade at all, and I always wondered why.

We left for Riverside the week after school was out. The station in Cincinnati was much bigger than the one in Terre Haute, with many more tracks running through it, and I'd never seen so many people in one place before. Our train was already standing on track eight, and I was afraid that we would miss it. "No need to worry, Bus," Daddy said, "this train is made up here. It doesn't leave for another fifteen minutes."

As we walked into the vestibule of our Pullman car, I looked for the name on the door. Mount Royal. I felt a little disappointed. I was hoping it would be Red Desert again. When we found our seats they had already been made up into beds for the night with the green curtains around them, and we had three berths this time; a lower berth for me and one for Mother across the aisle and an upper berth for Daddy above mine. I told them good night and hopped in my berth and undressed as quickly as I could. The train didn't leave until ten o'clock, and I wanted to see as much as I could as it pulled out of the station. I turned off the night light and raised the shade. There was nothing to see except a lighted day coach across from my window. People were putting suitcases on the racks above their heads, and then settling down in their seats, and I felt sorry for them having to sit up all night long in the day coach.

Just then our train gave a lurch, and we started moving slowly out of the station. I could see the top of the Union Central Building all lit up, and several other tall buildings still had lots of lights burning in their windows, and I wondered if people were still working there this late at night. We rattled over a crossing, and then we were on the bridge over the Ohio River, and it was beautiful. I could see the C & O Railroad bridge that crossed over to Covington. That was the bridge we used when we would sometimes take the streetcar to "go over the river" to Cincinnati.

The bridges had lots of lights on them, and when you looked at the dark water below, the lights seemed to jiggle up and down. It made me think of that night I had seen all those lightning bugs from the train window. When was that? Two or three years ago? I couldn't exactly remember.

Once we had crossed the river, the low Kentucky hills seemed to swallow us up, and I could see nothing but dark blurry shadows passing by, so I turned on the little light above my head. I reached over to the windowsill and picked up the chocolate Hershey bar I had put there when I was undressing. I bought it in the station before we left so I would have something to eat after I went to bed. I had just about finished it when I heard somebody say very quietly, "Hi, Bus! How you doin' down there?" I looked up at the ceiling of the berth, and there was Daddy's head looking at me upside down! I was so surprised I couldn't say anything. I just stared at him. Then finally I raised up from my pillow and laughed at him. "How in the world can you do that?"

"Shh, be quiet," he cautioned. "We don't want to wake anybody up." Then I could see what he had done. He had unhooked the top part of my curtain and had stuck his head through the opening to see if I was all right. He grinned at me. "What are you having, a midnight feast?"

"Yeah. You want a bite?"

"No thanks, son. I just wanted to make sure you were okay. I'll see you in the morning. Sleep well." His head disappeared, and the hooks went back in place.

I took the last bite of my Hershey bar and turned out the light. The train was going very fast now and there was nothing to be seen from the window. I lowered the shade to keep out some of the smoke and cinders if we happened to go through any tunnels. Up in front the engine gave a long, low, dying whistle, and that was the last thing I remembered before I fell asleep.

Riverside hadn't changed at all since my last visit, or if it had I didn't notice. Maybe the white paint on the house had peeled a little more, and there was a new set of wooden steps going up to the front porch. Everything else was the same, except for the baby. Billy had been replaced by a new one, and this one was named David Wallace. He had been born the summer before and was now toddling around on his own and had to be minded almost constantly. Sissy was his main nursemaid that summer, especially during the first week of our visit, because Allie was confined to her bed with malaria fever. Mammy would sometimes pile blankets all over her bed to keep her warm even on the hottest day, but she would keep shaking with chills just the same. The day we arrived I had been so disappointed when I couldn't see Mammy waving to us from the train window. When I asked her why she didn't, she smiled tiredly and said, "Honey, I have been too busy looking after your Auntee to think about much, what with the new baby and all." When I looked at her, she seemed tired, and there were many more wrinkles in her face than I ever remembered. But Dr. Harper had prescribed quinine for Allie to cure her malaria, and I guess it did, because she was up and around before too long.

I was sitting on the front porch one day near the open bedroom windows when I heard Daddy and Allie talking. "It was nice of you and Cally to do that," Daddy said.

"You mean naming the baby David Wallace?"

Daddy must have nodded his head because I couldn't hear him saying anything more.

"Why you know how fond we've always been of you, Wallace!" Allie must have been rocking the baby because I could hear the chair creek back and forth. "And I think it's a beautiful name, don't you?"

"Yes, Pug, yes it is. And I'm awfully proud that you used it because—" Daddy stopped talking for a very long time and then, "Because it looks like Polly doesn't want to—" There was a big silence in the room. Even Allie's rocker had stopped creaking. "Because, Pug, I don't think there's going to be anymore little Busters—or sisters for that matter."

"I know, Wallace." Allie's voice sounded very far away, and then finally I could hear the rocker start up again. "But I still feel that Polly is wrong to be afraid. Having a baby is the most wonderful thing in the world!"

I knew that this was something that I wasn't supposed to be listening to, so I scooted away from under the window and went down the front steps to the well trough, feeling confused inside, and wondering all the time what it was that made Mother afraid. But there was one thing I knew for sure—I was afraid to ask.

During the first part of our visit that summer Sissy was usually so busy taking care of David that I felt deserted. We would begin playing in the back yard, when suddenly Mammy would call out the back door, "Sissy, will you come and mind David for a minute?"

And Sissy, with a shrug, would go into the house, and I might not see her again until dinnertime. Kiddo and Bubba seemed to think they were completely grown-up now; they were either working in the field or maybe I'd see Bubba ride away on a horse and not come home until suppertime. I often wondered where he went, but he never told me. Of course, Billy was usually there. He was four years old now. But like Bubba and Kiddo seemed to feel about me, I felt Billy was still a baby. So those first days that summer didn't seem to offer much fun.

A few days after Allie was up and around the house following her bout with malaria I asked her, "Auntee, when have you seen Leroy?"

"To tell you the truth, Bus, I can't even remember." She was stringing beans on the front porch while Sissy was keeping an eye on David. "He's got a new little baby sister, didn't you know?" Then she added, "Come to think of it, I haven't seen much of Leroy since the baby came. He's probably staying pretty close to home helping Mattie these days."

A little later I decided to walk down to the railroad track, but I didn't really expect to find Leroy there, and I was right; he was nowhere around. I sat on the stile looking up and down the tracks hoping maybe a train might be coming. But I knew it wasn't the right time for one—even a freight. There wasn't a sound I could hear, except for a distant cowbell in somebody's pasture on the far side of the tracks. It was getting very hot sitting on the stile, and I was tired of waiting for a train anyway. So I climbed down off the stile and headed up the lane for the house.

When I came in sight of the well the first person I saw was Mattie Riley. She was bending over the water spout getting a drink. I yelled to her and ran on as fast as I could. "Mattie Riley! Mattie Riley!" I kept calling to her.

"Well, Lawd'n mercy, will you look who's here now!" She was beaming all over. I ran up to her and threw my arms around her big waist. She hugged me and patted me on the back and then pushed me away a little distance so she could really see me. "I do declare how this chile done growed!" She crossed her arms and cocked her eye at me. "How old is you now? Nine or ten?"

"Ten goin' on eleven!" I announced, feeling very grown-up.

"Ten years ole a'ready. My, my, how the time do get away," she said. "Why, you and my Leroy just about the same age. He gonna be 'leven just 'fore Christmas." Then she looked at me and laughed. "I'll have to start callin' you Mister Buster 'fore you know it."

I wanted to ask her why—that puzzled me for a moment—but the thought of seeing Leroy again was more important, and I hurried on excitedly. "Did Leroy come with you?" I asked.

"No, honey, he done stayed over to the house tendin' the baby." Then a huge grin covered her face. "Didn't you know that Mattie done got her a new li'l baby girl? She just four months ole."

"I know," I said. "Auntee told me this morning. But when can I see Leroy? Do you think he might be coming over here today? I sure would like to see him, Mattie!"

She looked at me for a minute, her eyes smiling with a sudden idea, and I could tell she was about to say something important. "I tell you what we do if'n you wants to." From the way she was smiling and speaking I already knew I would want to—whatever it was. "Miss Allie done promise me some pole beans and collards and I'se goin' up to the house to fetch 'em now. S'pose I see if'n Miss Polly let you come home with me for dinner, and then you can see the new baby and Leroy, too."

"Oh, yes, Mattie." That was the most exciting idea I'd heard since arriving at Riverside. "I'd love to see Leroy and have dinner at your house," and then I remembered to add, "and to see your new little baby, too." I grabbed her hand, "Come on, let's go ask Mother right now," and I began pulling her toward the house.

Mother and Allie heard us laughing as we came up the lawn, and they stood out on the front porch to see what was going on. I was half running, tugging at Mattie's hand so hard that she finally freed it and said, "Now you just slow down and hold your horses, chile. I cain't go no faster," and she lumbered up the steps.

"Miss Allie, I done come for the collards and beans." And then she turned to Mother. "I declare Miss Polly, you put a idea in this here boy's head, and he don't let go of it, do he?"

"What is it, Mattie?" Mother asked.

"Tell her, Mattie, ask her now!" I was looking first at Mattie and then at Mother. "Ask her, Mattie."

Mattie was looking a little embarrassed now as she said to Mother, "Ain't no big t'do, Miss Polly. He just wants to go see Leroy, and I tell him I'd take him over, if'n you say so, and he could stay and have some dinner if'n you say so." Mother seemed surprised and just stood there.

"Please, Mother, please, I'd really love to go. Can I go, Mother, please?"

"I be sho' that he got home safe." Mattie added, "Leroy can come back with him through the big pasture."

Mother looked at Allie, who smiled and gave a quick nod of her head. Then she turned to me. "Well, I think that's real nice of Mattie, and I guess it's all right if you really want to go." I started to yell and run around the porch, but Mother caught hold of me. "But before you leave, you go inside and put on your shoes and socks. I don't want you stepping on a sand spur and having it fester on you."

"Do I have to?"

"Do you want to go or not?" I knew by the tone of her voice not to argue anymore, so I went inside to find my shoes.

I put on my shoes and socks and ran back to the kitchen where Allie was filling a big sack with vegetables.

"Miss Allie, I sho' do thank you." Mattie was standing by the kitchen safe. "My pole beans ain't doin' nothin' a-tall this summer. I sho' is thankful for these!"

Mother came into the kitchen to see that I had put on my shoes. She looked at Mattie and smiled. "Now you be sure Buster minds what you say, Mattie." Then she turned to me. "And you mind your manners while you're there."

Mattie threw back her head and laughed. "No need to worry none, Miss Polly. I just gonna treat him like one of mine. He ain't gonna be no bother." She took my hand, and we went out the back door and headed toward the pasture gate.

We followed a cow path down past the barn and then walked in some wagon ruts that crossed the big pasture back of the orchard. It was getting awfully hot when we came up to a big barbed wire fence. I stood there wondering how in the world big Mattie Riley would ever get under it when she suddenly thrust the sack of beans into my arms and said, "Hold these for a minute." She went to one of the fence posts, lifted it up out of the ground, and made an opening for us to cross through. "Come on through here." She replaced the post, and the fence was standing straight again. "Mr. Cally done told me I could make me a place to get through this here fence. I can't do no stoopin' 'count o' this here misery I got in my back." She took the sack from me and walked on.

I was almost ready to ask if we could stop and rest for a while when Mattie said, "We almost there now." I looked up from the path and saw directly ahead of us a little cabin. At first I thought it was painted dark grey, but as we came closer I could tell that it had never seen a coat of paint; it had just turned that color from the rain and wind and hot summer sun. There was very little of what I called a front porch, but there was a big, wide opening—with no doors—that ran through the middle of the cabin with rooms on either side of it.

As I watched, an old hound dog came running through the opening and trotted out to meet us. Then I remembered something. That open space must be a dogtrot; at least that's what I remembered Cally called it—the dogtrot. On each side of the cabin there were two umbrella chinaberry trees, and under one of them, pushing a little homemade wagon back and forth, sat Leroy. I broke away from Mattie and ran to him shouting, "Hi, Leroy!" He just sat there and looked at me for the longest time; then finally he lowered his eyes and mumbled, "How long you been back here?" He didn't seem at all glad to see me, and I didn't know what to say next, so I just looked down at my feet and said nothing.

Mattie came up to the side of the little wagon and peered in. "The baby all right, Leroy?"

"Yes'm," he said, his eyes still on the ground.

"Take this here sack o' beans and collards to the kitchen then, while I show Buster the baby." He took the sack from her, ambled on up to the cabin, and disappeared into one of the doors off of the dogtrot. He hadn't looked at me again or said another word, and I was beginning to feel miserable about the whole visit.

"Come on over here and see my Emmie Lou." Mattie was holding up the baby for me to look at. "She a sweet li'l ole gal, if'n I do say so."

Emmie Lou looked just like every other little baby I had ever seen before, except her skin was sort of chocolate colored. Mattie kept holding her up for me to look closer.

"She looks like a nice little baby, Mattie." I didn't know what else to say. I was too upset wondering why Leroy had cut me off so. It had really hurt my feelings, so I finally asked, "Why is Leroy mad at me?"

Mattie turned to me with a surprised look on her face. When she saw I was really worried, she laughed. "Lawd, honey, he ain't mad at you. He just mad at his self 'cause you done caught him rollin' the baby in the wagon. He says that's a girl's job, and he don't want none of it, that's all." She looked at me and saw that I still wasn't sure. "I tells you now, he ain't mad, he just embarrass. He be all right when he get some dinner in him. Come on now, let's go on into the house." And she went up to the steps with Emmie Lou slung on her hip.

"I'se sorry Napoleon won't be here to eat dinner with us."

Mattie had crossed over to the little stove. "He gone to Enterprise today doin' some work for Mr. Moore." I had to think for a minute before I remembered that Napoleon was Mattie's husband. She looked in the stove, and then she yelled so loud I jumped.

"Leroy! Leroy, you get yourself out here and get this here fire started. You done let it go out. And I done told you and told you." She didn't have to finish because Leroy came running from the front of the house and started shaking down the ashes as Mattie went grumbling into another room with the baby.

Leroy took some kindling sticks from the woodbox, put them into the coals, and blew on them, and they burst into flames. He quickly put some more wood on the fire and closed the door to the stove. Then he turned toward me, and he was grinning broadly.

"Sho' am glad you came over today," he said. "Mamma ain't gonna stay mad long if'n you here." Mattie must have been right; he didn't seem the least bit mad, and after he was sure the fire was going good, we went out under the chinaberry tree to play until Mattie called us for dinner.

While we were talking and waiting to eat, I kept thinking that Leroy was different somehow. Of course, he was older and so was I, but that wasn't the only difference I noticed. I wasn't even able to explain the difference to myself, but I sensed it and knew it was there. For one thing he seemed more serious when he talked, more grown-up. Oh, he would still squeal when he laughed at something that pleased him or when he made a joke that he thought was especially funny, and once when I was telling him about our fire escape at First District School in Covington, he rolled over and over, laughing in the sandy dust just like the time I'd caught the fish that got away. But he would pause at times, as if he were thinking things over very carefully, before he'd ask me a question. And if I questioned him about anything that had happened since I'd seen him, he'd give me the strangest look and maybe just nod his head and not really answer at all. It never entered my mind that I might be different; it was only Leroy who had changed, and I didn't understand it.

"Leroy! Leroy, you and Buster come on in to dinner now." It was Mattie calling to us from the back cabin door. We ran on into the kitchen where Mattie had a pan of water waiting. "Wash your hands real good now, before we eat," she said, and she thrust a towel in my hands.

When I sat down at the table, I saw we were having collards and sliced tomatoes with cornbread and buttermilk. I picked up my fork, and then I put it right down again; Mattie was sitting with her hands folded and her head bowed for the blessing.

"God is great, God is good.
And we thank ye for this food.
Bless our home and bless our land,
And keep us ever near your hand."

She raised her head, picked up the big bowl of collards, and passed them to me. "Now then," she smiled, "just help yourself to what we got. Ain't a lot, but what we got is plenty of."

I took some of the collards and passed the bowl over to Leroy. "Mattie, that was real nice the way you said the blessing."

She looked at me with surprise on her big face. "Why, thank you, chile." She was cutting the cornbread into wedges. "The good Lawd, he been nice to me lots o' times, so maybe he deserve a nice blessin', too."

I looked over at Leroy who was crumbling a big piece of cornbread in his glass of buttermilk.

"Does that taste good like that?" I asked.

"Does to me," he said, and Mattie added, "Just try it yourself if'n you wants to and see if'n you like it."

I took a wedge of cornbread and broke it up and dropped some into the thick buttermilk, pushing it down with my spoon. Then I took a big mouthful; the cornbread had soaked up the buttermilk like a sponge, and it did taste wonderful. Mattie must have seen that I liked it. She was watching me carefully. "Pretty good, huh?" she asked.

"Best way I've ever tasted cornbread," I mumbled with my mouth full and kept on spooning it up.

After we'd finished eating, Mattie hauled herself up from the table with a groan. "Now you all go out and play while I clean up the table." She looked at Leroy. "Emmie Lou sleepin' like a li'l angel, so you go on."

It was hot in the cabin by now, and we headed for the thick shade of the chinaberry tree and sprawled out in the cool sand.

Leroy glanced up at me. "Been fishin' yet?" he asked and smirked at me.

"No," I told him. "Not yet. Auntee's been real sick with malaria fever, and Kiddo and Bubba never seem to be around anymore. I guess they think they're too grown-up for me now. It really hasn't been much fun for me so far this summer."

He raised his eyes to watch my face for a long while; then he picked up a handful of the cool sand and dribbled it through his fingers before he spoke. "You get use to that." He gave me a quick glance. "How old they now?"

I had to think for a minute. "I'm not sure, Leroy. Kiddo must be fifteen or sixteen by now, and I think Bubba is fourteen. Maybe that's not right, but it's pretty close."

"Close enough," and Leroy leaned back against the tree.

"Close enough for what?" I wanted to know.

"Ain't no sense worryin' about it. They already think o' theyselves as li'l gentlemen, and you caint do nothin' about it." He slanted his eyes up to me. "I been callin' 'em Mister Kiddo and Mister Bubba more'n a year now."

I suddenly remembered what Mattie had said this morning down by the well. What was it she had said? "Won't be long before I be callin' you Mister Buster." Something like that. Leroy was still leaning against the tree staring up through the thick branches. But he wasn't seeing anything; his face looked all closed up.

"Leroy." He was still looking up in the tree. "Leroy!" I reached over and nudged him to get him to look at me. "I want to know something, so listen to me for a minute." He was looking right at me now. "When did you start to call Kiddo and Bubba mister?"

He scooted back against the tree and began twisting a leaf in his hand; he seemed restless and looked down at the leaf he was holding. Then he mumbled, so low I could barely hear, "Soon as they pass thirteen."

"But why?"

"That's just the way it is, I guess."

"How do you know that?"

"Mamma done told me."

"But what did she tell you?"

He raised himself up from the tree trunk and crossed his legs and began making little marks in the sand with his finger. He didn't look at me. "Mamma say when any of you all gets to be thirteen, that's the day I starts callin' you all mister."

"But why?" I kept on. "I think that's silly."

"Don't you know nothin' at all?" He was looking at me now all right, almost shouting. "It's because you a white boy and I'se a nigger, that's why! You just don't know nothin' about nothin'!"

None of it made any sense to me, and I just sat there looking at him as he scratched away in the sand. Leroy could make me mad quicker than anyone I knew, and he had done it again. "Well, I may not know very much," I said, "but I can sure tell you one thing. When I get to be thirteen, if you start callin' me Mister Buster, then I'm sure gonna start callin' you Mister Leroy."

He laughed at me, but somehow it didn't sound funny. "Huh," he said. "That'll be the day!"

"You just wait and see, Mister Smart Aleck. You think you know so much!" I was so mad by now I got up and was walking toward the cabin, but I suddenly stopped. Leroy had started laughing, so hard now that he was rolling over and over under the tree, laughing and rolling and squealing.

"Mister Smart Aleck!" he squealed. "Mister Smart Aleck!" He rolled over one last time, then looked up grinning. "And I ain't even 'leven yet. Look to me like you done got a head start."

It wasn't until then that I realized what I'd said. I ran over and hit him as hard as I could. He grabbed my arms and held them tight, laughing at me all the while. And before I knew how it happened we were both on the ground, holding on to each other and screaming with laughter. We were making so much noise that it brought Mattie running out from the cabin.

"What's the matter with you young-uns?" she wanted to know. "Raisin' such a ruckus you done woke up the baby. What's the matter?"

"Nothin', Mattie." I looked up, trying not to giggle. "We're just playing."

"Well, for the Lawd sake, see can you play a li'l quieter." And she disappeared into the kitchen.

After she left, Leroy and I stretched out full length, side by side, under the tree. We were both hot and sweaty and every now and then one of us would break into a giggle. After we had cooled off for a while, Leroy jumped up and pulled me up with him. "Come on," he said, "let's go play back of the barn. It's a good place back there. And I show you my li'l ole coon, looks just like a bandy."

I followed him around to the back of an old barn. Leroy squatted down by a little cage. It was made of wooden slats roughly nailed together, and inside was a little black and white animal. He began talking to it. "How you doin' li'l ole coon boy? Guess you ain't gon' be stealin' no more eggs is you? You a regular li'l ole bandy, that's what you is."

I had never seen any animal like it before; it would stick its front paws between the slats and chatter away to Leroy, and Leroy would chatter back, squealing with happy laughter.

"What kind of animal is that, Leroy?" I wanted to know.

"It's just a coon, that's all. Pappa done catched him and pen him up like this so he won't steal no more stuff. He a cute li'l fella though, ain't he?"

"Why do you call him a bandy, Leroy?"

He looked up as if he couldn't believe I was so dumb. He shook his head and motioned me closer to the cage. "You sho' is a city boy, ain't cha? Looka here." He pointed to the little coon's face. "See that black streak 'cross his face? Right there?" He pointed to it. "It's just like a black mask that a holdup man wear. Just like a bandy."

"Oh, I see! You mean a bandit."

"That's what I been all a time sayin'." He shook his head in complete disgust. "Lawd, but you sho' is slow to catchin' on!

First it's fishin', then I hafta 'splain the difference between black and white, and now—" He shook his head again and walked slowly into the barn. He had made me feel stupid again, but after a moment I followed him inside.

We spent the rest of the afternoon in the barn, but neither one of us mentioned the number thirteen or the word mister again.

Leroy walked back to Riverside with me in the late afternoon. I guess Mother had been waiting for me, because she came out on the back stoop when she saw us walking up from the barn. She waved and called out, "Did you have a good time?"

"Sure did," I yelled at her. Leroy and I stood near the backyard gate not quite knowing how to say goodbye.

"Wanna go fishin' again sometime?" he finally blurted.

"Sure," I told him. He nodded several times, and with that he turned back the way we had come through the pasture.

That night after supper all of us were sitting on the front porch to catch a breath of fresh air before bedtime. It had been a very hot day, and even now Mammy said, "There isn't a leaf stirring anywhere." She and Allie were slowly waving palmetto fans back and forth; everyone else just sat around not saying much of anything at all, just waiting for it to get good and dark so the bedrooms could cool off a little. At the far end of the porch I heard Pappy ask, "Allie, is Mattie coming over to do the washing this week?"

"No. Pappa, she won't be here again till next week."

"Oh, pshaw!" Pappy sighed a little, and then, "That means I'll have to make a trip over there tomorrow or the next day. I want Napoleon to help me fix the fence in the lower pasture. One of those fence posts has almost rotted out." He sighed again. "I don't want Bessie gettin' on the railroad track."

The mentioning of Mattie made me think of Leroy. "Has Mattie got anymore children?" I asked.

"She's got a grown son, eighteen or nineteen I think." Cally was rocking slowly back and forth. "Lives over somewhere near Jackson, as I recall." Quiet settled down on the porch again, and the katydids took over. I listened to them answer each other for a minute, and then I asked, "Why does Leroy call Kiddo and Bubba mister?" I couldn't see anybody in the dark on the porch, but it seemed like the rocking and the fanning had stopped.

"I guess it's because they've gotten a little older now," Cally said and started rocking again.

"Mattie said Leroy had to start callin' them mister after they got to be thirteen." And then I added, "Anyway that's what Leroy told me today."

"Good ole Mattie," Allie sighed and began fanning herself again.

"Leroy said it's because they're white and he's a nigger."

"Buster, don't you ever say that again!" I could tell Mammy had stopped fanning and was sitting up very straight. "Don't you ever call one of Mattie Riley's children a nigger, you hear me?"

"But I didn't, Mammy." I turned to try to find her face in the dark. "I didn't. That's just what Leroy said. I didn't say it. All I called him was—"

"The very idea!" She sounded very upset. "They are good, hard-working Negroes, as honest as the day is long. Why, Mattie is almost like one of the family, and I don't ever want to hear you say that again!"

"But I didn't," I said again, but no one seemed to be listening. I decided it was the wrong time to say anything more about Leroy. And I knew for sure it was the wrong time to tell them about Mister Smark Aleck or Mister Leroy. But I kept thinking about it for a long time after I'd gone to bed that night.

The next morning Allie was sitting on the front porch stringing snap beans for dinner. Mammy was out in the kitchen, and no one else was around. I sat down on the steps and watched her for a minute. I was still worrying about Leroy.

"Auntee," I finally asked, not looking at her. "Was Mammy mad at me last night when I told her what Leroy said?"

"Aw, honey, she wasn't mad at you." She looked up from her lap of beans. "You mean when Leroy said he was a nigger?"

"Yeah," I mumbled. Then I went on quickly, "But he said it about himself, Auntee. I didn't call him that."

"I know you didn't. Leroy was probably just mad about something, just mad at himself, and everything else, not at you."

"But he sounded like he was mad at me just the same." I turned away from her because I still didn't understand, and I didn't know how to ask for an explanation. Leroy seemed to think that I didn't understand anything, and I was beginning to think that maybe he was right. Finally I asked, "But why did Mammy get so upset when I told her what Leroy said?"

Allie dropped a handful of beans she had been stringing and snapping into a big pot by the side of her chair. She looked out across the front lawn for a minute; she shifted in her chair and then turned to look at me.

"Bus," she took a big breath as if she were trying to solve a hard problem. "Honey, do you understand what white trash means?"

"You mean like the Calebbs?"

I had heard Mammy and Allie and Cally talk about the Calebbs for as long as I could remember. They never mentioned them in front of me or Sissy if we were around to overhear, but we had heard them many times when they didn't know we were listening. They lived in an old abandoned cabin on the other side of the Chunky River, and Mammy always called them "those shiftless, no-good Calebbs." I had never seen them, but I remember hearing Cally say to Daddy once, "Wallace, I don't think they even bathe more than once a year. You can smell them comin' for a hundred feet. They're just no damn good for nothin'!"

"You mean like them, Auntee?" I asked again. She had been quiet for such a long while that I was afraid she wasn't going to say anything more.

"Yes, I s'pose I do mean the Calebbs." She looked very sad for a while before she spoke again. "Because when we say white trash we mean the laziest kind of a white man we can think of." She became thoughtful for a moment, almost talking to herself. "I guess sometimes we shouldn't say it, when we really don't know folks that well, but, oh, I don't know. I guess it's just the easy way out."

She sighed and seemed to come back to the front porch once more. "But anyway, maybe that's the reason Mammy seemed to get upset last night. Mattie Riley and her family are such good hard-working people that you can't even think of them as—niggers—let alone say it. I guess when you come to think about it, nigger and white trash means just about the same thing."

Allie sat back in her chair and slowly went on stringing beans. I kept thinking about Leroy, and him always having to call white boys mister. Finally I looked up at her again.

"Auntee, when Leroy gets to be thirteen, do you s'pose anybody will ever call him mister?"

She glanced down at me. She had stopped rocking and stringing beans. There was a sort of soft hurt look on her lips as if she might cry. She slowly raised her eyes to stare out over the front lawn and was silent for a while. Then she sighed deeply, almost as if she were troubled. "I don't know, Bus," she finally said. "I just don't know. But maybe, maybe someday."

The Fourth of July was always a big day at Riverside. It meant spending most of the day at Chunky River, swimming and boating and diving, but most of all it meant eating, until we couldn't eat any more. As Mammy would say as she surveyed the boxes of food she and Allie cooked up for the Fourth, "Well, I believe that's enough to keep 'em from starving until we get back home for supper." And the boxes would always be filled with fried chicken, sliced home-cured ham, roasting ears to be cooked at the river, Lady Baltimore cake, and homemade boiled custard that had been frozen that morning. All of the food would be loaded in the wagon after breakfast, and we would follow along beside it until we reached the same place each year that Allie always called "the perfect spot" near the river bank. Then the food would be unloaded and set aside, and Mammy and Allie and Mother would guard it carefully while the children and menfolk went wading or swimming or fishing, or sometimes just lazying around until time to eat. All of us loved going to the river for a swim, but on the Fourth of July it was always the food that made it something special for us. We thought and talked about it for days ahead, we dreamed about it night after night, and when the day actually arrived we were usually so excited that we couldn't eat any breakfast at all. No wonder we were starving when the food was finally spread out on the ground near the river. That was the one day of the summer when we never had to be called twice; most of the time we were ready and waiting beforehand, looking to see where the biggest pulley bones were, checking up on the number of Lady Baltimore cakes, and making certain that the big freezers of ice cream were carefully stored under the shade trees. It was always the high point of the summer for me, and from the way they acted, I think it was for everyone else. It was a wonderful day, like no other day of the year.

And the Fourth of July was special for me this year for another reason: Daddy would be here to celebrate with us. Usually every summer, as far back as I could remember, Daddy would have to leave by the end of June and go back to Terre Haute or Cincinnati. But this year he wouldn't leave until after the big day. And as it turned out, this Fourth of July was the one that nobody in the family would ever forget.

It started out much like all the others. Billy and Sissy and I had been cranking the ice cream freezers since early morning, being careful not to waste any of the precious ice that Cally had hauled back from Stonewall the day before and stored in the root cellar protected from the heat with sawdust and burlap bags. Billy couldn't turn the freezer crank for very long, but he got to lick more of the dasher than either me or Sissy because "he was the littlest." The odors from the kitchen were making me wish I'd eaten more biscuits and ribbon cane syrup at breakfast. Sissy and I had just finished the last hard turn of the freezer handle and had called out, "Mammy, it's finished. I think you can come pack it now!" when I saw a strange wagon with a man, a woman, and a small girl turn in from the lane and drive up the front lawn. I nudged Sissy. "Who in the world is that?"

She looked over my shoulder and said with a big sigh, "Oh, law, it's that crazy Erda Mae Jones and her folks." She watched the wagon stop on the front lawn. "Now what in the world do you s'pose they want?"

Mammy was pouring big pieces of ice cream salt around the freezer and adding more pounded-up ice before she covered it with burlap bags. "Never you mind now," she said as she worked. "Erda Mae is going to spend the Fourth with us."

I don't think I have ever seen Sissy look so completely surprised and disgusted before in my life. "Well, will somebody please tell me why?" she asked. "I certainly have never had her for a friend. Everybody knows she's nothin' but boy-crazy."

Mammy turned on her quickly. "You hush up now, you hear me?" Then she stood there looking right at us. "If you must know, Miss Priss, her mother and daddy have to go to a family funeral this afternoon, and I told them to bring Erda Mae by here to spend the day with us." Then she added, "So you be nice to her today, you hear?"

I had only seen Erda Mae Jones once or twice before, and I didn't care one way or the other, but Sissy certainly must not have liked her much because she said right away, "Well, that has sure helped to spoil my Fourth of July already!" And then she whispered to me, "I just hope she stays out of my way, that's all I hope!"

Mammy kept urging us to go out in the front yard to say hello, but we didn't. We heard the wagon rumble out of the yard, and finally Erda Mae appeared on the back stoop. "Hi, Mary Evelyn," she called. "What you all doin' out here?"

"We've been helping Mammy pack the freezers." That was all Sissy said; then she added with a nasty smirk on her face, "We've already finished lickin' the dasher!"

Erda Mae had joined us in the back yard by now. "Oh, I don't anymore care about that old stuff," she smiled. "That's baby stuff." And she sort of sidled up to me. "I remember you. You live up north in some big city, don't you?" She was standing right in front of me looking up and down so hard. I began to feel uneasy. "Lemme see now. Your name is Buster, isn't it?" She was smiling all over me, a kind of grown-up smile that didn't make any sense to me. "I remember now. You're the one that talks so funny. I think it's real cute." I didn't know what to say because I wasn't sure if I was supposed to say anything, so I said nothing. Erda Mae kept on smiling and edging closer until her body was touching mine. She felt hot and sticky all over. I jumped away and walked around to the other side of the ice cream freezer. I didn't especially like the way Erda Mae smelled when she was standing that close to me. She was about to follow after me when Mammy called to us from the back door.

"Sissy, you and Buster come on in here and wash that ice cream from the dasher off your hands. We'll be ready to leave for the river just as soon as Pappy finishes tying up those oats in the pasture. Make haste, now!" Then she remembered Erda Mae and added in her company voice, "Come on into the house, Erda Mae honey, where it's cooler. I hope you remembered to bring your bathing suit."

"Yes'm, I did," I heard her call as she lagged along after us.

Sissy and I finished washing our hands in a pan of water that Mammy had set out on the kitchen table. Erda Mae was breathing down my neck so close that it tickled and made me shiver. I was just about to turn around and tell her to stop that when I heard the front screen door slam, and Kiddo came racing through the house yelling, "Daddy, Daddy, come quick!" Then he ran into the kitchen. "Where's Daddy? Where is he? He's got to come quick. Right now!"

"He's down at the barn hitching up the wagon." Mammy grabbed Kiddo and held on to him to calm him down. "Now what is this all about?" Mother and Allie and Daddy were standing in the doorway by now and crowding around Kiddo. When he saw Daddy, Kiddo ran up to him and pushed him so hard he nearly fell down. "Uncle Wallace, oh good Lord, come quick, please come quick. We gotta do something quick and I don't know what to do. And if we don't do something pretty soon it might—" Daddy took hold of Kiddo's arms and shook him so hard that his straw hat fell off. Kiddo's mouth flew open, but he stopped talking.

"Now," Daddy said very softly, "just tell me what happened."

His lips started moving again, but nothing came out. He finally gulped for breath and said, "Pappy, Pappy's been bitten by a cottonmouth!"

I don't know how long I stood by the wash pan, but the next thing I knew there was nobody in the kitchen except me and Erda Mae. And I remember thinking, "If she breathes down my neck now, I'm going to slap her." But she must have been as frightened as I was because she gave a little whimper and flew out into the back yard. I'm sure she didn't go home then, but I don't remember seeing her again for the rest of the day.

I ran out onto the front porch. Way down by the lane I could see Mammy and Daddy walking on either side of Pappy. Mammy had hold of one arm and Daddy was holding the other one tightly; he had something twisted around it. Kiddo was following after them, and Mother was standing in the middle of the front lawn, holding her hand up to her mouth. As they came closer I could hear Daddy talking in a very quiet voice.

"Just keep as quiet as you can, Pappy," he said, and then quickly he added. "No! No! Don't move your arm. I want to cut off the circulation in your arm, so just hold still."

"Will, honey, how in heaven's name did it happen?" I'd never heard Mammy call Pappy by his real name before.

"Not now, Mammy! Don't ask any questions now. Just let him save his breath." I had never heard Daddy speak that sharply at Mammy before. As they came up the front steps past me I got a quick look at Pappy. His face was awfully white; sweat was dripping down his forehead and cheeks, and he looked scared. His right hand and wrist were awfully red and looked puffy. They passed by me as if I wasn't even there, and Mother went in after him. Kiddo came up the steps, and I ran to him.

"When did it bite him, Kiddo?" I asked. "Were you with him down there?"

He just looked at me. I don't think he even heard what I said. He finally opened his mouth to answer something, but just then the sound of something running fast came from the direction of the barn. It was a horse and somebody on it, whipping it and riding it hard. It was Bubba, and he kept shouting something to the horse as he rapidly disappeared down the lane, headed for the railroad.

I was really frightened now, and afraid that I might start crying any minute. I whispered to Kiddo, "Where is Bubba going?"

"Probably down to Stonewall to try to find Dr. Harper."

I didn't ask any more questions. If Bubba was going for Dr.

Harper then surely Pappy must be dying. I ran down the steps and sat under a big tree, all scrunched up and not moving.

Daddy came quickly out of the front door. "Kiddo, go tell Cally to get up here fast. I need him." Kiddo started across the yard. "And if you can't find him, you hurry on back. You'll have to help me." And Kiddo was gone.

After Daddy went back in the house I sat there wondering—help him with what? Help him do what? What did he want Cally or Kiddo for? Were they going down to the Jennings' pasture to try to find the snake and kill it? I scooted back against the tree trunk, and as I did I felt something moving on my arm. I yelled and looked down and saw a big red ant sitting there. I shook it off and shivered with fright and relief, and then I looked carefully all around me to be sure that nothing else was crawling near the tree.

A cottonmouth moccasin! Next to a rattlesnake that was one all of us feared the most. A garden snake was harmless, "but stay out of its way just the same," Allie always warned. A black snake or a king snake or a chicken snake wasn't too poisonous, but a cottonmouth!

"Come on out on the porch, Pappy." It was Daddy's voice coming from the house. "Sit him down in that big chair, Cally. The light is much better out here." I don't know where Cally had come from, but he had followed Daddy out to the porch and was holding Pappy's arm. They got him seated in a big chair, and Daddy knelt down by his side. He looked up into Pappy's face and said, "This is gonna hurt like hell, but it's got to be done." Pappy wasn't even shocked when Daddy said hell; he just tightened his mouth and nodded his head. Mammy was standing right behind the chair now with some bottles and bandages in her hands.

Daddy took out his little pearl-handled pocketknife, struck a match, and held the blade in the flame for a long time. He looked up at Pappy one more time. Pappy nodded yes. Then Daddy struck the knife blade right into the middle of Pappy's finger and cut straight up toward his hand. I could see the blood begin to run out. I could hear Pappy give a low hard grunt. I heard Mammy cry out, "Oh, dear God!" And then I saw my daddy do a very strange thing. He dropped the knife and leaned over to kiss Pappy's finger. Except he wasn't kissing it, he was sucking it. He would suck and spit, suck and spit, until I finally got so sick I turned away and vomited on the grass. I felt hot and cold and dizzy, and there was a roaring in my ears I couldn't stop.

When I looked up again only Kiddo and Sissy were on the porch; they were sitting near the window of the front bedroom, and I could hear voices from the inside. I crept up the steps and sat as close as I could to Kiddo. "Is Pappy dead?"

He turned and looked at me. Then he put his arm around me and made a halfway smile. "'Course he's not dead. He's just lying down in there while they tie up his finger."

"But Daddy cut his hand wide open and all that blood was—"

"Not his hand, Bus." Kiddo's voice was very quiet now, very gentle as he talked to me. Sissy had come over and sat down in front of us to listen. "It was just his finger where the cottonmouth bit him. He had to cut it open like that, so he could suck out as much of the poison as he could."

"Is Pappy going to be all right?"

"I sure hope so." He didn't sound very sure about it though, and I looked up at him. He smiled again and tightened his arm around me. "Yeah, I think he's gonna be fine, Bus." But he still didn't sound like it.

Sissy tugged at Kiddo's knee. "Kiddo—how come Pappy got so close to a snake? Wasn't he being careful to watch out for one?" The folks were always warning us to be careful and watch out for snakes wherever we went.

"Sure he was." Kiddo stood up, and as he talked he began to show us how it happened. "You know those sacks of oats he was tying up down near the Jennings' pasture?" Sissy nodded. "Well, he was reaching down to lift one up, and this old cottonmouth was all coiled up right under it, and Pappy couldn't even see it until it was too late." He looked at us for a minute and then, "It caught him right in the middle of his finger, and he—"

Kiddo's face got very pale. "—he had to raise up his whole arm and sling it real hard before that old cottonmouth would let go."

I sat there in the sunshine and shivered. Sissy leaned over and said. "Did you kill it, Kiddo?"

"Good Lord, no, Sissy!" Kiddo got very mad. "I was so scared all I could think about was getting Pappy back to the house. That snake just crawled away somewhere—I don't know where!"

Allie came out on the front porch just then and sat down to fan herself. She looked very tired and kept rubbing her lips over and over.

"How is he doing, Mother?" Kiddo asked.

"He's lying down now. Mammy gave him a big drink of whiskey to keep him quiet until Dr. Harper gets here." She looked up at all of us then, and I thought she was about to cry. "But he's awful sick. That hand is just—" She tightened her lips and took a big breath. "You children will have to be quiet and stay right around the house today. Stay within calling distance if we should want you for anything." She had a sudden thought. "Oh, my Lord, I've forgotten all about Billy! Where is he?"

"Right there at the edge of the porch." Sissy pointed to where Billy was playing on his tricycle. "Don't worry about him, Mother. I'll take good care of him all day."

Allie got up and started into the house. At the door she stopped. "Oh, if any of you all get hungry just go into the kitchen and eat anything you want from the picnic." And she closed the screen door very quietly.

The three of us just sat there not looking at anything at all. It was getting awfully hot on the porch, but I didn't feel like moving out of the sun. I heard Sissy whisper something to Kiddo and looked up just in time to see him shake his head. I wanted to ask them what they were whispering about, but before I could I heard Daddy's voice coming from the front bedroom. He was talking very loud.

"No, no, Pappy, don't try to get up. Just lie there and be real quiet."

"You let me get up from here, Wallace!" It was Pappy's voice, although it sounded so strange I wasn't sure at first. "Now confound it, I told you to let go of me. You think I'm afraid of that dern snake?"

I heard Mammy's voice almost crying now. "Will, honey, please, please lie back down and be quiet."

"Confounded woman! You think it's a joke, don't cha? And you like jokes, don't cha?" Pappy was almost yelling by now. "Well, I'm gonna show all of ya—every dern one of ya—I'm gonna get up from here and I'm gonna get me a big stick and I'm goin' down there and kill that dern cottonmouth moccasin. Now you lemme up from here!"

Daddy's voice broke right in then. "All right, Pappy, all right. But just listen to me for a minute first, will you? Now just listen!" And Pappy got quiet.

"Now I'll tell you what we'll do." Daddy sounded like he was talking to a baby. "If you'll just lie here real quiet for a—now wait a minute, dammit—if you'll just rest here for a little longer, then you can get up and I'll go with you, and we'll both go look for that snake, and we'll find him and we'll kill him, too!" Daddy paused for a minute and then said, "What do you say? Will you do that for me?"

Pappy mumbled something that I couldn't hear, and finally Daddy said, "You bet your boots, Pappy. I promise you I will."

I don't know what it was that Daddy promised, but it suddenly got very quiet in the bedroom, almost as quiet as we were on the front porch. I simply couldn't believe that it was Pappy I had heard talking that way. I looked up at Kiddo. "What is the matter with him?" Kiddo just shrugged his shoulders, and Sissy looked as startled as I did.

In a little while Mother and Daddy came out on the porch and sat down on the swing. Daddy had taken off his collar and he reached up with his fingers to wipe his forehead and slung the sweat off on the floor. Then he lit a cigarette and said, "Whew!" That was all he said.

"What's the matter with Pappy?" Kiddo asked. "Is he—is he delirious?"

Mother spoke up quickly. "No, he's a little confused right now, that's all. He just isn't real sure of everything right now."

Daddy started chuckling to himself and then turned to Mother. He looked at her, and finally he laughed out loud and said, "He sure is confused all right." He looked at us and laughed again. "Pappy is lying in there as drunk as the Lord!"

I don't think any of us believed him at all. I just sat there and stared at him with my mouth wide open. Finally Kiddo spoke up. "Pappy? Is drunk?"

Daddy glanced at Mother who was beginning to smile a little, then he leaned over to us. "Well, you see, Kiddo, after I'd cut open his finger and we got him inside, Mammy poured a little whiskey on the open wound so it wouldn't get infected before she bandaged it up." He looked at Mother again and giggled. "Then she saw a glass by the bed, and she poured it half full of whiskey and made Pappy drink it down. Poor Pappy—probably the first drop of liquor he ever had in his life. Oh, it quietened him down all right—at first. And that's all Mammy wanted it to do. But when that whiskey really hit him, he got as wild as a billy goat; he was goin' down there and kill that dern snake or be damned!" Daddy began laughing harder as he remembered. "Last thing he said before he passed out, he made me promise to help him find that snake and stomp it to death." He shook his head, still laughing.

He looked at the three of us sitting there, still waiting to hear more. Then he reached over, got one of Mother's hands, patted it very gently, and smiled at all of us. "Pappy is going to be pretty sick for a while, but I'm sure that he is going to be all right."

Dr. Harper said practically the same thing when he finally got to Riverside just before sundown that evening. He had been at his own Fourth of July picnic just outside of Stonewall, and Bubba wouldn't leave town until he found him and brought him back. He drove up in his Model T roadster and went right into the sickroom. Sissy and I were sitting in the dining room eating some of the fried chicken—we had two pulley bones apiece—when we heard him come in the house. "Right in here, Dr.

Harper," we heard Mammy say, and they went in and closed the bedroom door. Then we could hear nothing, and everything in the house seemed to be waiting and listening. Sissy and I even stopped making a wish on our first pulley bone and sat there alone in the lamplight. I thought that the front bedroom door was never going to open again, but when it did Mammy was saying, "Thank you for coming, Dr. Harper. And I'll do exactly what you said."

"Mr. Briggs," I heard him say to Daddy, "the best thing you could have done was use that tourniquet right away. And, by the way, did you ever think about studying surgery?" Dr. Harper laughed. "That was a pretty good piece of work, using just a pocketknife. But seriously, it certainly did help to keep a lot of that poison out of his system." Then he leaned over and nudged Daddy in the ribs. "Mrs. Neal's remedy was about the worst thing she could have done, but I don't think it did too much harm." Then he laughed. "Looks to me like you could use a little of the remedy yourself."

Dr. Harper said good night to everyone. Bubba cranked up his roadster for him, and he drove off down the lawn. It was good and dark by then.

Mammy came through the dining room and went into the kitchen carrying a pan of water and some towels. Daddy was following right along after her. I heard Daddy whispering to her, and then she said, "There's no reason why not, and Polly doesn't have to know anything about it. It's right up there in the safe—just help yourself." Then I heard Mammy open the back door and empty the pan of water. A little while later Daddy came into the dining room and sat down at the table with us. He had a plate with some cold chicken and ham and cornbread on it, and he began to eat as if he were starved. When Mammy came through the dining room on her way back to be with Pappy, she stopped and watched Daddy eating; then she put her hands on his shoulders and patted him. "Wallace," she said, "you're a good man. We've all got our faults and who hasn't, but you're a good man. I don't know what I would have done without you today. When I saw that hand of Pappy's and knew we might not be able to get a doctor at all, well, I just—I—" she stopped and tightened her hold on his shoulders. "Thank you Wallace—and thank God you were here. I'll never forget it."

"It's all right, Mammy," he reached up and touched her hand gently. "I'm just glad it wasn't any worse."

"Glad what wasn't any worse?" Mother had come into the room and sat down by Daddy's side. Then she said, "Oh, you mean about Pappy." Daddy nodded his head and suddenly started eating fast.

"Oh, honey, I was so proud of you today. You just took over and seemed to know exactly what to do." She looked up at him, and her eyes were shining in the lamplight. "Dr. Harper told Mama you did just the right thing when you—" She stopped and gave Daddy a big kiss right on the mouth. Then she pulled away a little and began to sniff, almost like a rabbit. She stiffened and said, "Wallace, do you mean to tell me on top of everything else that you have been—"

"Yes, he has!" It was Mammy who finished it for her, and she said it very plainly. "Yes, he has, and with my blessing!" Mother looked completely shocked. "Any man who has done what Wallace did today deserves a drink, if he wants it, so don't get your back up, Polly!" Mammy started on out into the hall, but she turned in the doorway. "And if I were you, I'd sit right there and see that he has plenty to eat before he goes to bed." She went on in to Pappy and closed the door.

Pappy was in bed for more than a week, and when he did get up and around, I often heard Mammy say, "I don't know, it seems to me it's taking an awful long time for Will to get his strength back." And all of us were a lot more careful in watching out for snakes after that, especially if we thought that it might be a cottonmouth moccasin.

Daddy had gone back to Cincinnati more than two weeks before, and Pappy had been out of bed sitting on the porch for over a week when the turn-around plate was broken. Mammy broke it, and the reason we were all so mad about it was the plain fact that Mammy did it on purpose. No one could deny that—all of us had seen her do it, and the longer I thought about it, the madder I got. Oh, sure, all three of us were to blame, I guess—Sissy and Billy and me—the way we whined and carried on so every day at dinner, or every night at supper, but still that was no reason for her to smash it up the way she did.

The turn-around plate was a very special plate, and we loved it. It wasn't very good china—it may have been mail-order variety for all I know—but in its own way it was special. The turn-around plate was only one piece out of a set of eight, and it had a flaw. But it was the flaw that made it so desirable to all of us kids. This particular plate had an uneven bottom; there was a high place in the middle of it, which caused the plate to turn around and around if you twisted it, and this is what we loved to do. I think it was Sissy who discovered the secret first. It was at her place at supper one evening, and as she tried to cut her food, it would turn away from the knife or fork she was using. She laughed and began spinning it around and said, "Look, I've got a turn-around plate. It's almost like a merry-go-round." And from that time on, we always called it the turn-around plate.

We all wanted it—we fought over it—and sometimes Sissy and I even drew straws to see who would get it for dinner or supper. Of course, Billy never had a chance between the two of us, and finally he began to set up a howl for the turn-around plate, too. One night at the supper table Mammy made an announcement. She said, "Now I want you three children to listen to this." She was looking at me and Sissy and Billy. "I'm getting sick and tired of you all quarreling over who's going to get the turn-around plate. The whole thing is getting to be ridiculous, and I'm not going to put up with this anymore." Her mouth was screwed up tight, and I could tell that she had reached the end of her patience. "So, from now on, we'll take turns. Billy can have it first—he's the youngest; then it goes to Buster; and then, Sissy, you'll have it last."

Sissy set up a protest right away. "I don't see why I have to be the last one to get it," she whined. "I'm the one that found it first. I'm the one that called it the turn-around plate! I don't see why I—"

"I just told you, Mary Evelyn!" Mammy was getting that look again. "Because you're the oldest and Billy's the youngest and Buster's in between. Maybe Buster ought to have it first anyway, because he's a visitor, and visitors ought—"

"He's not a visitor." Sissy was really howling for her rights now. "He's not! He practically lives here all summer just like everybody else. But he don't have to mind the baby, or help in the garden, or do any of the things that—"

"That will be enough out of you, young lady!" It was Allie's voice, and she was speaking very firmly. "All of us are tired of coming to the table and hearing you children quarrel over that silly plate. Now you can either take your turn or just do without it altogether!"

That put an end to the argument for that evening. Mammy put the turn-around plate in front of Billy, and Sissy and I sat glaring at him and then at each other. Within the space of a few minutes we had become almost enemies. I was angry with her for saying that I didn't do anything around the house to help, and since it was true, I hated her all the more for saying it; she was angry with me because I smirked at her when Mammy said she was to get the plate last. Only Billy was happy, and he sat there twirling it around and around, ignoring us completely, which made both of us furious.

But it worked. There was peace over the plate, at dinner and supper, for almost a week. It was an uneasy peace as far as the three of us were concerned; when Billy had it, Sissy and I paid very little attention to him or what he did with it; when it came our turn to have the plate we would announce loudly, "I've got the turn-around plate today," and proceed to flaunt it in the other's face, turning it around many more times than was necessary even for our own enjoyment. Then came the day when the dinner table peace was completely destroyed.

I was on the front porch pushing David Wallace back and forth in the buggy—probably through a sense of guilt—when Allie called us all in for dinner. She took up the baby, thanked me for looking after him for a while, and plopped him into his baby bed until the meal was over. I followed her on into the dining room and sat down at my place just as Pappy appeared from the kitchen and took his place at the head of the table. It was my day to have the turn-around plate, and there it was right in front of me. I looked at Sissy and grinned and gave it a big spin. Mother put her hand down and stopped it. "Be quiet now. Pappy's going to say the blessing." I bowed my head and closed my eyes, and Pappy began praying over the food. It was a fairly long blessing, and I opened my eyes once to peek, but I felt Mother's hand tighten on my arm and I shut them again. Pappy finally got to his amen; then everyone began to talk at once as the food was being passed. I forked a big pulley bone before the platter of fried chicken got to Sissy, but she didn't seem to mind. I passed up the squash—which I didn't like and wouldn't eat unless Mother insisted—and passed it on to Sissy, who spooned some onto her plate. I helped myself to three big slices of tomatoes and twirled my plate to see if I could make the red slices end up right in front of me. Nothing happened! My plate wouldn't turn at all. I tried again, still it wouldn't move.

"Hey, what's the matter with my turn-around plate?" I yelled to the table in general. Everybody stopped eating and looked up; everybody but Sissy. She was eating very fast, and as she forked up a slice of tomato, she accidentally hit the side of her plate. It turned around one full circle!

"You've got my turn-around plate!" I yelled again. "Today's my day for it. This is my day to have the turn-around plate."

Mammy was confused for a minute. "Why, Buster, I'm sure I put it at your place, right next to Polly. Billy had it last night at supper and I—" She suddenly stopped because Sissy was snickering.

"You took my turn-around plate." I was reaching over to get it. "You're not supposed to have it until supper tonight. It's my turn to have it."

"Just change plates with Sissy," Allie said. "Then everything will be all right."

"She's got ole squash on her plate. I don't want any of that ole squash." I turned to face Sissy. "Scrape all that squash off that plate. You knew it was my turn to have it, and you knew I didn't like that stuff anyway. Scrape it off!" I was determined to have it my way. "And keep your own chicken. I don't want it—I want my pulley bone. Here—put it on that plate." I was handing her my plate and trying to change the food at the same time when my arm struck the ice tea pitcher, and the whole thing spilled all over the table, running into the chicken. There was a dead silence for a moment, a frightening and guilty silence. Then I started again. "Now look what you made me do!" I screamed.

"I didn't make you do that," Sissy yelled back at me. "You did it yourself."

"I did not."

"Did too!"

"That will do!" Mammy's bark was like a command. "I have had all I'm going to take from you two—and I mean it!"

She marched around the table between the two of us. She picked up the turn-around, scraped all the food off it, walked over to the fireplace, and slammed it against the stone hearth. It broke into several pieces; then she stooped and gathered them up in her hand. She looked at them and then at us. She was smiling as if to say, "I told you what would happen."

"Now this is what happens when children can't act like decent people." She looked at us. "I don't want to hear another word—ever again—about that fool plate." She went into the kitchen, and we could hear the broken plate falling into the woodbox.

Billy started howling. I swung around to face Sissy. "Now look what you've done! I hate you, I hate you. You had no right to steal my plate. You're the cause of it."

"You're the one that upset the tea and made the mess, not me!"

I was so mad that I was crying now. "You had to be the smart aleck and steal it, and you stole it while Pappy was prayin', and I hate you, I hate you!"

I pushed up from the table and my chair fell backwards.

Mother grabbed my arm, but I jerked away and ran sobbing out into the front yard. I sat down under a tree and kept sobbing and pounding my fist into the ground. The turn-around plate was broken, and it was all Sissy's fault, and I hated her. And I hated Mammy, too. She didn't have to break it like that; she could've put it up in the kitchen safe until we promised to behave ourselves. She could've given us another chance, but she broke it to pieces right in front of our eyes, and I hated her, too. And I was getting hungry. I hadn't eaten a bite of dinner, and that was Sissy's fault too. I decided I'd never speak to her again; I'd get even with her, and Mammy, too.

I stopped crying and wiped my nose with my hand. I looked up and saw Mother standing on the front porch watching me. "Do you think you're ready to come in and eat some dinner now?" she asked.

"I don't want any! I'm not hungry."

"Well, we're going to put the food away, so if you want anything you'd better come and get it now." And she went back into the house.

She didn't care either. They were probably putting all the food away right now; they didn't care if I was hungry or not. None of them gave a darn! Well, all right. I didn't give a darn either. I'd sit right there until— Then the big idea struck me as I sat there sniffling under the tree. I didn't have to sit here all day with nothing to do and no one to play with. I'd go over to Mattie Riley's; she'd give me something to eat, and Leroy would be there and he'd understand that it wasn't my fault that the turn-around plate was broken. But suppose they weren't home? I thought about that and shivered in the hot sun. Well, at least I could go over there and see, and I made up my mind that I would.

Inside the house it was very still; there was no sound of dishes being washed and put away; Pappy had probably gone upstairs to rest. I didn't know where Sissy was, and I didn't care. I went up the steps and on into the front hall. I could hear Mother and Allie talking from the front bedroom, and I knew they were stretched out on the beds to take an afternoon nap. I stood just inside the doorway and listened.

"David asleep?" It was Mother's voice.

"Sissy has him with her in the back bedroom." Allie must have turned over because I heard the bed creak. "Did Buster ever eat anything?"

"Not that I know of," Mother laughed. "He hasn't gotten over his mad yet. Just give him time."

They were both silent for a moment; then I heard Allie sigh. "I wish Mama hadn't lost her temper though. Now I've got only seven plates left in the set."

I tiptoed through the dining room headed for the back door, but I stopped when I reached the kitchen. Sitting on the stove under the warmer was a plate of food: chicken and several biscuits with thick pieces of ham between, some tomato slices, and a good-sized helping of green beans.

I looked at it and felt the water start in my mouth. And I think it was at that very moment, looking hungrily at that plate of food, when I decided how I would get even with all of them, Sissy and Mammy and Mother, too. I'd run away. I think I almost said it out loud—"I'll run away!"

I went over to the big kitchen work table and found several folded sugar sacks; I took one and hurried over to the stove and stuffed the chicken and ham biscuits inside. I knew I couldn't take the green beans with me, but I gobbled up the slices of tomatoes where I stood, and then eased myself out the back door, closing it very quietly behind me. I stood on the stoop for a long while undecided, until I had really made up my mind. I walked slowly out into the back yard, watching the windows carefully to be certain that no one saw me. I opened the back gate only a little so that it wouldn't squeak and slid through the small opening. Then I ran faster than I ever had, back of the barn and down the path that led across the big pasture to Mattie Riley's house.

I didn't know what I was going to tell her if she asked me why I was there, and she would certainly see the sack of food and wonder about it. "What you doin' with that there sack of food, Buster?" And I knew if I said that I was running away, she'd get just as angry at me as she always did at Leroy and take me right back to the house again. By the time I had climbed through the barbed wire fence that separated Riverside from the Riley property, I had just about decided I had run away too quickly without thinking the whole thing through. But it was too late now.

Just as I came in sight of Mattie's cabin there was a big crepe myrtle bush by the side of the path, and I dodged behind it, because Mattie was standing over an iron kettle in the front yard washing clothes. I watched her as she stirred the clothes around with a stick, and at first I didn't see Leroy at all. But then she ambled over to the far side of the chinaberry tree and said something I couldn't quite hear, and Leroy poked his head out from behind the tree.

"Yes'm," I heard him say, and Mattie went back to the washing, satisfied. Then I could see that Leroy was pushing the little wagon back and forth with Emmie Lou in it. He had probably stopped pushing and Mattie had reminded him to keep it up.

The afternoon sun was bearing down hard on my head and shoulders, and I could feel the sweat trickling down my back, and there wasn't any shade nearby if I wanted to stay hidden from Mattie's big eyes. I was beginning to feel miserable, mostly because I was hot and hungry, but I was also feeling a little uneasy about running away from home. Nobody back at the house knew where I was, and I suddenly realized that Mother would be awfully worried; probably Mammy and Allie would be, too. Maybe even Sissy. But then I thought, "Naw, she won't give a darn—she'll probably be glad."

I looked out from behind the myrtle bush, and Mattie Riley was walking up to the cabin. She didn't pause but went right up to the steps and disappeared in the kitchen. I stuck my head out from my hiding place. "Psst," I hissed to Leroy as loud as I dared. He didn't even look up; in fact, I think he was half asleep. "Psst," I tried again, and then I called, "Leroy!"

He looked up for a minute, stood very still, and then went on pushing the wagon.

"You dumb thing," I muttered to myself. "Can't you hear anything at all?" It was getting too hot to keep squatting behind the bush, so I just stepped out in full view for a second and almost yelled, "Leroy!"

"Who that?" He stopped pushing the wagon and looked around wildly. "That somebody callin' me?" He looked scared.

I stepped out from behind the crepe myrtle bush again, put my finger up to my lips, and motioned for him to come over to me. He looked up toward the cabin, and when he couldn't see Mattie anywhere about, he came racing down the path and sat down beside me so that we were both hidden from view.

"What cha goin' round like that for yellin' and then hidin' yourself and scarin' the livin' shit outta me for? What'sa matter you, boy?"

"Hush up and be quiet." I put my hand on his arm, and he jerked it away angrily.

"Don't be hushin' me none! Comin' round here tryin' to act like a ghostie." He looked at me for a moment, then added, "What you doin' over here anyway? You come over here by yourself?"

"Yes, I did, and I'm not trying to act like a ghost." I peeked around the crepe myrtle and saw that Mattie Riley was still in the cabin. I looked at Leroy straight in the eyes, took a big breath, and told him. "I'm running away from home!"

He didn't say anything at all. He just stared at me. Then he slapped his leg and threw back his head and started that squealing laughter of his. He got the first high note out of his mouth before I could stop him, and when I finally did, he jerked his hand away and just sat there watching me. Finally I said, "I mean it, Leroy. I'm not joking. I'm not going back to that house—ever!"

"What cha runnin' away for?"

"They didn't even give me any dinner." I showed him the sack of food. "So I just grabbed up some leftovers and ran off over here." I hesitated for a minute and then added, "I didn't know where else to go."

Leroy pulled a red bloom off the crepe myrtle bush and

twisted it around in his fingers over and over. Then he looked up at me, and he was grinning in that special way that always made me angry. "What you done that they wouldn't give you no dinner?"

"I didn't do anything at all. It was Sissy's fault, she was the cause of it, she was to blame for the whole thing!" And I began telling him about the turn-around plate, how each of us had special times when we used it, how Sissy had stolen it from my place at dinner, and how Mammy had snatched it up and broken it. "So you see," I ended, "it wasn't my fault at all. And I hate every one of 'em, and I'm not going back there!"

After I'd finished, Leroy didn't say a word. He sat there looking at the ground. "You gonna get awful hungry if'n you don't go home no more."

"I don't care!"

"You will when your stomach starts to growlin'."

I held my sack of food up in his face. "I've got my dinner right in here!"

"Won't last long."

He was saying exactly what I had been thinking for the last hour, but every time he spoke up to disagree with me, I became more stubborn, more determined to go through with it.

"I'm going anyway." I didn't know what else to say; nothing was going the way I thought it would, so finally I said, "I just thought you'd like to know."

Leroy looked up at me. "Where you plannin' to go?" he asked.

I hadn't really given it any thought, but I wasn't going to let him know that. "Somewhere down by the river," I told him. "I'll find a place to stay—you needn't worry about me," I assured him.

"There's a ole shack on this here side of the river. You ever see it?" I shook my head. "Your cousin Bubba use it sometime when he out huntin' or just foolin' round." He suddenly got very excited and leaned toward me on his knees. "You wants me to take you down there? It's near about a mile from here."

"Sure I do." I was breathing a sigh of relief inside of me. If

Leroy was going with me—even for a little while—I knew that everything would be all right. "Come on, let's go!"

Leroy stuck his head out beyond the crepe myrtle bush, and I peered over his shoulder. Mattie was still nowhere in sight.

Leroy poked me in the side and whispered, "We gonna light out from here fast as we can while Mamma still in the cabin. Run fast as you can till we gets to the barn. She can't see us after we gets there." He peeked out once more and then yelled. "Let's go!"

Leroy was gone so fast I couldn't begin to keep up with him. He had already disappeared behind the barn before I had covered half the distance. When I rounded the corner he was sitting on the ground leaning against the barn door, breathing hard. I sat down by his side to catch my breath.

"Lee-roy!" It was Mattie Riley's singsong call coming from the direction of the cabin. We sat very still, trying not to breathe at all. Then she called again, short and loud and angry. "Leroy! Where you at?"

"God a'mighty, let's get the hell outta here fast!" Leroy pulled me up, and we ran down through the pasture toward some tall pine trees that grew on the edge of a wooded slope. He kept calling to me over his shoulder as we ran, "Hurry up, Buster, hurry up!"

I had been running so fast that my chest was beginning to hurt when I tried to get a good breath, and my right leg felt as though it might buckle under me at any minute. I couldn't hurry any faster, so I slowed to a half-hearted trot. When I looked up, I couldn't see Leroy anywhere. I stumbled on until I finally reached a big pine tree and sprawled under it to rest.

"Come on over here. It's cooler." Leroy was sitting under a low-hanging oak tree, watching me and smiling as if nothing unusual had occurred.

"—catch my breath for a minute." I nodded and gasped.

Leroy crawled over to me. "You feelin' all right?" Again I nodded. "It ain't but a little piece to go now. Just over yonder—down past that li'l ole hill in the river." And he pointed through the thick trees.

I sat there leaning back against the pine tree, trying to breathe easier. Leroy leaned over and put his hand on my chest and watched me with a worried expression. "Feel like a drum beatin' in there. You sho' you is all right?" Then he put on that nasty grin. "Or is you just plain scared?"

I knocked his hand off and sat up. "You just shut up, Mister—" I was about to say Mister Smart Aleck, but I stopped too late. Leroy started howling and stood up in front of me.

"You is just bound and determined to make me a mister, ain't cha?" He kept looking at me and laughing all the while. But it wasn't a teasing laugh; I could tell that he was enjoying everything—me, himself, the idea of running away, the cool shade of the woods—everything.

"Come on and show me where this shack is." I got up and started toward the river, but both of us were smiling as we headed through the trees toward the shack.

As we came to the bluff overlooking the Chunky River, I could see the shack, and that's all it was—more like a lean-to shed, except that it had nothing to lean against. It was made of old discarded lumber, pieces of wrinkled tin that might have once been cracker boxes, and scraps of wooden shingles. It was not only weather-beaten but dirty, and surrounded by giant oak trees whose thick leaves allowed very little sunlight to come through. It was a dismal place, and I couldn't imagine spending the night there even with Leroy along for company and comfort, much less staying in it alone.

I stopped at the edge of the bluff when I saw the shack. Leroy walked on a few steps, then turned and motioned to me impatiently. "Come on," he said. "Let's go and take a look inside."

I stood there trying to think of any excuse for not going inside. "I bet there are snakes in there," I cautioned.

"Then we gotta get 'em out if'n we gonna spend the night there."

That made me feel some better when he said *if* we were going to spend the night—not much, but a little. Even so, I didn't want to go inside the shack, and I just stood there, dumbly, looking at it.

"You gonna stand there all day till it's plum dark?" Leroy was getting tired of waiting for me, and I'm sure that he could tell I was frightened. "We gonna look around in that shed or not?"

Suddenly I thought of the sack of cold chicken in my hand. At least that would give me an excuse to delay going inside the shed, for a short time, at any rate. I raised the sack up toward Leroy. "I'm hungry. I didn't even have a bite of dinner, Leroy." I crossed over to a sandy knoll above the shack and sat down. "Come on. Let's eat what I've got here, and then we can explore the shack."

I thought it might work, and it did. I had never known a time when Leroy wasn't hungry, and he crossed over to me and sat down quickly. "That's a good idea," he said watching me untie the knot in the sack. "You ain't afeared o' nothin'—snakes or ghosties or nothin' much else—if'n you got a li'l more food in your belly."

I reached in the sack and pulled out a ham biscuit and a chicken thigh and gave them to Leroy. I began eating a ham biscuit myself, intending to make it last as long as possible, so I could postpone looking inside that dark and frightening shack. But I couldn't eat slowly; the moment the salty ham biscuit hit my mouth I realized how hungry I really was. I ate all of it quickly, swallowing before it was half chewed, and reached for another before Leroy had even finished his.

"You wasn't foolin' none." He looked at me gulping down the food. "You looks like a half starved chicken gobblin' up shit."

"Told you I didn't have any dinner." I was pulling the juicy meat off a chicken leg. "And you don't have to talk like that. Can't you wait until I get through with my chicken anyway?" I kept on eating, but I could see that special smirk spreading across Leroy's face.

"Oh, 'scuse me, Mister Buster. I so sorry I done spoil your dinner." He was grinning at me nastily and enjoying every word. "But I thought all nice li'l white boys knew just what chickens eat. They's all the time eatin' shit. That's why we's all the time sayin' chicken shit, chicken shit!"

He doubled up with laughter and began rolling in the sand,

repeating the words over and over. I kept right on eating and paid no attention to him; the food tasted much too good for any of his words to stop my hunger. I threw the chicken leg away and reached for the last ham biscuit. Leroy sat up and watched me eat the last crumb and then lick my fingers. "You sho' enough was hungry." He had stopped laughing.

"I told you so, didn't I?" I felt highly satisfied and lay back on the sand staring up through the low-hanging branches to the sky. "When you're really hungry nothing much can spoil your appetite. You ought to know that. You're always hungry—at least you always say you are." I turned over to look at him. "But I don't see why you had to use those dirty words to try to make me sick at my—" Leroy grabbed my arm so tight that it really hurt. "What in the world are—"

"Hush up, be quiet," he whispered and slowly crawled over to the edge of the knoll and peered down at the shack below us. At first I thought he was playing a joke, but when I saw his tense body—he wasn't moving a muscle—and his frightened eyes, I knew something was very wrong. I crawled over by him and peeked down at the shack. I could see nothing unusual at all. "What's the matter?" I whispered.

"Somebody in that shack!"

I looked again and strained to listen. I couldn't hear anything at all. "I don't hear anything. What makes you think someone is—"

Leroy's hand clutched my shoulder so tight I nearly cried out. The door of the old shed opened very slowly, then closed again. Both Leroy and I looked up, checking to see if it was the wind. We looked around at the leaves above us; they weren't moving at all. We looked back at the shed door again. Nothing happened. I started to say something, but Leroy shook his head, frowned at me, and put his mouth right over my ear.

"It ain't the wind. Somebody or sompin' is in there!" His words whispered right in my ear, making my neck tingle, and I shivered all over. Then his next words scared me so that I stopped breathing.

"God a'mighty, Sweet Jesus!" The door opened again, and a

man stooped to come out. He held a rifle in his hand. He was a big man with a black mustache and the dirtiest, ugliest face I'd ever seen. He wore an old faded brown hat pulled down over his eyes and an old leather jacket pulled on over his overalls. He walked around to the river side of the shed and disappeared from our view. I wanted to run—I think Leroy did, too—but I couldn't move. All I could do was let out my breath and start shaking. Then we heard him call out in a rough voice: "I don't know where you varmints are—but I know you're out there someplace."

I had stopped breathing again. Leroy was shaking now, too. And then in the next moment I knew I was going to die. I could see the barrel of his rifle sticking out from the corner of the shack. It was pointed toward the knoll where we were stretched out listening and not daring to move. He came slowly into our view again, crouching low and swinging the barrel of his gun back and forth, and, with his next words, I knew I was going to die.

"If any one of you dares to come any closer, I'll let you have it with both barrels!" He looked wildly around for a moment, stood in the doorway, and shouted, "I've given you fair warning!" And he stepped into the shack and closed the door with a bang.

I don't suppose I'll ever know whether it was the banging of the door or his disappearance into the shed that caused us to move. Leroy didn't grab my hand—he didn't have to; we jumped up in one movement and ran. I ran almost as fast as Leroy; we didn't look back, we didn't turn, we didn't speak, we just ran. We ran until I was lost. I had no idea where we were. I didn't care as long as we were further away from that man with the rifle. I looked up and saw Leroy was running up a path a little ahead of me, and I tried hard to catch up. He stopped suddenly, and I ran headlong into him, nearly knocking him down. He looked about him to get his bearings, and then began following a barbed wire fence I hadn't even noticed before. But now I recognized it and knew where we were. It was the fence that separated Mattie's property from ours, and there was the back pasture that led up to our barn. I scooted under a wire fence and didn't even know that I had snagged my leg until much later.

I couldn't run anymore, but I kept walking as fast as I could through the pasture. I had nearly reached the barn before I realized that Leroy was still with me, trotting along by my side. When I saw him I stopped in the middle of the pasture and sat down right on the path. I thought for a minute I might be sick; the whole pasture was going around in front of my eyes, my heart was choking me, and I looked at my leg and saw blood trickling down. I wiped it away with my hand, but I didn't feel any pain at all. I looked up at Leroy and tried to smile but it turned into a shaky sob. "Who—who was that?" I choked.

"Never seen him before in my life." Leroy was still breathing hard, his eyes were rolling wildly, and he was looking in all directions at once, searching to see if anyone was following us. "Come on," he was still whispering. "Let's get on up to your house." We sort of reeled on up to the barn and came at last to the back gate. As I swung it open, I saw Mother and Allie sitting under the shade of the big black oak tree, and I started sobbing with relief as I ran to them.

"Some old man tried to shoot us down by the river. I don't know who he was, and Leroy didn't either. He had a gun and he said that he—" I dropped by Mother's chair, put my head in her lap, and bawled like a baby. I couldn't stop; I knew she was startled. She kept asking questions, and I kept trying to answer, but the words wouldn't come out. For a long time Mother stroked my hair and kept repeating, "It's all right, Bus. Everything is all right now. Just calm down, honey. Everything's going to be all right." And finally it did seem all right; I felt safe and protected, and that dirty, evil old man seemed far away. I raised my head and looked at Mother.

"It's true, Mother. I'm not making it up. Ask Leroy." And then I remembered what I'd done to hurt her. "I didn't mean to run away, and I'm sorry. I'll never do it again, I promise!"

She looked even more startled when I said that. "Run away?" she asked. "Where have you been? Where did you run away to?" She and Allie were staring at each other. "We wondered where you were," Mother looked somewhat dazed, "but we thought you were playing around the house somewhere." She looked at me and then at Leroy. "Leroy, come over here." He sidled slowly to me. "Now you two tell us what's been going on. Let's have the truth now."

I started telling them about taking the food and deciding to run away to get even with Sissy and Mammy. Mother's mouth tightened up at that, and I hurried on to tell about going over to Leroy's house and then running away from Mattie's to get to the old shack. While I was explaining how frightened we were when we saw that man with the rifle and what he had said, Mother turned to Leroy and raised her eyebrows like a question.

"Yes'm, Miss Polly," he blurted out. "It's the God's truth. That's just what he said. And he all a time pointin' that gun left and right. He done scared the livin'—" He stopped and froze, and then finished quietly, "—scared us near about to death."

Mother still looked uncertain; she knew that something very strange and frightening had happened to us, but I suppose she found our story as hard to believe as we did. It still seemed like a bad dream to me. She looked at Allie. "Allie, is there a shack down by the river? I've never seen one. Where is it?"

"It's about a half mile from where we go in swimming, Polly." Allie was looking at both of us, and there was a strained, worried expression on her face. "Bubba sometimes goes there in the fall, during hunting season, to get in out of the cold or the rain." She thought for a moment, then shook her head. "But I've never heard him or Kiddo mention anything about someone else using it." She got up quickly. "One thing I do know. I don't like this one bit. Just as soon as Cally and the boys come in from work we'll get to the bottom of this." She turned to Leroy. "You'd better get back home, Leroy. Mattie'll be worried sick." He started toward the gate. "And, Leroy, mind you now—you go straight home, you hear?"

"Ain't gonna waste one speck o' time, Miss Allie," he said, and from the way he flew out the gate, I felt sure he wouldn't stop running all the way home.

Mammy and Pappy were sitting on the front porch when we

went in through the house, and Sissy was rolling David Wallace back and forth in the buggy. Allie began questioning Pappy about the shack and asked him if he knew of anyone who used it for any reason at all. He told her he didn't, and then Mammy got very curious and wanted to know what all the questions were about. Allie told her what had happened. Sissy stopped pushing the buggy, her eyes got very big, and she came over to sit on the steps with me. I had to repeat the story all over again with everyone asking questions until I got confused and said, "I've told you everything I know, and I don't want to think about it anymore."

There was a long silence. Sissy scooted over close to me and took my hand in hers, and we sat there half smiling at each other without saying a word. We were no longer enemies, and no apology was needed for us to know it.

"I'm going to have Cally get to the bottom of this." Allie was very upset. "That old shack has never been anything but an eyesore. That man was probably a tramp that had been walking the railroad tracks." Mother and Mammy nodded in agreement, but Pappy said, "Tramps don't carry guns, Allie, at least the ones I've seen!"

"I'll have Cally and the boys tear that shack down, that's what I'll do!" Allie was very firm about it. But when she told Cally the whole story later that evening and ended by saying she wanted the shack torn down, he reminded her that it wasn't even on our property, that it probably belonged to Mr. McLemore.

"Then ask him to tear it down," Allie snapped. "I'm not going to have railroad tramps or bums living that close to the farm."

Cally went down to the shack early next morning to investigate. He found the sugar sack where Leroy and I had eaten our food and a good many footprints inside and all around the shed, but there was no other evidence that anyone had been there. For a few days everyone was uneasy, and if any stranger was seen walking down the lane to or from the railroad, we all stopped talking and watched till he was out of sight. But after a week, the man and the rifle were almost forgotten.

We were going back to Cincinnati in three days, and Leroy had come over to spend the day with me. Mammy had fixed us a picnic lunch that we carried out under the big oak tree in the back yard. After we had eaten the last scrap, we sprawled out in the sand to rest for a while. We didn't seem to have much to talk about; Leroy finally looked up at the sky and muttered, "Look like it gonna rain." There were black thunderheads forming over in the west, and it wasn't long before I felt a drop of rain hit my arm.

"Let's go inside," I said. "We'll find something to do." And we ran for the back door. Mother and Allie were cleaning up the kitchen. "You all stay in the house till the rain's over," Allie smiled at us.

"Can we play upstairs on the sleeping porch?" I asked.

"I don't see why not." Allie was stacking plates in the kitchen safe. "Just don't make too much noise. Pappy will probably take a nap in the east bedroom." She smiled at Mother. "And if this rain keeps up, Polly and I just might take a snooze ourselves. So don't be too noisy up there, you hear?"

"We won't," I yelled as we raced through the dining room. And I heard Mother say, "Huh! No more than a bunch of wild Indians they won't!"

Leroy and I ran up the stairs and out onto the front sleeping porch, and there was Sissy curled up on a bed reading a book. Leroy stopped dead when he saw her, and she looked up at us. "What you all doin' up here?" she asked.

"Mother and Auntee said we could play up here," I told her.

"Not while I'm reading the Bobbsey Twins!"

"Well, I guess Auntee said we could." The rain was pouring down now, and I knew we couldn't go back outside until it stopped.

"I can't read with you all making a racket," she said. "Go find someplace else to play." She turned back to her book.

Leroy was still standing in the doorway. "Come on, Leroy," I said in a huff. "Miss Priss is on her high horse today." And we walked back toward the stairs. The door to the west bedroom was closed, and I suddenly thought it might be a good place for us to play. "Come on, Leroy, we can stay in here for a while." I opened the door and we started in but stopped on the threshold.

There was a man crouching by the fireplace with his back to us. He was wearing an old brown hat and leather jacket, and as I stood there unable to utter a sound he turned toward us. It was the same ugly old man we had seen in the shack, but he didn't have a gun—or at least I didn't see one. He looked at us and grinned; two or three of his front teeth were missing, and he was the most horrible-looking man I had ever seen. I heard Leroy let out a groan deep down in his throat just about the time I screamed, because the man was coming toward us, still grinning. We backed out into the hall just as Sissy came storming in from the sleeping porch.

"What's the matter with you all?" she pouted. "I told you I couldn't read if you're making a lot of noise out here! What are you—" She was facing the door by now and saw the man standing there. She just stopped and stood there looking at him stupidly, her mouth hanging open.

"Children!" It was Allie's voice from downstairs. "I asked you to be quiet. Polly and I are trying to take a nap. You hear me?"

"It's all right, Mother. The kids are just excited. I'll keep them quiet." It was the dirty old man talking, just as if he had known Allie all his life.

"See that you do." Allie's voice floated away downstairs. I stood there looking at the old man. He took off his hat; he rubbed his teeth with his fingers, and they came off black; he took off the old jacket and looked at us. "Now will you kids please be quiet? I've still got to learn the lines for this silly old play, or Miss Etheridge will give me the devil. Now be quiet!"

I knew it was Bubba from the sound of his voice and the grin on his face, but I was still so frightened I couldn't move or speak. He stood there watching all three of us. Leroy was sitting on the floor with his back pushed tight against the wall; Sissy and I were standing close together starting to breathe again, when she began to smile and said, "It was you they saw down at the shack last week, wasn't it?"

Bubba sat down on the floor and began talking to us in a quiet voice. "Now listen, you all. I want you to promise me you won't say anything to the folks about this if I tell you." He looked at all of us. I just kept staring at him, trying to decide if he really was the man I had seen in the shack. I looked at Leroy, who hadn't moved; he looked like he was paralyzed, but his eyes kept rolling wildly from me back to Bubba.

"You promise?" Bubba whispered again. I nodded my head, but none of us spoke.

"Well, you see, school starts next week, and Miss Etheridge has asked me if I would be the villain in the play she's going to put on in September." He turned to Sissy. "You remember that day we went into town with Daddy to get some groceries and stuff for Mother?" Sissy nodded. "Well, that's when she gave me a copy of the play, and she asked me to learn as many speeches as I could before school starts." Bubba suddenly looked very embarrassed before he spoke again. "You know I don't memorize things by heart very quick, so she gave me a copy ahead of time, and that's what I've been doing." He turned to me and Leroy. "I didn't even know you all were anywhere near the shack that day I was down there practicing. I had been inside studying my speeches, and they sounded silly to me." He began to grin at us. "And then I put on that old hat and jacket of Daddy's and smeared dirt on my face and started walking around with my rifle in my hands, and it began to make more sense." He giggled softly. "I guess I was getting better than I thought 'cause I must have scared the hell out of you all!"

I thought of how frightened I was that hot afternoon down by the river, how we had run until we were exhausted, and how I had cut my leg on the barbed wire fence. When he giggled at our fear it made me furious.

"I don't see anything so funny about it," I said. "Goin' around scaring people half to death. I hope they go on and tear down that old shack." I couldn't have said anything worse as far as Bubba was concerned. His face got hard as stone.

"Now you listen here, Bus. I've spent a lot of time this year patching up that old shack. It don't leak anymore, and I use it lots of times." His voice got quiet again, and he looked at me with a pleading on his face. "It's sort of my secret place, you know, where I can always get away from the folks, or anybody else. Just for a little while."

"Like my fishin' place under the Chunky River bridge!" It was the first thing Leroy had said, and I looked at him with surprise. He wasn't smiling in agreement—he still sat half frozen—but he seemed to understand what Bubba meant.

"That's right, Leroy!" Bubba was surprised and pleased. "A place that you sorta think of as yours; it just belongs to you."

"That's right." Leroy was beginning to relax now. "Don't nobody else know about it 'ceptin' you." He began to smile a little. "Lawd God, but you sho' done scared the livin' shit out of us."

Leroy looked up quickly at Sissy. "'Scuse me!" Bubba giggled; I frowned; Sissy opened her eyes wide and then clapped her hands over her mouth to smother her shocked laughter.

"Well, I sure didn't mean to scare you 'cause I didn't even know you were anywhere around." Bubba looked at all of us again. "Now will you all promise not to tell anybody? I have to get off by myself to practice these lines in the play, and—" He sounded embarrassed again. "—and I'd feel awful silly if the folks started listening and watching me. You won't tell 'em, will you?"

I was so relieved to learn there would be no dirty stranger coming to kill us that I decided it might be a fine secret between us. Leroy and I both agreed not to tell anyone. But Sissy sat there on the floor looking too smug. Finally she said to Bubba, "I won't tell anyone either,"—she had a strange expression on her face—"but you'll have to say part of the play for us before I promise."

"Oh, Sis, come on!" But she just sat there shaking her head. "If you want me to promise not to tell—"

"Oh, all right." Bubba stood up. He knew that Sissy wasn't

going to change her mind, and he was mad about it. "Come on in the bedroom." And he stalked angrily through the doorway.

We followed him into the room, and he closed the door. He made us sit on the side of the iron bed and he walked over to the wall and took his rifle down from where it hung. He walked over to the fireplace. "Now, I don't want you kids to say a word till I've finished, and I don't care whether you like it or not. You just keep quiet. And I don't want to hear any gigglin' either." We sat in a row on the bed, stone-still.

He leaned the rifle against the mantel and bent over into the fireplace. He was doing something to his face; I couldn't tell what. Then with his back still turned to us, he put on the old hat and jacket. When he turned around there was the dirty old man again; his front teeth were blacked out, and he had smeared soot all over his cheeks where his beard was beginning to grow. I turned to Leroy, and we smiled weakly at each other, half remembering, half believing. Then he began to speak, and it was the same nasty, high nasal voice we had heard that terrible afternoon.

"I know you varmints are out there somewhere!" He moved slowly toward the bed where we sat. "I can't see you, but I know you're there." He backed over to the corner of the room and crouched down. "I've got the girl tied up inside my cabin, and if you come any closer, I'm gonna let you have it with both barrels!" He said a lot more, but I heard very little of it. I knew it was Bubba, but he was mean and coarse and ugly, and I thought he was a wonderful actor. After a while he stopped and said, "That's all I know by heart." And he hung the rifle back on the wall.

Sissy drew a deep breath. "I think you're gonna be good, Bub. You even scared me a little, and I knew who you were."

"I think I'll get a little better as I go along." He smiled shyly, but he looked very pleased. "If I don't have to worry about the folks watching me practice." He looked at Sissy.

"I'm not gonna tell," she assured him. "But I can't wait to see their faces when you do the play."

"You sho' is good, Mister Bubba." Leroy was grinning so

much I thought he might begin rolling on the floor squealing. "You scared me might as bad as before."

We never did tell anyone of the secret of the old man with the rifle, and the shack never was torn down. After we got back to Covington, Mother received a letter from Allie, and she told all about a play that Bubba had been in that fall. "He was really good," Allie said in the letter. "He played the part of the villain and almost stole the show. He was made up to look like the worst old tramp I've ever seen. Some of the younger school children who didn't know him seemed afraid of him." Then she finished by saying, "I guess he got the idea from that old tramp who frightened Buster and Leroy so bad last summer. Thank goodness, we were never bothered by him again."

CHRISTMAS—1926

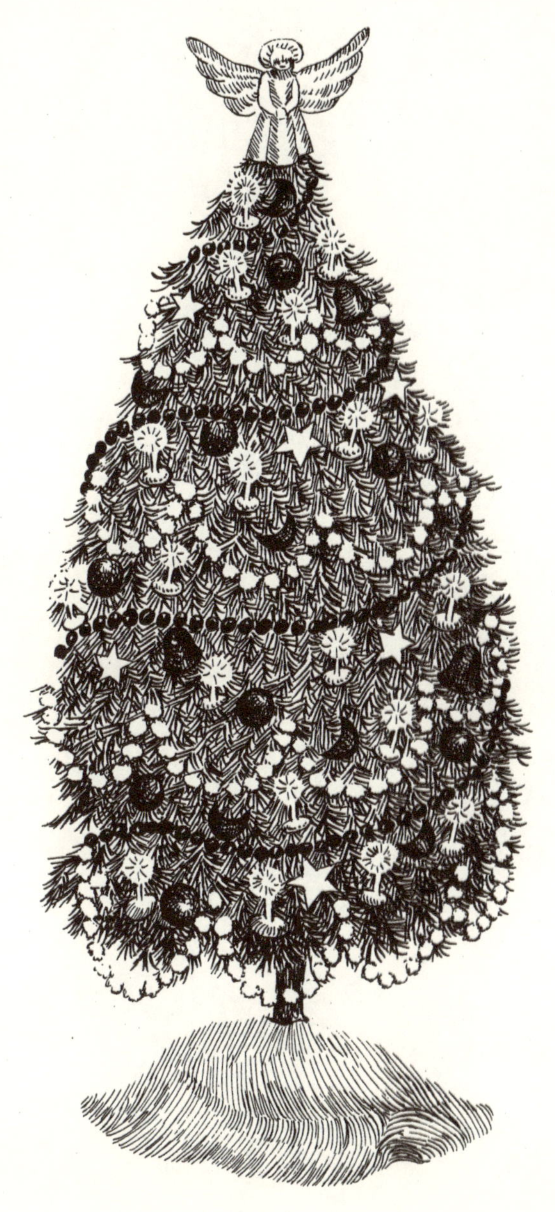

Two days after Thanksgiving Mother got a letter from Mammy. She read it quickly and would occasionally look up at me with a smile on her face. Then she turned back to the center page and read that again.

"What does Mammy have to say?" I asked. "Is everything all right at Riverside?"

"Everything's just fine." She looked up smiling again. "Matter of fact, this letter is mostly about you. Mammy and Allie have invited you to spend Christmas at Riverside. What do you think about that?"

I could feel the excitement rising in me. "You mean we're going to spend Christmas with them?" I couldn't imagine anything more wonderful.

"Now wait a minute, Bus—they just ask if you could come. They didn't invite us." Mother's eyes looked like a little girl's, and she leaned toward me. "Anyway, Daddy couldn't get away for more than two or three days, and I certainly wouldn't leave him here alone for Christmas."

I felt a great surge of disappointment. "Then I won't get to go either."

"I don't see why not, that is, if you really want to." She folded Mammy's letter and put it back in the envelope. "We'll save this for Daddy to read and see what he says when he gets home this evening."

I couldn't ever remember feeling so excited and happy and frightened all at the same time. All I could remember about Riverside at Christmas was burning my neck with a sparkler, and I wasn't even sure that I remembered; perhaps I had just heard it told so often that I thought I remembered. I had never been away from Mother and Daddy before in my life, and the thought of traveling on the train all alone was a little frightening. But it was the kind of fright that makes you anticipate wonderful things to come!

I stood at the window that evening waiting for Daddy to come from the post office. When I saw him coming up the street

I ran to open the front door, and all of my pent-up excitement exploded in one breath.

"Mammy and Auntee have asked me to come to Riverside for Christmas. Mother just got the letter this afternoon, and she saved it for you to read, and she says we'll see what you say, and I think I'd really like to go, don't you think so, too? And she says that—"

"Whoa now, slow down there!" Daddy was laughing and trying to hold me still. He looked up at Mother and said, "Now if you two will let me get my coat off and sit down, maybe I can make heads or tails out of what you're saying!"

He took off his overcoat, held his hands over the gas grate to warm them for a minute, and then sat down in his big rocker. "Now then," he smiled, "tell me what this is all about." I ran over to his chair. "Mammy has asked me if I can come to Riverside—"

"I think it's wonderful of them," Mother interrupted.

"—and I really think I'd like to go if—"

"But I've been worrying about that long train trip—"

"—you think it's all right, Daddy, 'cause I—"

"Hold it, hold it!" Daddy held his hands up. "I can't hear either one of you, you're talking so fast!" He looked at Mother. "Polly, why don't you just let me read the letter for myself." Mother crossed to the library table to get it.

"Do you think I really could go, Daddy? I mean—"

"Will you let me read the letter, son?" Daddy was getting a little annoyed at all the confusion around him. He unfolded the letter and read it through slowly. Then he turned back to the center page and read it again aloud.

"My main reason for writing is to ask a favor of you and Wallace. Allie and I have been talking it over, and we both would love for Buster to come spend Christmas with all of us this year. Of course, we'd love to have you and Wallace, too, but we know that Wallace can't get away for two weeks during the Christmas mail rush. And I'm sure you wouldn't leave him alone at Christmas. I know it's a long trip for a 12-year-old to make alone, but Bus is growing up so fast now, I'm sure he'll be all right. Allie and

I think it will be wonderful for him and Sissy to have one more Christmas just to be little kids again, along with Billy and David, who, by the way, are just the right age for Santa Claus this year. I do think Sissy and Bus would enjoy planning the Santa Claus for them, don't you? Please let me hear from you right away, and please let him come."

Daddy read a little more of the letter, but I wasn't listening. I was sitting in front of a big roaring fire in the front parlor at Riverside helping Sissy decorate a Christmas tree. It reached clear to the ceiling, and Sissy and I were looping long strands of tinsel all around it.

"Well, well, this is certainly a surprise." It was Daddy's voice. I looked up. He folded the letter and handed it to Mother. "Well, well," he said again slowly and rubbed his face.

"What do you think, Wallace?" Mother looked rather uncertain. "About the trip I mean?"

Daddy sat staring at the gas grate and began talking in that quiet way that he called thinking out loud. "Well, let's see now." He hesitated a minute. "If he had to change trains, that would be out of the question, of course. But the Southern runs straight through from Cinci to Enterprise, so that's no problem." He looked at Mother. "We'd put him on a Pullman, of course, and I would tip the porter real good to look after him and see that he got off at Enterprise all right."

"Don't you think I'd know when I got to Riverside?" I felt insulted. There they sat talking about me as if I weren't there at all. "I've made that trip as many times as you have!"

Daddy laughed and winked at Mother. "Well, Polly, what do you say if we let this young man make a long trip by himself, huh? What do you think?" They looked at each other and then at me.

"You mean I can go?"

Daddy cocked his head at me, looking very serious. "I think it might be a good idea for you to be on your own for a while," he said. "Yep, I'll make your train reservations first thing next week."

I broke into a war whoop and began running around the

room. I hugged Daddy, ran over and kissed Mother, and kept shouting, "Oh, boy, goin' to Riverside for Christmas, goin' to Riverside for Christmas!"

The next three weeks were the longest of my life, and I remember only a few things clearly. Mother seemed to be constantly checking on my clothes: Did I have enough? Would I be warm enough? Would my corduroy knickers be too warm for Mississippi? Could she get everything in one big suitcase? One evening after supper Daddy sat watching her checking some shirts against a long list in her hand. He frowned and said, "I, God, Polly! The boy's not going to Europe to spend the entire winter!"

"You just go on and read your paper." She didn't even look up from sorting some shirts. "You don't know anything about packing for a trip."

"Oh, no, of course not! I've only been doing it for about fifteen years."

"What?" She looked at him with real awareness for the first time. Then she smiled. "Oh, honey, I'm sorry. It's just that I want everything to be right for him."

"I know, I know," he said, smiling broadly. "And it will be, if you'll stop fussing about it so damn much!" And he turned back to his newspaper. He looked over at me and winked, and I winked back at him, for my daddy and I had a secret together that Christmas.

Leroy Riley had told me many times that someday he hoped he could own a pocketknife. "Not just any ole pocketknife but a good un. Like them Boy Scouts has got, with them two blades in 'em." His face would light up whenever he talked about that knife. When I knew that I was going to Riverside for Christmas, I also knew that I just had to get a pocketknife for Leroy. It would be a present for his thirteenth birthday and Christmas, too. I had saved half of my fifty-cent allowance for the past two weeks, but I knew that wouldn't be enough to buy a good one. Finally, the week before the trip, I decided to tell Daddy about it. Mother was busy in the kitchen, and I took him to my bedroom and closed the door.

"What's this secrecy all about, son?" he asked as he sat down on my bed.

"Can I ask you to do a favor for me?" I sat on the floor and looked up at him.

"Well, now, that depends. What kind of favor?"

"Daddy, I want to buy a Christmas present for Leroy Riley." He looked puzzled. "You know, Mattie Riley's boy, the one I go fishing with at Riverside."

"Oh, yeah, I remember now." He looked at me over the top of his glasses. "He's the one you ran away with that time, isn't he?"

I swallowed hard and whispered, "Yes, sir."

"What kind of a present do you want to give him, Bus?"

"A pocketknife, Daddy. Leroy has always wanted a pocketknife with two blades. I guess it's sorta like a Boy Scout knife." I looked up at him and hurried on. "I've saved fifty-cents out of my allowance for it, but I'm sure that won't be nearly enough." There was a puzzled frown on his face now. "I could pay you back out of my allowance, or you could just not give me any allowance at all until I'd paid you for it."

"Son—" He seemed very surprised. "Isn't a Boy Scout knife a pretty big present to give to a little colored boy?" He cleared his throat. "I don't think Mother is sending anything that expensive to Kiddo and Bubba or Sissy for Christmas. Seems to me that—"

"I don't want Mother to know anything about it!" I broke in.

Daddy raised his head, took off his glasses, and looked straight at me. "Why not?" His voice was quite stern now. "Why don't you want your mother to know about this?"

"I don't think she—" I stopped in confusion, and then finished feebly. "I just don't think she'd understand."

"I'm not at all sure that I do." Daddy put his glasses back on and peered at me. "Think you could try to explain it to me?"

"Well, I—" I looked at my Daddy who was watching me very carefully now. I knew exactly why I wanted to give Leroy a knife, but I didn't know how to explain what I felt.

"Daddy, Leroy is one of the best friends I've ever had. He's the one who taught me how to fish when I was real little." Daddy put his hand over his mouth and coughed, but he kept looking right at me. "But that isn't the real reason, I guess. He's awful poor, and he doesn't have any special thing he can call his own—I mean that didn't belong to somebody else first." I knew I wasn't saying it right; it didn't even sound right to me. I looked into Daddy's eyes and said, "I want to give him the knife and write on the card, 'Happy Birthday to Mister Leroy and Merry Christmas from Buster.'"

I could see that he didn't understand what I was saying even before he spoke. "Why would you want to write that, son?" he asked. I was suddenly remembering the day Leroy and I were sitting under the chinaberry tree at Mattie's cabin and he said, "I been callin' 'em Mister Kiddo and Mister Bubba ever since they done pass thirteen. Mama done told me to."

"Daddy, Leroy is gonna be thirteen years old sometime early this month—maybe he already is by now." Then it all came out in a rush. "He told me about a year ago that he would have to start callin' me Mister Buster when I got to be thirteen. Well, he'll be thirteen before I am, so I want to give him a present and write 'To Mister Leroy' on it. 'Cause I told him once if he had to call me Mister Buster, I'd sure start callin' him Mister Leroy." I paused for a breath and then finished very quietly, "It's sort of a secret joke between us, but I don't want this to be a joke. I want it to be real."

I was afraid to look up. When I finally did, Daddy was staring out the darkened window. He finally turned to me, took one of my hands, and held it for a long while. Then he shook it and said, "I'll get that knife for Leroy, son. And it'll be a secret just between us." He smiled. "Something like your secret joke with Leroy—only this will be for real, too." He got up very suddenly and opened the bedroom door, and I could hear him blowing his nose all the way to the living room.

Friday was the last day of school before the Christmas holidays, and my train left that night at ten o'clock. It began snowing right after my lunch, and I couldn't keep my mind on anything Miss Rawlings was saying. I'd look out the classroom window at the big heavy flakes falling and wonder how we would get to the depot that night. Finally the three o'clock bell rang, Miss Rawlings wished us all a Merry Christmas, and I flew down the stairs and out of the school building. It was snowing harder now; it came up almost to the top of my shoes, and I was beginning to worry. I love the snow, but if it kept up all night until train time, would we be able to get to the station? Or worse still, would the train be able to get through the snow?

Daddy was already at home when I got there. He had taken the afternoon off from work.

"Will we be able to get there through all this snow?" I asked breathlessly.

"No trouble at all, Bus." Daddy sounded very calm and reassuring. "Anyway, we're going to leave early and have our supper at the station restaurant, so we will be there in plenty of time." He looked at me and grinned. "How does that sound to you?"

"Sounds like fun to me!" I watched him as he opened his wallet to see if my train tickets were safe, and it suddenly struck me. I was the one who was having the wonderful trip home for Christmas, but he and Mother had done all the work, all the planning, and had taken care of all the details so I could just enjoy the trip. I needn't have worried about the snow or anything else; they would take care of it.

"I guess I'm going to miss you all this Christmas," I said, and for a moment I felt insecure and a little homesick already.

"I know you will," Daddy smiled. "And we're going to miss you, you bet!" Then his voice took on an excited tone. "But think of all the fun you'll be having with the folks, and all the stories you'll have to tell us when you get home!"

"Yeah." I half smiled. "I guess I will."

I had never before seen the Southern station so crowded with people. We had to wait in line for a table in the restaurant, and after we had eaten supper, we came out into the waiting room, which was packed with Christmas travelers. People who came from outside were covered with snow, carrying packages wrapped like Christmas presents, rushing from ticket windows to train gates to waiting platforms, talking and laughing and joking. Nobody seemed to mind the cold and dirty station. And, strangely enough, the snow seemed to turn it into a warm and friendly place.

They opened the gates to track 8 at nine-thirty, and the three of us walked down the platform looking for car 37. "Here we are, Bus," Daddy said, and a porter was waiting by the steps to take my bag and packages. I followed him up the steps to the vestibule and stopped. Daddy and Mother were right behind me; they bumped into me.

"Look!" I cried, pointing to the car door.

"What's the matter, Bus?" Daddy was puzzled.

"Red Desert! It's Red Desert again, Daddy!" I traced the letters with my finger.

"Yes, I see it is, son," he said, but he still didn't understand.

"We rode the same ole Pullman from Terre Haute all the way to Riverside several years ago!" I said. Mother and Daddy just looked at me. "Don't you remember that time we had the hot box and Mother thought we'd missed the train?"

Daddy opened the door and held it for Mother. "I guess I don't remember, son," Daddy laughed. "But I'm glad you do. One thing for sure, you won't have any hot box this trip."

"Good ole Red Desert," I smiled as I walked down the aisle to lower berth 7. I felt a little less lonely.

My berth was made up and ready for the night. The porter had put my big bag under the berth, and I saw Daddy hand him two one-dollar bills and take him to the end of the car. Mother kissed me and hugged me very hard. "Have a wonderful Christmas, Bussie Boy, and give the folks my best love." She hadn't called me Bussie Boy in years. I looked at her, and there were tears in her eyes as she hurried away down the aisle.

Daddy came back from talking to the porter. "All set, Bus?" He was smiling. I managed a nod of my head; I was afraid to speak. Then he pulled a small white box out of his pocket and handed it to me.

"I had the card printed like you wanted it, son. Now all you have to do is sign it yourself before you give it to Leroy." He bent down and kissed me hard on the cheek. "Merry Christmas, boy!" And he was gone down the aisle. I stood outside the berth and watched him till he was out of sight. I had never felt so lonely in my life.

The porter stopped by my berth. "Anything I can get you, young man?"

"Oh, no, thank you." I opened the curtain to lower 7. "I think I'll hop in bed before we pull out of the station."

"That's a good idea," he smiled and leaned over the bed. "Now if you wants anything during the night, your bell is right here." He pointed to it. "Right there between the windows. Good night!"

"Thank you," I said and closed and buttoned the green curtains. I put the package Daddy had given me on the windowsill and undressed as quickly as I could, trying not to remember I was alone. I was nearly undressed when somebody bumped into my curtain, and I sat there scarcely breathing. I heard the porter say, "Here you are, sir!" Someone was climbing up the little ladder to the berth above mine. Everything was very quiet again—too quiet, it seemed to me. Then I saw why; the windows were closed tight against the cold air. I had never before ridden in the train in the winter. I finished undressing and snuggled down under the thick blankets. I picked up the white box on the windowsill and opened it. There was a brand new knife inside with a card tied to the handle. The card, in big black printed letters, read, "Happy Birthday to Mister Leroy and Merry Christmas from______," with a blank space for me to sign my name. I put the lid back on the box, snapped the rubber band around it, and held it tightly in my hand. I tried to force it into my mind, but that made it worse because my eyes began to sting and I gulped to hold back the tears. Just then the train gave a jerk—and I was starting the long trip back to Riverside for Christmas.

I didn't see Mammy standing on the back stoop waving a towel when we passed Chunky River bridge, because I was standing in the Pullman vestibule right behind the porter. He had carried my bag and packages out there early so I'd have plenty of time to get off. "It's just a flag stop for passengers that got on the train north of Birmingham," he told me, "and they just stop long enough for me to get your bags off." The train was slowing down; he opened the door and lowered the steps just as we came to a screeching stop. He lifted my bags down, then turned to help me down the steps. He looked up and down the little platform, then turned to me. "You is shore some of your folks comin' to meet you?" He looked concerned.

"Oh, yes, somebody will meet me I'm sure."

The engineer gave two shrill blasts on the whistle, and the train was moving; the porter waved from the vestibule door and called, "Merry Christmas!" and the train rumbled on south.

I looked around the platform; there were several men in overalls sitting on the station waiting bench who eyed me curiously. There were a good many people coming and going around R.J. Williams General Store, but there was no sign of any of the folks from Riverside. I knew I couldn't walk the mile to the house and carry my bag and packages, and I certainly couldn't leave my bag on the station platform. I walked hesitantly up toward the men sitting on the bench. They turned and stared at me.

"Excuse me, sir," I addressed the one closest to me. "Have you seen Mr. Neal or Mr. Gunn? They live over at Riverside. Have they been around the station today?"

"No, sonny, ain't seen Mr. Neal at all." He screwed up his mouth and spat a big brown blob of tobacco juice on the platform. "Course nobody ain't seen Mr. Gunn for weeks now, 'cept on Sa'day night or Sunday maybe. He's working at the creosote plant up near Meridian, drives up there every day with old man Jennings." He spat again and squinted his eyes. "What you lookin' fer them fer, sonny?"

I didn't like him; he frightened me. He looked almost as dirty and ugly as Bubba did when he was practicing for his play. I decided I wasn't going to tell him anything and turned back to stand uncertainly by my bag and packages.

"I seen you get off that train, boy." He was standing up now, and the other men were watching him with more interest. "Where'd you come from, sonny?"

"I'm Mr. Neal's grandson." I was beginning to panic. "I got on the train in—"

I heard a horse and buggy pull up at the front of the station and a voice call out, "Whoa there, hoss." I looked up, and there was Mattie Riley laboriously climbing down from the driver's seat. I forgot bag, packages, and everything else and rushed down the platform yelling, "Mattie! Mattie Riley! It's me, Buster!" She was lumbering toward me as fast as she could, and when I reached her she grabbed me and hugged me up tight to her breast. She smelled delicious and warm and safe, and she made me feel exactly the same way. She finally let go, and I clung to her arm as she began talking.

"Miss Allie and your Mammy right smack in the middle of fruit cakes and Lady Baltimores, and they couldn't leave 'em. That's why they done sent me to fetch you. You been waitin' long?"

"Not very long, Mattie." I grinned at her. "But I was getting a little worried."

She threw back her head and laughed. "Well, no need to fret yourself, chile. Ole Mattie right here with you." She looked around. "Where you have your bags and stuff?"

I pointed back down the platform. "That's good." She started forward. "Let's go fetch 'em to the buggy and get started home."

As we walked down the platform I felt Mattie's hand tighten on my arm, and she began to walk faster. "Don't pay no mind to that man standin' there, Buster—let's just get your things and get on home!" She was looking straight ahead of her, a hard scowl on her face. She picked up my bag, I gathered up the two packages, and we turned in the direction of the buggy. Out of the side of my eye I saw the man was still standing by the bench; as we passed him, he called out to me, "Well, good for you, sonny, I see you done found your mammy." It angered me so I turned to him to speak, but Mattie jerked my arm so hard I dropped one of my packages. The man was laughing at me as I picked it up and hurried on to the wagon.

"Who was that man?" I asked after we were settled in the buggy and started on the road to Riverside.

"That's ole Jake Collins." Mattie's mouth was a hard straight line. "He don't do nothin' but drink moonshine and whore around on Sa'day night. Nothin' but white trash." She let out a big "huh," and then added, "Wouldn't s'prise me none if ole Jake Collins turned out to be that man what scared you and Leroy half to death in that ole shack." I looked up guiltily, but her face was still tight with anger. That surprised me so that I quickly changed the subject.

"Mattie, how come Leroy didn't ride over with you?"

"Now son, you know Leroy might nigh as well be me." She slapped the reins on the back of the horse. "I brought him and Emmie Lou over to Miss Allie's with me today to help out with the chores. But where is he at?" She looked at me and half grinned. "You prob'ly know as well as I does. Huh! Gone fishin' or settin' on that stile. I 'speck he done run down there to watch your train go by."

I felt a twinge. If Leroy had been there watching my train come in, he would have waved, and I had missed him. "It sure will be good to see him again, Mattie." Then very casually, I asked, "How old is Leroy now?"

"Done had his thirteenth birthday week before last!" Mattie almost giggled. "Thinks he's a growed man hear him talk!"

I put my hand on my pocket. I could feel the outline of the little white box with the knife and card inside. I held onto it tightly as we turned into the lane leading to Riverside.

Mammy and Allie had heard the buggy as we headed up the front lawn. They were standing on the porch; Allie was waving, and Mammy came down the steps to meet us. "Oh, Bussie Boy, Bussie Boy!" Mammy was almost crying as I jumped down from the buggy and ran to meet her. As she hugged me she said, "Thank the Lord you got here safe and sound. Polly would never forgive me."

"Cain't be callin' him Bussie Boy much longer, Miz Neal." Mattie was grinning at us as she got the packages out of the buggy. "He pert near big as my Leroy. Spit and turn around twice and he be a growed man!"

"Have you got a kiss to spare for me?" Allie was standing on the porch with her arms wide open. I ran up the steps and hugged her. I had never seen her look so pretty; she had a blue shawl around her shoulders, her skin was soft and clear, and her eyes were shining. She had gained considerable weight since I had seen her, and to me she looked beautiful. I told her so.

"You sure are pretty, Auntee," I said. She laughed and kissed me.

"And you know what, Bus?" Her eyes were almost dancing. "I feel pretty, too!"

We stood on the porch smiling at each other until she put her arm around me and we started into the house. When we got inside I asked, "Where's Sissy?"

"She's over at the school." Allie was leading me to the back bedroom. "They're having a Christmas party for her class this afternoon. But she'll be home by four or five o'clock. And won't she be happy to see you, you bet." She sat down on the bed. "You and Billy are going to sleep in here, and Sissy will be in with us. Now why don't you change your good clothes and come on into the kitchen with Mammy and me. We're making our Christmas cakes." She got up and crossed to the doorway and stood there for a minute looking at me. "Oh, Bus, you don't know how glad I am Polly let you come. This will be a wonderful Christmas; I can just feel it in my bones." She stood there so long I thought she was about to say something else. But she only smiled and sighed and walked into the kitchen.

Pappy and Kiddo and Bubba had gone to Meridian that morning with Cally to do some Christmas shopping, and they wouldn't be back before dark. Billy was spending the afternoon with Victor Jennings, so that left only David Wallace in the house, and he spent most of the time in the kitchen licking the cake pans after Mammy and Allie got the cakes in the oven. I watched them work for a while; Allie would sit at the kitchen table cutting up the fruit for the Lady Baltimore cake, and Mammy would beat the batter over and over, her mouth screwed up in a tight knot. The wood fire in the stove was roaring away, and it seemed awfully hot after a while, so I said, "I think I'll go out for a while. It's so pretty today." They were busy with the cakes and only half heard me.

I walked through the front hall; as I passed the parlor door I saw Mattie Riley, down on her hands and knees, cleaning out ashes from the parlor fireplace. I started to ask her about Leroy, but I decided against it and went out to the front lawn. The sun was a weak yellow disk in the sky, but I couldn't believe how warm it was; it almost felt like summertime, but there were no leaves on the oak trees, and none of Allie's flower beds were in bloom. The lane down to the railroad track seemed very empty and bare, and suddenly I thought again of Leroy. I had his present in my pants pocket; maybe he was still sitting on the stile, and if he wasn't, maybe he might be fishing under the Chunky River bridge. It was worth a chance; I didn't want anyone else around when I gave him his knife. I ran down the lane toward the tracks, thinking he wouldn't still be there but hoping somehow he would. The bushes and trees were bare all around me, making the lane seem much wider and more open than I remembered. I saw him long before I got to the stile. There he sat, hunched over with his head almost between his legs. I began to tiptoe through the damp clay as soon as I saw him; I was determined to surprise him if I could, and then I heard the whistle. A freight train was coming, and Leroy had waited there for it. As it got closer I kept walking toward him; he was intent on the approaching train and had no idea that I was anywhere near. I waited breathlessly until the caboose was passing, and then I jumped on the stile.

"Hey, Mister Leroy!" I yelled in his ear.

He jumped like he'd been hit, lost his balance, and fell off the stile. He just sat at the foot of the stile looking at me, as I climbed up and sat down on the top step. I grinned at him and said, "Guess I scared the livin' shit out of you this time, didn't I?"

He just sat there staring at me for a while; then his face broke into a wide grin. "Where you come from, white boy?" His teeth were shining in the pale sunlight, and his eyes had a nasty gleam. "I been settin' here all afternoon waitin' for your train to come by, and you ain't even on it! How'd you get here, that's what I wants to know."

"Oh, I was on that train all right." Then I tried my best to talk and to smirk the way he did so often. "Maybe your eyesight ain't so good no more since you got so much older."

I thought at first he was going to get mad, but then he rolled over in the dirt and started his squealing. He raised his laughing face to me and said, "I do believe you beginnin' to smarten up, white boy. I do believe you beginnin'."

Somehow I knew this was the right moment. I reached in my pocket to be sure it was there; then I climbed down the stile and sat there beside him. I pulled the little box out of my pocket and handed it to him. "Merry Christmas, Mister Leroy."

He didn't say a word. He just looked at it and then at me. I was suddenly embarrassed, and to cover it I said, "I hope you like it, Leroy. I think you will."

He hadn't moved, and I began to think he never would. So to urge him on I said, "Go on, Leroy, open it."

He finally looked up. "This here for me?" His voice seemed far away.

"Course it is. Open it up and you'll see."

He took the rubber band off and slowly lifted the lid of the box. He turned it over, and the knife fell out on the ground. He could see the printed card tied to the handle, but he didn't touch it; he bent over closer to read it but still wouldn't touch the knife. He read it two or three times, his lips moving over every word; then slowly he looked up at me. "This here for me?" I nodded. "It's for real? It ain't no joke?" He picked up the knife and examined it carefully; he read the card again, and then pulled out one of the blades. When he saw the second blade he was dumbfounded. "God a'mighty, it's got two blades."

"Well, I thought that's what you always wanted, a knife with two blades."

He held it up to the sun and watched it as it gleamed. "It's a whittlin' knife for sho'!" He seemed to think I wouldn't understand what he meant. "I can might nigh whittle anything I wants

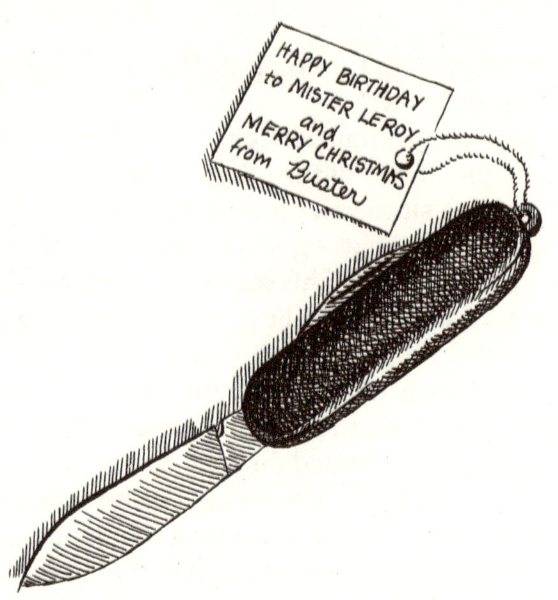

with this here ole knife." He looked at me suddenly and his eyes got hard with fear. "You ain't gonna take it back, is you?"

I thought of the trouble I'd had explaining the knife to Daddy, how careful I had been not to lose it during the train trip, nearly wearing out my pocket reaching in to be certain it was still there, and now Leroy was asking if I was going to take it back. It made me really angry with him.

"What kind of a friend do you think I am?" I must have been shouting. "I don't go to all the trouble to buy somebody a Christmas present and lug it all the way from home and then decide to take it back." I was far more hurt than I realized. "But if you don't want it, I'll be glad to give it to somebody else."

"No you don't!" He held the knife right against his chest, so close that I was afraid he might cut himself with the sharp blade. "Ain't never had nothin' like this before, and ain't you or nobody else gonna take it away from me—ever!"

We sat there staring at each other—eye to eye. Slowly I began to realize that Leroy loved the card, too—he had read it several times before he had even touched the knife. But most important—and it was almost like an explosion in my head—Leroy had probably thanked people many times before for small gifts or favors all his life and then had seen them snatched back from his friendly grasp. I think I realized for the first time that day why Leroy was wary—of me or anyone else; the chip on his shoulder was his protection. His rolling and squealing were his real outlets to freedom—the only times his guard was completely down. He had shown this to me many times, openly and freely; I was his friend, and the friendship was almost more than he could bear.

I sucked in my breath, afraid that I would spoil everything. "It's yours, Leroy. I brought it just for you. Nobody else." Either my face or my voice must have told him the truth. He loosened the card from the handle, looked at it closely, folded it carefully, and put it in his pocket. Once more he held the knife up to the sun.

"Sho' is somethin'." He sighed and lay back on the ground, holding the knife high above him. "Sho' do shine, don't it?" And I'm sure he had forgotten I was there, until his eye caught mine again. He jumped up quickly and plopped himself on the top of the stile. "Know the first thing I gonna do with this here knife?" He had folded up the big blade and was releasing the small one. "Gonna make us a special sittin' place on this here ole stile. Which side you like to set on?"

I had no idea what he was talking about. He indicated the wide wooden top step.

"Which side do you like best?"

"This side," I said and pointed to the left.

He started cutting into the wood, and I watched him as he worked, wondering what he was planning to do. He would dig out little pieces of wood and then cut deeper into the grooves he had made. He worked very carefully, with great concentration, and he would not be hurried. Once I asked him, "What are you making, Leroy?" and he merely grunted, "Just hold your horses." He kept his body doubled over the top step, with his face so close to his work that I really couldn't see what he was doing. Finally he drew a big breath, blew some wood shavings away, and raised himself up to peer at the top step. He nodded with obvious satisfaction.

"There now," he said. "That's your side from now on. Cain't nobody set there but you!" I climbed up a step or two to look. He had carved my initials on the left side—B.B. in big capital letters—and I was amazed at how smooth and even the letters were. "Hey, Leroy, this is really good." I turned to him. "I didn't know you could print like that."

"I cain't." He giggled. "My schoolteacher say she cain't hardly read what I writes. She don't like me much, I guess 'cause I don't go no more'n I have to."

I looked at him and then back at the big carved letters. "Then how can you carve letters this good?"

"I been practicin'," he explained. "I done ruined Mama's best kitchen knife tryin' to do some carvin'." He laughed. "She think she done lost it. I ain't never told her I done broke it." He looked down at his knife and wiped the blade clean. "Now that I got me a sho' enough knife, you gonna see some real carvin'!" His face was so alive with joy it made me glad just to look at him.

The short winter day was clouding over; it was getting late, and Sissy was probably home by now, or would be soon. I stood up. "We'd better get back to the house, Leroy."

"Ain't goin' nowhere till I done finish my side," he said and started to work again.

I climbed over the stile and turned to him. "Well, I'll see you tomorrow or the next day. Sometime before Christmas anyway."

"Sho' will." He stopped carving and looked up, smiling. "Seem to me like Christmas done come a'ready!"

I started up the lane toward the house. I turned once to look back; Leroy was still working away intently, carving his initials on his side of the stile.

There was a fly crawling on my nose; I brushed it away, turned over, and dozed off to sleep again. But once more the fly had landed right on the end of my nose. I sneezed and woke up. There was no fly on my nose—there never had been. Kiddo was bending over my bed, brushing a little feather back and forth across my face, and he was grinning broadly. "Wake up, Yankee Boy, wake up! You plannin' to spend all of your Christmas holiday in bed?"

I was still only half awake, but I couldn't help laughing. "How long have you been standing there?"

"Long enough to know that you're the hardest person to wake up I've ever seen. I was just about to get a dipper full of water to pour on you." He started toward the door. "Maybe I'd better—"

"Don't you dare!" I yelled and jumped out on the cold floor. I rummaged around and found my clothes and raced into the front parlor to dress. There was a great roaring wood fire sending out a delicious warmth. I pulled a chair up close to it and sat down to dress. By the time I had pulled on my stockings and laced my shoes, my front sides were roasting and my back sides were freezing. I stood up and twisted my buttocks to the blaze to finish dressing. I was still buttoning my shirt when Mammy came in carrying a big cup of hot chocolate.

"Drink this up before breakfast," she said. "It'll warm you up. I've set a place for you and Sissy at the kitchen table by the stove where it's nice and warm. When you finish dressing by the stove come on out here. Make haste, now!"

I had drifted to sleep the night before with Leroy's face in front of me. He had carved so many initials on the stile it looked like my Chinese puzzle at home. And when he had finished with the stile, he started carving on the crossties of the railroad track, until a freight train came puffing across Chunky River bridge and he ran for safety. When it reached the place on the tracks where Leroy had been carving, the crosstie gave way, and the freight cars just tumbled over and lay quietly on their sides. Apples and oranges and peppermint candy canes spilled out of the car and rolled down the bank by the stile. Leroy got up from his initialed seat and I got up from mine, and together we began gathering up the fruit and the candy that lay strewn around the red clay bank. While we were doing all this, a big green fly lit on my nose and I tried to brush him away. That's when I woke up to find Kiddo by my bed.

When I had finished dressing by the fire I hurried out to the kitchen. It had turned very chilly during the night, but the kitchen was warmed with the wood stove fire and filled with the odor of sausage and grits. Mammy was turning batter cakes in the big iron skillet and stacking them up on two plates in the warming oven. Sissy was already sitting at the table, and I sat down across from her.

"Mornin', sleepyhead," she grinned.

"You didn't have to wait for me, Sis." I was remembering that Mother had said to be sure and mind my manners while I was at Riverside.

"Huh." Mammy was lifting the last batter cakes from the skillet. "She didn't have to wait long. She hasn't been up more than ten minutes herself. So there's no need for you to feel bad about sleeping late." She brought our plates to the table filled with the brown crispy cakes. She put her hands on her hips and stood looking at us; then her wrinkled face lit up in a big smile. "I may not have any fancy presents for you this year, but don't say I never gave you anything special." She looked at the plates in front of us. "They're the best I've made in a long time, so eat up."

Sissy and I covered them with fresh churned butter and ribbon cane syrup and ate up; we needed no further urging. Between mouthfuls, Sissy looked up. "Kiddo and Bubba are taking us out to the south pasture today to get our tree."

"If the weather holds," Mammy added.

"I know." Sissy forked another big bite and wiped her mouth. "They've already picked out two or three trees they think are pretty, but Mother said we could decide which one we could decorate best."

"I want one that reaches clear to the ceiling," I mumbled with my mouth full of batter cake.

"Oh, I'm sure one of them will, if it's full enough. That's what we'll have to decide today. Anyway, we'll decorate it tomorrow, so's it'll be ready for Christmas Eve. Then tonight we're going to the Christmas pageant at church, and after the pageant they'll have a Santa Claus for the little kids, you know, like Billy and David."

"Will he give out presents, too?"

"Probably just things like candy canes or chewing gum, things like that."

We had just finished eating when Kiddo and Bubba marched into the kitchen with Billy right behind. They all were dressed in heavy sweaters and toboggans; they walked right past us to the back door and Bubba called over his shoulder.

"We'll see you all later; we're going out to pick out the tree now!"

Sissy and I jumped up from the table, almost upsetting the syrup pitcher. "Now you just hold your horses till we get our coats on." Sissy carried our empty plates over to the dishpan. Then she turned to Bubba, who was still by the open door. "Anyway, Mother said Bus and I could pick out the tree we wanted, so there!" She stuck out her tongue, and Bubba made a lunge for her.

"Close that door and get out of here if you're going." Mammy was laughing. "I want to get on with my baking."

I ran into the bedroom and found my Mackinaw jacket and cap and put them on as I went out the back door. Out by the barn the horse was hitched up and waiting; Kiddo and Bubba were in the driver's seat with Billy sandwiched between, and Sissy was on the tailgate swinging her legs. I jumped out of the barn lot.

There was a sharp cutting wind out of the northeast, and the sky was the color of dull lead. We bumped over some old wagon ruts, and my teeth began to chatter, not so much from the cold as from the wagon ruts. I recognized them. Leroy and I had stopped there to sit down and catch our breath when we thought the old tramp from the shack was chasing us. I turned to glance up at Bubba; he was searching out the pasture for trees they had picked out.

"You're cold?" Sissy was watching me.

"Nope, not really. I guess I'm just glad to be here with you all." And I was. The cold didn't matter. The gray sky and the pasture land were all a part of Christmas, and these were the people I knew and loved best. I suddenly thought of Mother and Daddy sitting at home by the gas grate and wondered what they would be doing right now. I remembered Daddy saying to me, "We're going to miss you, you bet, but think of all the fun you'll have with the folks," and for one tugging moment I wished that they were here with us. Now the wagon was rolling along parallel to the fence that separated the Riley property from Riverside. I smiled as I thought of Leroy and wished he might be here with me, too. But he would be much too busy today, whittling and carving up everything in sight. I laughed out loud.

"What's so funny?" Sissy was laughing, too, and Kiddo had turned to look at us.

"Nothin' funny, really." I colored up with embarrassment. "I'm just glad you all invited me to spend Christmas with you."

"Well, don't worry. We'll never do it again." Kiddo was looking at Bubba. "Whoever heard of spending Christmas in bed, unless you're sick." He leaned over toward Sissy. "You better be careful, Sis. Don't get too close to him; you'll catch the sleepin' sickness!"

Billy looked at me, then at Kiddo. "Is Buster sick?" he asked, and they all started laughing, so he decided it was safe for him to join in.

We jolted across several deep gullies on the upper end of the pasture, and I tightened my grip on the side of the wagon. It was here that most of the evergreens grew, lots of pines and some cedar trees as well. I began to look around carefully to see if I could spot any of them that Bubba and Kiddo had chosen as possible Christmas trees. We passed a pine tree that was beautifully shaped, and I nearly called out for them to stop. But I realized as I looked again that it was much too tall, probably fifteen or twenty feet.

"Whoa, there," Kiddo called to the horse, and Sissy and I jumped out of the wagon. She ran up a sandy slope ahead of us and circled a cedar tree. "I don't know if this is one of 'em you all picked out, but it sure is a beauty. Look how full it is, Bus." I had followed her up the slope. "What do you think of it?"

I walked around the tree, looking at it from all sides. It was perfectly shaped from any angle and was free of that rusty color so many cedar trees have in winter. But I was afraid it would be too tall. "How tall do you think it is, Kiddo?"

"Just about eight or nine feet, I'd say."

"Would it fit in the parlor?"

"I guess so."

Sissy and I circled the tree again. Halfway around we met Billy coming the other way. "Do you like it, Billy?" I asked.

He looked up to the top of the tree. "I like it a lot," he said. "But do you think Santa Claus will like it?" He looked very serious. "What would happen if he didn't?"

"I just betcha he'll love it!" Sissy was grinning at him, then she ran over and hugged him. "Just you wait and see if he don't!"

Billy broke away and ran to the wagon calling excitedly to Kiddo and Bubba as he ran. "This is it! This is the one we want! Sissy says he'll like this one so let's get this one, Kiddo. Santa will like this Christmas tree."

We were all smiling at Billy's excitement, and then somebody, one of us, started laughing. I don't know which one. At first I thought we were laughing at Billy, then we were laughing at each other, with each other together, laughing at Billy's joy, which soon became our own, laughing for the joy of Christmas.

Kiddo and Bubba got the axes from the wagon and started chopping at the base of the tree. Billy danced around from one side to the other, watching them, hopping from one foot to the other. He began to sing "Jingle bells, jingle bells, jingle all the way," and Sissy joined in. When the tree finally fell with a whoosh, Billy ran to the top of it, picked up a small branch and declared, "I'll carry this part!" And suddenly we were all helping; Kiddo and Bubba grabbed the trunk, Sissy and I the middle branches, and, still singing, we hauled it into the wagon. Kiddo called, "Giddap," and we were headed back to the house.

I looked at Sissy sitting by me on the tailgate and whispered somewhat shyly, "Merry Christmas!"

"Yeah." She put her arm around my shoulder and smiled. "It looks like it sure enough is gonna be!"

All the way back to the house I was worried, afraid that our Christmas tree would be too tall. Kiddo and Bubba hauled it off the wagon around to the front porch and nailed two boards on the bottom to make a stand for it. When they had finished it, Kiddo called out to us. "You all open the front doors so we can get it into the parlor." Sissy and I swung both doors wide as they carried it in. I held my breath as they turned it sideways to get it through the parlor door, but they made it and set it in the corner between the windows. It was a tight squeeze as they slowly stood it up on its base, for the topmost branch was almost touching the ceiling. I heaved a sigh of relief and murmured, "Oh, it really is beautiful." Sissy stood with her arms folded, eyeing it doubtfully. "I'll never be able to get my Christmas angel on the top. It'll hit the ceiling. The tree's too tall." For a minute she looked as though she might cry.

"Oh, I bet it will." Kiddo stepped up to take a long look. "I'll bet it'll fit right on that top branch, with maybe an inch or two to spare."

"Well, I'll just make sure right now," Sissy said, and she ran out into the hall and up the stairs. When she came back, rather breathless, she was holding a white paper angel with tinfoil wings spread wide. She straightened the wings to her satisfaction, handed it to Bubba, and said almost pleading, "See now if it will fit down right over that tip-top branch." He took it from her carefully and climbed on top of the library table. "Hand me that chair, Kiddo," he said. "I can't reach it from here."

Kiddo put the chair on top of the table and held it steady. Bubba eased himself up, still holding the angel. Slowly, almost on tiptoe, he leaned over toward the top branch, pulled it toward him, and slid the angel over the pointed top. Very carefully, as if he were afraid to let go, he pushed the top of the tree straight again, stepped off the chair, and jumped down to the floor. He hit the floor so hard that the tree quivered as if it were still living, and the angel swayed slightly to and fro, almost as if she were hovering and had found at last the exact place, the only place where she could make her glorious announcement.

All of us watched the little miracle and said nothing. Even

little Billy stared open-mouthed and was silent. Bubba was the first to speak. "Looks like she's found her perch!"

"She's beautiful."

"It's a close fit, but it looks good."

"I never thought my angel would look that pretty."

"Is it alive, Sissy?" Billy broke the spell, still peering uncertainly at the angel, and, as I turned to watch him, for a fleeting moment I thought it might be really alive, just as we were alive with the wonder and the magic of the tree. Then the moment was gone; we were all talking and laughing at once.

"I made it in school, Bus," Sissy said. "It was my Christmas project."

"Looks real good, Sis." Bubba grinned. "I couldn't have done better myself."

"Well, I don't know, now." Kiddo was walking to the far side of the room, scrutinizing the angel from every angle. "Maybe if we bent the wings a little more or maybe painted 'em white to match her skirt."

But Sissy didn't even get ruffled. She just stuck out her tongue and smiled at him. Then the smile changed suddenly into an impish grin. "You better be nice to me, Kenneth Gunn, or I'll plunk myself down right smack between you and Margaret Harper at church tonight." She giggled. "I can just picture you and dear Margaret tryin' to bill and coo with me sittin' right between you."

Kiddo's face turned the color of cranberry sauce, but he fought right back. "Oh, I don't think I'll have to worry too much about that." His eyes got very big and solemn. "'Specially if Mr. Jack Del Buno happens to be at church tonight."

I looked from Sissy to Kiddo. They were playing some kind of game with each other that I didn't quite understand. Their faces showed no real anger, but they seemed very wary of each other, and suddenly they both decided to let the matter drop. But I wasn't ready to.

"Who is Margaret Harper and Jack—what'd you say his name was?" I asked.

"That's Sissy's new boyfriend." Bubba was grinning and

enjoying their embarrassment. "And Margaret Harper is the Margaret Harper of Stonewall. She's Dr. Harper's oldest girl, and right now she's Kiddo's one and only. She can do just about anything and everything, to hear him tell it. Why, she even plays the piano for all the picture shows down at Stonewall—plays just like an angel. Like this." And Bubba ran to Allie's piano, raised the lid, and started banging and singing, "I love you truly, truly dear," all the while rolling his eyes at Kiddo.

Sissy began laughing when she saw Kiddo make a lunge for Bubba seated at the piano. Kiddo got his arm around Bubba's neck, and I thought there was going to be a free-for-all rough-and-tumble right in the parlor, but Allie's voice stopped it.

"What's going on in here?" She was standing in the door smiling at all of us. "And who's been banging away on my piano?"

"They're teasing each other about their girlfriends and boyfriends," I laughed. Then I looked at Kiddo. "Are you going to marry her, Kiddo?"

Allie let out a whoop of laughter and sat down in the big rocker. "I hope not for another few years anyway." She was sitting there rocking back and forth smiling happily at all of us when she suddenly spied the angel on the tree. "Oh, Sissy, it really is lovely. It's going to set the tree off to perfection." She reached over and grabbed Sis and kissed her. Still looking at the tree, her eyes lit up with a sudden thought.

"Tell you what. Since you all have already got the angel in place and the tree is up, why don't we just decorate it right now, right after dinner. What do you say?"

Billy started jumping up and down, clapping his hands. "Right now, right now." He made it into a song.

"Oh, yes, let's do," Sissy cried out. "Then we can enjoy it all day tomorrow." She swung Billy up in her arms. "Then it'll be ready in plenty of time for Santa Claus."

"Is Santa Claus in here?" Little David Wallace had heard our commotion and was standing in the doorway, wondering if Christmas had already arrived.

Allie picked him up and hugged him to her. "He isn't here yet, but we're sure going to be ready for him when he comes tomorrow night." David bounced up and down on her lap.

"Comes tomorrow night, comes tomorrow night!" he kept repeating happily, looking at each of us in turn and nodding his head to be certain we understood.

I looked at Allie sitting in the big rocker. David was snuggled up to her breast; Billy was hanging over one arm of the chair with his head on her shoulder. I kept thinking of a picture I had seen somewhere, on a Christmas card maybe, and Allie's face and the face of the woman on the Christmas card got all mixed up. Then her face looked like my mother's, and I felt a momentary pang of loneliness, but it was gone in a second, for when I looked again Allie was smiling right at me.

"Having a good time, Bussie Boy?" Her eyes were peering into mine as if she knew.

"I sure am." She kept looking at me. "I was just thinking about Mother. Wonder what she's doing right now?"

"Probably getting things ready for Christmas just like we are." Allie was a very wise woman; she knew exactly what I was feeling at the moment. She leaned toward me and said, "Now tomorrow you can sit down and write her a long letter and tell her how we decorated our tree. I think she'd like that, don't you?"

"I'll sit right in here by the tree tomorrow so I can see it and remember to tell it all."

I didn't wait until the next day to write the letter; I wrote it that afternoon as I watched them and helped decorate the tree.

When dinner was over and the dishes put away, Mammy and Allie started popping corn, great bowls full of it. As soon as one batch was finished, Allie would fill the big popper again with the bright yellow grains and start all over. "We'll need several batches, Mama," I heard her say. "It's going to take a lot of popcorn to decorate the tree, and I don't want it to look skimpy." The rest of us sat on the floor in the parlor by the fire with two big baskets of chinaberries between us. One basket was filled with the chinaberries in their natural color, a dark greenish purple.

Our job was to string them on long pieces of black spool thread until we had enough to decorate the tree.

Allie and Mammy came in to join us when the popcorn was finished. They set the big bowls on the floor, pulled two chairs up to the fire, and began stringing the popcorn in the same manner. It seemed like hours passed without a spoken word except when Sissy or I would come to the end of a thread, look up, and say, "Mammy, will you thread my needle for me?" Or Allie would turn to Mammy and say, "Mamma, I think I'm going to alternate this next string with popcorn and berries. Think that might look pretty?"

"M-m-m," Mammy would mumble as she held a needle up to the light to thread it, sticking the end of the thread between her thumb and finger before trying to insert it into the eye of the needle.

When all the popcorn and chinaberries were strung to Allie's satisfaction, she turned to Kiddo. "Son, go bring me that big cardboard box in the top of my wardrobe, and you all can start hanging the ornaments I made from last year while Mamma and I make some more."

When Kiddo returned with the box, Allie set it in front of her chair and lifted out piece after piece of tin foil, most of it silver, some few pieces of gold. "I've been saving this nearly all year from Prince Albert tobacco cans and wherever I could find it. I think I've got enough to make up a couple dozen more ornaments." She handed the box to Bubba. "You climb up on the table, Bub, and start tying these older ornaments near the top." I watched, fascinated and somewhat mystified, as he reached in the box and took out some ornaments. They were different sizes and shapes. Some were covered in silver tin foil, some few in gold. Little strings were threaded through the top, and he tied them carefully to the tree branches. The firelight caught them as they twirled, and they shone silver and gold. I stared open-mouthed. "Did you make all those, Auntee?" I asked.

"Mammy and I did last year. Sissy helped with some of them, too." She looked up and smiled. "You like 'em?"

"They're beautiful. I've never seen anything—what are they made of?"

"Come on over here, and I'll show you. You can watch me make a new one." She looked at the amazement on my face. "Then maybe you can make one for yourself."

She reached into the box and took out a dried corncob and with her scissors cut it squarely in two equal pieces. Then she selected a piece of heavy gold foil from the stack and covered the cob with it, carefully shaping the foil so that none of the cob would show. She stuck a threaded needle into the top of the cob, drew it through, and snipped off the thread, leaving two or three inches of it sticking out on each side. She began to ruffle the foil at the bottom of the cob, ran a pin through one of the red chinaberries, and stuck it into the end of the cob. When she had finished she held it up by the thread, dangling it in front of my eyes.

"There now, what would you say we've got?" It looked like a little gold Christmas bell with a red clapper at the bottom; she had done it so quickly, so expertly that I couldn't quite believe I'd seen her do it.

"Why, Auntee, that's—why, that's gorgeous. Why, it doesn't even look homemade!"

She and Mammy started laughing at the same time, and Allie reached over and hugged me hard. "Bus, that's probably the best compliment I'll have this Christmas." She handed me a corncob. "Here, now you try one."

"Oh, Auntee, I'd ruin it. I couldn't make one."

"Sure you can." She handed me a piece of silver foil. "Use this, Bus. We've got more of it than the gold. Don't try to make a bell at first. Look here now. Just cover the whole cob with tin foil, then twist the ends up tight like this," she began to demonstrate, "and you can tie a piece of red or green ribbon on each end, and see how pretty it looks?"

She held it up, and it was pretty; it resembled a gaily decorated party favor, or a little Christmas gift tied up on both ends.

We made several, working together; Allie would use the gold foil and turn out a little bell, and I would wrap the cobs in foil and tie the ends with ribbon. When we had used up all the foil, I counted the ones we had made; we had nineteen new ones lying on the floor.

When I finally looked up from my work, Bubba and Kiddo and Sissy were draping the long strings of popcorn and chinaberries all around the tree. Billy was helping on the lower branches, and even when he didn't loop the strands evenly Sissy would say, "Oh, that looks pretty, Billy." Then when he wasn't watching she would quietly change it to suit herself.

When the last ornament had been made and tied in its place, when the last string of popcorn had been used to festoon the bottom, we all stood back to admire our work. There were no candles on the tree yet; Allie said she had only one set and she was saving those to use on Christmas Eve. But the flickering light from the fireplace and the pale afternoon sun from the front windows caught the little handmade ornaments and turned them into spheres of beauty. Small currents of air made them turn slowly, first one way, then another, reflecting the light from the sun and the fire; the loops of popcorn looked like snowflakes strung together; the red and dark green chinaberries were like endless strings of beads. And Sissy's white angel looked down calmly from the topmost bough.

"I have never seen a prettier Christmas tree in all my life," I wrote Mother later that afternoon, sitting by the fire. "And Auntee made all of the decorations herself, except I helped her, and all of us together strung the popcorn and chinaberries. I wish you could see it right now, but I'll try to tell you all about it when I get home next week. The train trip was nice, but I got a little homesick that night in the berth. I miss you and Daddy very much, but I'm having a very good time.

Love, Bus

P.S.— Please tell Daddy that Leroy is going to have a nice Christmas. I sat on the stile with him one day and watched a train go by."

❦

When dark came that evening it had turned bitter cold; Mammy said it must be below freezing and went to each room building up the fires. She decided she wouldn't go to the church pageant so she could tend the roaring fires, but Allie said, "No, Mamma, you go along with Pappa. Billy and David Wallace won't want to miss the Santa Claus, and somebody will have to stay with them. I'm a little tired tonight anyway, so you go on." She smiled faintly; there were little shadows under her eyes. "Cally and I will stay here and keep warm by the fire."

Supper was early—we had finished just after first dark—when Kiddo and Bubba lit two lanterns and carried them out to the barn. In a little while I heard the horse and wagon rumble around to the front porch. We bundled up in our warmest clothes; Billy and David were dancing up and down the front hall. Mammy found it almost impossible to button their jackets, and finally Allie bent down to them. "Now, boys, you mind whatever Mammy says tonight, and be very quiet while the pageant is going on. Keep your toboggans on till you get inside. It's awfully cold out there." She kissed them and raised up slowly, a tight pinched look on her face. "And be sure to thank Santa Claus for anything he gives you." Then she was smiling again and herding all of us out the front door.

Bubba helped Mammy and Pappy up on the wagon seat, holding his lantern high to guide them. Then he lifted David into the back of the wagon, and the rest of us crawled in. It was piled high with straw, and we sank down gratefully, huddled together to keep warm. As we started down the front lawn I looked back; Allie was standing in the hall with a lamp in her hand, and Cally stood beside her with his arm around her waist. The rest of Riverside was dark.

Our lanterns made the only pool of light as we turned into the main road to Enterprise. There was no moon or stars; heavy clouds hid every familiar landmark. I knew we were fording the Jennings' branch only because I heard the horse snort when he pulled through the icy water. Everything was silent except for the wagon wheels turning and creaking through the red clay road. Bubba was seated beside me, and for a moment I thought he had spoken to me, but he hadn't; he was only humming. I listened without moving, and then I recognized the old familiar carol. I turned to him in the darkness—I could barely make out his face—and whispered, "Sing it for us, Bubba." He stopped humming for a moment. Then his clear true voice seemed to fill the shadows all around us: "Silent Night, Holy Night, all is calm, all is bright."

There was one lone light bulb burning above the station platform when we reached Enterprise. The wagon rattled across the railroad tracks, and we finally pulled up in front of the First Methodist Church. It was a small white frame building located in that part of town everyone referred to as Old Enterprise. There were several Model T touring cars and one Chevrolet sedan, plus the usual assortment of buggies and wagons, pulled up in front. The church doorway was lighted by an overhanging light bulb with a green shade, and there was a big Christmas wreath of pine boughs hung on the front door. Bubba helped Mammy and Pappy down, and they herded us up the steps and into the church vestibule. A pretty, dark-haired girl was standing just inside the doorway.

"Good evening, Mrs. Neal, Mr. Neal. Merry Christmas to you all."

"Why, thank you, Margaret." I knew right away she must be Margaret Harper, so I looked at her with considerable interest. Mammy was using her company voice now. "And how is the Doctor and Mrs. Harper?"

Margaret Harper smiled. I thought she was much prettier when she smiled. "They're just fine, thank you, Mrs. Neal. At least I think Daddy's all right. I haven't seen him all day. He had to drive over to Quitman this morning to be with Mrs. Walters. Her baby's two weeks overdue, you know." She kept looking at the church doors as more people began to arrive. "I was wondering—I mean, didn't Kenneth come with you?"

"He'll be along any minute." Mammy was smiling now and more at ease. "He and Carlton are just seeing to the horse."

"I have to play for the pageant, Mrs. Neal. But tell Kenneth

I've saved a place for him down on the front row by the piano." She smiled happily again at all of us and turned to go. "It was nice seeing you again, Mrs. Neal, and I'll see you after the pageant, of course."

Mammy and Pappy started down the aisle with Billy and David Wallace in tow; she found a place on the second row from the front and motioned for Sissy to join them. Sis hung back, looking over all the pews, and finally said to me, "Wait here, Bus." She ran down the aisle, whispered something to Mammy, who looked at her, then at me, and nodded. Sissy returned halfway up the aisle, beckoned to me to join her there, and we slipped into an almost empty pew. After squirming out of our coats, I began to look around. The church was filling up rapidly now; more than half of them seemed to be children, laughing and talking, being shushed and made to sit down, then starting all over again when new arrivals came in. The pulpit was covered with straw, and a little wooden cradle had been placed in the center of it. Margaret Harper was seated on a piano stool, and I saw Kiddo leaning over from the front pew talking with her. As I watched him, he suddenly seemed like a grown-up stranger. I couldn't find Bubba anywhere, and as I kept looking for him, a young man squeezed past me and sat down on the other side of Sissy. I turned to her.

"I can't find Bubba anywhere." She didn't even hear me; she was whispering to the boy next to her, and her cheeks were all flushed with excitement. I looked at him closely; he had dark eyes and black curly hair, and his skin was very tan even in winter. I couldn't guess his age, but he seemed to be several years older than Sissy. He became aware of me staring at him, and he smiled and stuck out his hand. "You must be Buster from Cincinnati. Merry Christmas." He was shaking my hand. "I'm Jack Del Buno. I'm a friend of your cousin here."

"So Kiddo has been telling me." I turned beet red; I closed my mouth and looked straight ahead at a lady's hat in front of me. I had wanted to sound very grown-up and had merely succeeded in sounding foolish. I needn't have worried; when I looked again they were whispering and nodding and had forgotten I was there.

The lights in the church were suddenly clicked off, leaving only two small lights burning above the pulpit. The room became very quiet except for a few whimpering babies. A gray-haired man in a black suit mounted the step to the pulpit and stood there waiting for complete silence. I had never seen him, but when he began talking I realized he must be the minister.

"Brothers and Sisters," he began, "I welcome all of you to our Christmas service. I don't know how you folks feel about it, but I can't think of a better way to celebrate the holy birth of our Lord, Jesus Christ, than to tell it, relive it again in song and story. Some of the children in our Epworth League have been rehearsing the last two weeks to bring you this holy pageant tonight, and I'm sure we all thank them from the bottom of our hearts." I could see many parents nod their heads and smile in agreement. The minister held up his hand. "But I must single out one person who has been such a great help to me and the children. Miss Margaret Harper has made several trips from Stonewall to help with the music, and I want to thank her especially for her efforts in helping to make this pageant possible tonight."

I looked over at the piano. Margaret was smiling shyly, and Kiddo was sitting like a stone statue, his ears fiery red. I giggled. Sissy turned and frowned at me.

"And now, Brothers and Sisters, let's watch again that holy night so long ago, when our Savior was born."

Margaret began playing "O Little Town of Bethlehem." A boy and girl came out one of the side doors back of the pulpit dressed as Mary and Joseph and knelt on either side of the wooden cradle. I didn't know the boy, but the girl looked familiar. There was a pale blue scarf thrown over her head, and she looked down into the cradle. I couldn't see her face, but I felt certain I had seen her before. One fat little boy followed by two others entered the pulpit from the opposite door as Margaret Harper began to play "We Three Kings of Orient Are." They were dressed in long full skirts and wore vests covered with rows of rickrack braids. Their heads were wrapped in colored towels to look like turbans. The little fat boy carried a smoking incense burner, and as he knelt above the cradle, the smoke got in Mary's eyes and she sneezed. The scarf fell off of her head, and my mouth flew open as I recognized her. It was Erda Mae Jones. I nudged Sissy in the ribs. "Look who's playing the Virgin Mary!"

She glanced up curiously, then whispered in my ear, "Erda Mae must be in seventh heaven." She giggled and seemed like her old self again.

Erda Mae frowned at the little fat boy as she adjusted her scarf again, but he paid no attention to her warning look. Two boys were entering from the opposite door, dressed like biblical shepherds and carrying long crooked sticks. A third boy, taller than the others, followed them, struggling desperately to bring on to the pulpit a live sheep. There was a rope around the sheep's neck, and the boy was pulling frantically to get the reluctant animal into the manger scene. The Three Kings of the Orient and Joseph seemed frozen with embarrassment, but as the tug-of-war between sheep and boy became more pronounced, I saw Erda Mae as the Virgin Mary cover her mouth to stifle a laugh. With that, all the other children began to smile and snicker and enjoy the obvious battle between the two. The other shepherds dropped to their knees, hiding their faces, as the third shepherd finally pulled the sheep into place and hung tightly onto his neck.

Taking her cue, Margaret Harper started playing the introductory notes of "Silent Night," and all the characters around the cradle began singing softly. As they reached the line "Roun' yon Virgin Mother and Child," the sheep began a rhythmic bleating. "Holy Infant so tender and mild, ba-a-a-a, Sleep in heavenly peace, ba-a-a-a." Long before the second verse was over, the shepherds, the wise men, and Mary were convulsed with laughter. Only poor Joseph continued to sing, staring stonily out over the auditorium. The parents in the congregation were scarcely breathing. Some few were horrified; others, only slightly less displeased with the constant bleatings of the sheep, made their feelings known by head shakings and tongue cluckings. The children all over the church, however, were enjoying the whole thing without restraint, pointing and laughing at the sheep each time he joined in with the others. When the last agonizing "Sleep in heavenly peace" had died away almost unheard above the laughter, the children burst into spontaneous applause for the singing sheep, and in another moment everyone was applauding, for the sheep, for all the work that had gone astray, and for the children in the pageant who had stood their ground so nobly.

It was obvious to everyone the pageant was over, but the children in the pulpit remained rigidly in their places as the applause continued. Finally the minister mounted the pulpit and knelt among the children, patting them on the shoulders and stroking the soft wool of the little frightened sheep. Then he rose, turning to the congregation and held up his hands. When the church became quiet once more, he smiled broadly. There was a joyous lilt in his voice, and he suddenly looked very young.

"If our Lord Jesus were here in person tonight—as I know He is in spirit—He would have been the first to lead the applause for these children and for this poor frightened sheep." His eyes roamed over the congregation, and he became gently serious. "This is not the time for a sermon, but we have all been witness to a wonderful little sermon this night—just now. He always suffered little children to come unto Him, and it made no difference to Him whether they were laughing or crying. I know that He would have loved their laughter tonight, for He is the real spirit of love and joy. And His birthday, which we are celebrating tonight, was a happy joyful time. He would not be offended by your laughter. He would be the first to laugh, probably the longest and the loudest." A quick eager grin appeared on his face. "Tell you what! Why don't I offer a birthday prayer for Jesus right now, and all of you children can listen in. We'll even let you older folks listen in, too, if you want." He raised his head and looked at the light above him.

"Dear Jesus, we are all happy tonight as Your birthday comes 'round again. We hope You enjoyed our pageant as much as the children did, but we're sorry the little sheep was frightened. Maybe he was just as frightened as some of the people we've read about in the Bible—on that night long ago when You were born. They didn't understand what a wonderful thing was happening, just as this little sheep didn't understand what was happening tonight. We are so thankful for Your birthday, and I hope that You will love us always—whether we are laughing or crying."

None of the people around us had bowed their heads. They were watching the minister and smiling, some few with tears in their eyes. He suddenly looked at them and, after a moment, gently whispered, "Amen."

No one moved, in the pulpit or in the congregation; the sheep stood perfectly still nibbling at some straw in the cradle. The children in the nativity scene were smiling quietly as they watched the sheep. Suddenly, unexpectedly breaking the quiet, an old man in one of the front pews shouted joyfully, "Amen!"

Then the church began to buzz with talk and laughter. The minister thanked the children in the pulpit and helped the tall boy take the sheep out the side door. When those in the pageant had joined their parents in the congregation, the minister walked over to the piano. "Now we will sing some of the wonderful old Christmas carols that Margaret has chosen for us tonight." He turned to her. "But if you don't mind, Margaret, let's begin with 'Joy to the World.'"

I was singing away happily, mumbling over the words of the second verse that I didn't know, when I felt someone squeeze in tightly by my side. I tried to make room and turned to look at the late arrival. It was Erda Mae Jones, minus her blue scarf. Her hair was no longer straight as I remembered it but curled into tight ringlets, and I felt sure she had on lipstick and rouge. She smiled broadly.

"Hi! Mamma told me you might be here tonight." Then she began to simper. "So I thought I'd come sit with you for the rest of the doings." She leaned over me to nudge Sissy. "How do you like my hair, Mary Evelyn?" And she patted her curls.

Sissy looked at her, frowning slightly at the interruption. I could tell that she still didn't like Erda Mae. "It's all right, I guess," she said. Then she added, "But if it rains tonight all your curls will come out."

Erda Mae flounced back across me. "Huh! I guess she's just jealous, that's all."

I kept trying to sing the carols, but Erda Mae was breathing down my neck again, harder than ever. "When did you get here?" she whispered in my ear. Her breath was bad.

I drew away and put my finger to my lips, pointing to the piano.

"Oh, phew—who cares," she said, but she started singing a few notes. They sounded very off-key to me.

We were in the middle of "Jesus, Jesus, rest your head" when I became aware that Erda Mae's hand was resting on my thigh. She would slide it down to my knee and then bring it slowly back up my thigh. I brushed it off like a fly and pretended not to notice. She was very quiet for a moment; then she placed her hand—with her blue scarf covering it—between my legs and began stroking me slowly at first, then more rapidly. I held on tightly to the hymnal, ignoring her as best as I could, until my groin gave an involuntary jerk I had never known before. I felt my neck and face become red with excitement or embarrassment—I couldn't tell which—and I knew that I was suddenly breathing much harder. In the next moment I felt naked and ashamed, and I didn't know why; there was a hard knot in the middle of my stomach, and I knew that I wouldn't be able to get another breath in my body. I seemed to be stinging all over, and I dropped the hymnal with a loud thud on the floor.

Sissy turned to me, and, gulping for air, I stammered stupidly, "I guess I dropped it." She turned back to the book she was holding with Jack Del Buno and went on singing, and I turned to Erda Mae. Her eyes were slits—smiling—but she hadn't moved her hand, still wrapped up and knotted in her scarf. I thought of what the minister had just said, and I suddenly remembered where we were. I looked at this curly-headed girl smiling in a way that I had never seen. I looked down at the scarf covering her hand, still secretly moving between my legs. I grabbed it and threw it at her, and slapped her hand—which was still moving and searching—so hard that I could feel the sting through my pants.

"You stop that now, Erda Mae!" She turned on me the angriest pair of eyes I had ever seen, sullen but blazing. Sissy was looking at me very strangely; Erda Mae turned to her and spoke loudly. I was sure everybody in church heard her.

"Your cousin hurt me. What in the world is the matter with him?" She got up from the pew, looked back at me with her eyes still blazing, then turned and walked demurely down the aisle to sit with her mother and father.

My face was on fire; I knew I was going to be sick right there in the pew in front of Sissy and Jack Del Buno and the whole church. I got up mumbling something about needing a drink of water, stumbled out to the vestibule of the church, and stood there in the cold air sucking great mouthfuls.

I don't know how long I had been standing there breathing so noisily, but suddenly I heard someone say, "What's the matter, sonny. You havin' a spell?"

I jumped and turned around. And there stood Santa Claus. At least it was Santa Claus in a red suit without his cap or his long white beard. There was a dirty white sack limp at his feet, and he was holding a small bottle of liquid to his lips. He wiped his mouth with the back of his hand and looked at me sharply. "Say, ain't you the kid I seen gettin' off the train the other day?"

I looked right into his eyes and recognized the man from the station platform, Jake Collins. I was still too upset to speak; I nodded my head.

"What's goin' on in there, sonny, that upset you so?" He grinned with tobacco-stained teeth. "They havin' one of them holy roller meetin's?"

I couldn't believe it! Was this the man who was going to play Santa Claus for the children tonight? What was it Mattie Riley had said? "He don't do nothin' but drink moonshine and whore around on Sa'day night."

Jake Collins—Santa Claus? Then I remembered Erda Mae Jones and her searching hands, and I shivered uncontrollably.

Everything this evening was out of focus. The wrong Santa Claus, the wrong Virgin Mary—this wasn't the way Christmas was supposed to be. I shivered again.

"You all right, boy?" Jake Collins reached for my arm. I drew back against the wall.

"I just got a little dizzy inside—too hot."

He peered at me uncertainly for a moment, then held up his bottle and squinted at the remaining contents. "Well, maybe the fresh air'll help you, but this is gonna see me through tonight." He gulped down the last of the moonshine and threw the bottle into the churchyard. He wiped his grinning mouth again. "Makes you sorta buzz inside, and you can be Santa Claus or anybody else you've a mind to."

He bent down to the sack at his feet and pulled out a red cap and a white beard; he fitted the beard tightly around his ears and pulled it down till it covered his mouth and chin. He set the red cap jauntily on his head so the white tassel hung over his shoulder. He looked at me and winked. "Don't never tell none of the little kids what you seen ole Santa doin' tonight," he said, and he laughed loudly for a moment.

He picked up the white sack, slung it over his shoulder, and was ready to go into the church when Bubba suddenly pushed open the door. "Where have you been, Bus? You all right? Sissy's been worried about you." He looked worried, too.

"He's just gettin' some fresh air, Carlton." Jake Collins spoke quietly. "He got a little dizzy inside, but he's all right now."

Bubba turned to him and called, "You're looking mighty good there, Jake." He nodded toward the door. "The kids are in there waitin' for you. As soon as you hear them start singing 'Jingle Bells,' you go inside saying 'ho, ho, ho.'"

Jake shifted his sack to the other shoulder, opened the door a crack, and stood there waiting. I could hear faint laughter and chatter from the children, and the man playing Santa Claus muttered to himself, "Now let's do it right, Jake, goddamn ya!"

The first notes of "Jingle Bells" began; he swung the door open wide, let out a roaring happy "ho, ho, ho," and strode down the aisle of the church. I stood there listening to the shouts of the children after the door closed.

"Come on, Bus. Let's go in and watch the fun." I looked up at Bubba; he was completely unconcerned.

"Do you know what that man's been doing?" I was outraged. "He's been standing out there drinking moonshine whiskey!"

"I know, Bus, I know."

"Well, I don't think he ought to be in there—"

"Now just take it easy." His mouth got hard. "You sound like all the old fuddy-duddies around Enterprise." He glanced at me, and suddenly his voice became gentle. "Jake Collins is a nice man. He started drinking about three years ago when his little boy was killed. He just can't seem to get over it. But he loves to play Santa Claus—does a darn good job of it, too. And someday—just maybe—" His voice trailed away. Then he grabbed my hand and said gruffly, "Come on now. Let's go in and watch."

As we rolled home in the wagon afterwards, I kept thinking about Jake Collins. I tried to picture his little boy and the kind of man Jake would have been if his little boy was still living. I couldn't. But I could see him quite clearly sitting on the station platform that day I stepped off the train. Once again I heard him saying, "Who you lookin' fer, sonny? Where'd you come from?" and I remembered how frightened I was. I wondered if he had seen something in me that reminded him of his own son. Then I thought with a start about seeing him again in the church vestibule; I was surprised and shocked to see him drinking whiskey, but I hadn't been frightened at all. He had certainly made a good Santa Claus for the children that night; he was a good man after all. But what about Erda Mae Jones? I tried to think kindly of her, too, but nothing came of it, except I could feel my face getting red again and I was glad it was dark. I just didn't understand her, and I wondered if I ever would.

Sissy woke me early on Christmas Eve morning. I had spent a restless night, turning and twisting, dropping off to sleep, waking with a jerk, and finally dozing off again. Toward morning, I slept deeply, with no dreams, and I was still somewhat groggy after she shook me awake. "You got to get up right away, Bus, and see what we got for Christmas last night!"

I suddenly wondered if I had slept through Christmas Day. "What is it? What's the matter?" She ran over to the window that looked out over Allie's summer garden.

"Well, get up and take a look. Just take a good look." Sissy was so excited I knew before I reached the window.

"Snow!" She breathed it almost like a prayer. "It must have started late last night after we'd gone to bed. Oh, I wish I'd stayed up all night to watch it. Isn't it beautiful, Bus?"

I looked out the window. There wasn't much on the ground that I could see, maybe an inch or so, and I was turning to tell her about the snows we always had in Terra Haute and Covington, when I saw her eyes. They were filled with wonder; she was looking at a miracle; she knew it was snow, but she still couldn't believe it. "Haven't you ever seen snow before, Sissy?"

"Only on Christmas cards and calendars." She was lost in the beauty of it. A few little lazy flakes were still floating down, and her eyes would follow each one hungrily until it settled into a thin white blanket already covering the garden. "Mammy says it hasn't snowed here in fifteen or twenty years, and she says she can't remember a white Christmas ever in her life!" She drew a deep quivering breath. "Oh, I think it's the most beautiful thing I ever saw."

I was wide awake now with the cold; my bare feet felt as if they were frozen to the floor. "I've gotta get some clothes on," I chattered. "I'm freezing."

She turned and ran to the bedroom door. "Then hurry up and get dressed so we can play in it before it melts. Pappy says the sun will be out before noon." She ran out, then stuck her head in the door again. "And Mother's gonna make us some snow ice cream if she can scrape up enough of it."

I hurriedly threw on my clothes and was pulling on my Mackinaw and cap when Sissy bounded back in dressed in a heavy sweater and toboggan. "Come on, slowpoke. Kiddo and

Bubba and Billy are already having a snowball fight out in the front yard. Come on!"

We raced through the dining room into the hall. I heard Mammy yelling, "Aren't you even going to have any breakfast?" But we were already out the door, and as I went down the front steps, a big wet snowball splattered my face.

"Gotcha, Yankee Boy, gotcha!" Kiddo was almost dancing as he threw one snowball after another. "I guess we'll invite you for another Christmas if you promise to bring snow with you every time!"

Another snowball hit the side of my head, and as I turned I saw Bubba dodge behind an oak tree. Billy and little David were far down the lawn, jumping up, falling down, rolling over in it, squealing with joy.

They'd stop for a moment to watch the snowball fight between Kiddo and Bubba, grin with a surprise at their older brothers acting as childlike as they, then start running around in crazy circles again, breathless with excitement. I even saw Pappy lean over in the back yard, gather together some snow, shape it into a ball, and throw it right at the back of Sissy's head; it hit her on the shoulder. She turned laughing to see who had done it, but Pappy ducked behind the fence. She put her hand to her heart and fell on the ground as if dead. I ran over to ask if she was hurt, but before I could, she reached up and pulled me down on top of her, and we rolled over and over in the snow, down the lawn like a human barrel. It seemed to me the whole family had suddenly gone wild.

Sissy was lying flat on her back looking up at the sky. "Not gonna last much longer, I guess." I looked up where she was pointing. The sun was trying to break through some pearl-gray clouds above us, and off in the west I could see a little scrap of blue.

"Let's go see if Auntee got enough to make some snow ice cream!"

We raced wildly around toward the back yard. Allie was already there, scooping up the wet snow with a water dipper, putting it into a big white bowl. We stopped by the back stoop when we saw her, and I burst out laughing. She was wearing an old overcoat of Cally's and a man's old black hat pulled down over her ears. She looked like a tramp bent over in the snow, and she was as excited as any of us.

"Bring me the vanilla extract in the kitchen safe," she called out, "and about a half a cup of sugar. And, oh yes, find me about eight or nine of those empty jelly glasses and set 'em on the back stoop. Make haste, now! This stuff won't last much longer."

We scampered into the kitchen, and by the time we had found what she wanted, the whole family was gathered around the back stoop waiting. "I'll have to make it out here, and we'll have to eat it out here, too. Wouldn't be anything but mush if we took it into the kitchen."

She deftly poured a few drops of vanilla into the bowl of snow, added some sugar, and whisked it around, quickly mixing the flavoring into the snow. She spooned a little of it into the jelly glasses and handed one to each of us. "Now eat it fast before it melts completely."

It was cold, slightly sweet, and disappeared immediately as it hit my tongue. There was no chance to bite into it or suck it, but it was a tasty treat for all of us.

The sun was coming through strongly now, and the back yard was beginning to show large patches of sand and red clay. Before we had finished the last watery spoonful, Mammy called out, "Bring those glasses in with you when you finish. And I want you children to take your shoes off in the kitchen before you go through the house. They're wet and muddy, and I don't want you tracking up. I've got a big fire going in the parlor. All of you—you too, Allie—go in there and get your feet warm. I don't want you taking your death. You hear me now!"

We trooped into the kitchen, took off our shoes, and left them by the stove. Then we headed for the front parlor and sat on the floor in a circle around the fire with our feet stuck out to the blaze. Billy and David kept jumping up from the fire, running to the windows to see if it might start snowing again. But the sun was eating up the clouds rapidly now; the only remaining snow patches lay in the shadows of the house and tree trunks, where the sun hadn't reached it.

"Ever had snow ice cream before, Bus?" Kiddo asked.

"If I have, I don't remember it."

Sissy sighed contentedly, stretching her feet close to the fire. "If I lived up north where you do, I think I'd have it for every meal."

"Maybe you would, but I doubt it." Kiddo was staring into the fire. "It's too much trouble for the little taste you get out of it. I bet you'd get tired of it pretty soon."

None of us answered him; it didn't seem worth the effort. We were lazily warm in the circle now, staring into the flames, each one of us finding whatever we wanted there. One of the logs shifted slowly, and a spark jumped out on the hearth rug. Bubba leaned over and flipped it back into the fireplace. I felt as though I could go to sleep again right there and sleep until Christmas morning.

"There's somebody comin' in a horse and buggy!" Billy was staring out the front window.

Bubba got up and ambled over to look out. He didn't say anything, but he turned and looked over at me strangely.

Sissy twisted her body so she could see him. She called out impatiently, "Well, you gonna tell us who it is or not?"

He looked out the window quickly again. "It's Erda Mae Jones and her mother!"

I felt my stomach tighten up, and my heart started a hard pounding.

"Now what in the world do they want?" Sissy got up and glanced at me with a puzzled expression on her face as she headed for the front hall.

Kiddo and Bubba went out to the kitchen along with Sissy, to get their shoes, I guess, or to tell Allie she had company. I sat there where I was by the fire, not moving, hardly breathing, hoping, I think, that if I didn't move I might be invisible to anyone who came into the parlor.

I heard Allie come through the front hall and open the front door. I heard her say, "Why, Miz Jones, Erda Mae, what a nice surprise, and Merry Christmas to you all." There was a pause and then, "Come in, come in. Wasn't that snow a wonderful sight this morning? I can't remember when we ever had snow before, but my, wasn't it beautiful while it lasted." Another pause and then Allie's voice had concern in it. "Why, Erda Mae, what's wrong with your hand, honey? How did you hurt it?"

"That's what I've come to see you about, Miz Gunn." Mrs. Jones sounded tight-lipped to me. I was glad I couldn't see her face. "Erda Mae swears to me that your nephew—Buster? Is that what you call him?—well, anyway, she swears he hit her hand so hard last night at the church service that it's all swollen and bruised this morning something awful. Well, you can see for yourself! I just couldn't believe he'd do a thing like that without good reason. And Erda Mae says she don't know why in the world he did it. Says he just hauled off and—"

"Now just a minute, Miz Jones." Allie's voice had somehow lost its friendliness and had become firm and strong. "Buster is right here in the parlor. So you two just go right in, and we'll hear what he has to say about this."

There was another pause, longer this time, but finally I heard Mrs. Jones speak sharply. "What is the matter with you, Erda Mae? Quit hanging back like that. You walk right into that parlor, you hear me? I want to get this whole thing straightened out. Now you just march right in there, young lady!"

Erda Mae was the first person to come through the doorway. She still looked as sullen as last night, but she certainly seemed more subdued; she was no longer flouncing. Mrs. Jones and Allie followed her, and I turned slowly and stared at them before dropping my head again. "Buster." Allie looked at me sharply. "Get up honey, and say hello to Erda Mae and her mother."

I rose up in my stocking feet; I looked from one to the other and finally managed to stammer, "Hello." Erda Mae seemed to be examining the roses in the carpet; she refused to look at me. Mrs. Jones's face was filled with questions I knew I couldn't answer to her satisfaction or mine either. Allie waited out the silence for a while; then she spoke up briskly.

"Buster, did you hurt Erda Mae's hand last night at the church pageant?" When I raised my head she was looking right at me, her eyes never moving from my face. I couldn't look away; I couldn't speak either, but I finally managed to nod a yes.

Allie looked down at Erda Mae who was rubbing her shoe across the faded roses. "Will you tell us why you did that?"

I looked again into her warm brown eyes. There was no scolding there; she only wanted to know the truth, and I knew in that one moment I couldn't tell her the truth. I didn't know how. I wasn't certain that I knew the truth myself, and even if I did, I knew I wouldn't be able to find the right words to tell her so. But I knew I had to say something.

"I didn't mean to." I could feel my face turning red. "Honest, Auntee, I didn't. I mean, Erda Mae started it all." Erda Mae was staring at me now with tight, hard eyes. "I mean she was teasing me, and I didn't know—and then she started—" I was making a mess of the whole thing. I glanced at Erda Mae. She wasn't smiling, but she looked like a hungry cat licking its lips. She was enjoying this; whatever she had told her mother, she was enjoying every minute of this. I couldn't think anymore. I was only feeling now, and it all came out in a raging gush.

"You think you're so smart, Erda Mae, always trying to act so grown up, curlin' your hair and puttin' rouge on your cheeks!" I was beginning to sob, and that made me madder still. "Don't you ever try to sit by me again. If you do I'll hit you again, harder than ever. You're mean—and I hate—I hate you!"

I was crying so hard I couldn't see; I flew into the back bedroom and slammed the door behind me so hard the whole room shook. I flung myself on the bed, sobbing and shaking uncontrollably.

It was a long time before I could stop crying; even then a dry sob would occasionally make my shoulder and chest heave. I could hear voices in the parlor, some of them sounded loud and angry at times. Then, after a while, I thought I heard a buggy drive away, and the house got very still. I suddenly realized I was icy cold and finally climbed under the patchwork quilt to get warm, but I still kept shivering miserably. I heard the bedroom door open, but I didn't turn over or look up. The bed creaked as a heavy body sat down on the edge of it. A hand reached out and touched my shoulder.

"Bus?" It was Kiddo's voice. His hand went on patting my shoulder, and I was afraid I would cry again. I turned to him; he was smiling, and he brushed the hair out of my eyes. Then he said, "Feelin' better now, Bus?"

"No! Oh, I guess so." I had to tell someone; maybe Kiddo would understand. "I did hit her hand—Erda Mae's, I mean. But I didn't start it, Kiddo, I didn't! She was—" I stopped. I didn't know what to tell him—or how to tell him.

"We know you didn't, Bus. And I think Mrs. Jones knows it now, too." I looked up quickly. "No, Erda Mae didn't say anything." Kiddo laughed a little, remembering. "Every time her mother would ask her why you hit her like that, Erda Mae would start blushing and say she didn't know. Finally Mrs. Jones walked up to her and said, 'Have you been acting smart with that boy, Erda Mae? After all I've said to you?'"

Kiddo's face got very gentle looking. "Finally Erda Mae started crying and yelling at her mother. Said if she didn't stop asking her about it she'd be sorry. Said she'd do something worse. I guess that's when Mrs. Jones slapped her, and Erda Mae ran out of the house and on up the lane."

Kiddo nodded toward the parlor. "Mrs. Jones stood in there and looked so confused I couldn't help feeling sorry for her. Said she was afraid she had spoiled our Christmas and apologized for it." He giggled suddenly. "Then she got in her buggy and lit out after Erda Mae."

"Kiddo—" I was afraid to ask. "Do you think Auntee and Mammy will forgive me?"

"Nothin' to forgive, Bus." He smiled, almost grinning at me. "Mammy's been saying for some time now that she thinks Erda Mae is growing up too fast. Maybe she is." He sort of winked at me. "What was she doing to you anyway, huh?"

"I don't know, Kiddo. I thought at first she was just bein' silly, but then she was feelin' my legs, and then—" I was almost stammering as I tried to tell him what had happened and how mad I felt. But from the look on his face I knew that he understood.

"Come on, Bus." He threw the quilt back. "It's nearly dinnertime, and you ought to be hungry by now. You haven't even had any breakfast yet."

I swung my legs over the side of the bed and sat up. "Kiddo." I looked down at my legs.

"Yeah, Bus?"

"You know, if we hadn't been in church and Erda Mae's breath wasn't so bad, I think I might have liked it."

For the rest of the day I was pretty subdued myself. After dinner I sat in the parlor for a long time looking at the tree, wondering if I'd ever feel the same about Christmas again. Mammy had seemed angry during dinner, but I knew it wasn't because of me; when I'd catch her eye she would be smiling, or if she happened to pass back of my chair she would pat me on the head. Sissy came into the parlor once and asked if I wanted to go outside and play. I shook my head. She came over to my chair.

"Don't worry about Erda Mae. She's—well, she's just fast. Everybody in school knows it. I guess maybe she can't help it though." She put her arm around my shoulder. "Now come on. Just forget about her. Daddy bought a lot of fireworks in Meridian, and soon's it's good dark we're gonna shoot 'em off!"

Allie's voice came from the direction of the kitchen. "Mary Evelyn, honey, come watch David for a minute. We can't even get the dressing made with him underfoot." Sissy shrugged her shoulders and left the room. I turned toward the dying fire and then looked again at the Christmas tree. I suppose it was still beautiful, but the parlor suddenly seemed stifling hot—breathless with the afternoon sun streaming through the front windows. I got up and went into my bedroom, put on my Mackinaw and cap, went out the front door, and headed down the lawn for the railroad tracks and the stile. Just as I reached the well trough I saw Leroy coming up the lane. He waved his hand and started running toward me. I didn't stop; I kept on walking in his direction. I had to get away from the house for a while. I wanted to be alone. I wasn't even happy at the thought of seeing Leroy.

"I was just on my way up to show you what I done made for Emmie Lou for Christmas." He grinned as he came up to me. "Looka here," he said, and he held out a little stick doll that he had whittled from a piece of pine wood. "Course I ain't near about finished yet. But I bet she gonna like it."

"Yeah," I answered shortly, barely looking at the doll as I kept walking toward the stile. "She probably will."

I didn't realize how curt I must have sounded until I became aware that I was now walking down the lane alone. I turned around; Leroy was standing with his hands on his hips watching me with a hard look in his eyes. "You sho' is actin' like a white boy today. You don't give a shit if'n she like it or not."

I was opening my mouth to say I was sorry, but he must have sensed I was upset because he walked slowly down the lane to me and looked into my face. "What's the matter with you today, Buster?" I turned and kept walking toward the stile. He trotted along by my side. "Somethin' wrong up at the house?"

"No," I said, but I was walking too fast and talking too loud. I knew it, and Leroy knew it. He asked no more questions, and when we had reached the stile we settled into our side-by-side places. I noticed before I sat down that Leroy had been hard at work in our carved initials since that first afternoon. They were much deeper and smooth to the touch. I squirmed my bottom around to one side to look closer. I could lay my finger into the straight line of the B.

I smiled. "If we sat here long enough we'd probably have our initials printed on our butts."

Leroy didn't look up. He was busy whittling away on the bottom part of the stick doll. "Maybe so—but I ain't gonna sit here bare-ass in the wintertime. No suh!"

He was angry or hurt—maybe a little of both—and he made no effort to hide it. I watched his face as he worked steadily and surely on the doll; his lips were pressed tightly together, and his eyes were blank and withdrawn. He was seeing nothing more than the shape of the wood in his hands.

"I'm sorry, Leroy." I knew he would never speak about it unless I did. "I didn't mean to snap your head off. I'm sorry."

He turned to look at me, holding the doll loosely in his hand, the knife blade gleaming in the afternoon sun. "You gotta right to feel the way you wants to, I reckon. Ain't none of my business how you feel."

"It is so your business." I was mad now—at myself, and, in some way I couldn't quite understand, at Erda Mae. I blamed her for making Leroy angry with me, which didn't make any sense at all, so I blurted out, "Doesn't make any sense at all!"

"What don't make no sense?"

"You and me—sitting here feelin' bad, almost quarreling over some silly girl!"

Leroy looked at me. It was impossible for him to follow my roundabout, jumbled thought, and it showed plainly on his face. He closed his knife and put it in his pocket.

"Boy, you sho' can mix me up." He rolled his eyes at me and then said, "You talkin' about Emmie Lou? She still a baby. She ain't no—."

"No, I'm not talking about Emmie Lou!" I was almost shouting again.

"Well, then, who in the hell you talkin' about?"

"Erda Mae Jones—that's who. She's the cause of the whole thing, and I hope I never see her again!"

Leroy's face was screwed up in a complete puzzle; he was silent for so long that I turned to apologize again, and he nearly broke out laughing when I really looked at him. He was shaking his head as if to clear it, and then he began speaking—slowly one word at a time. I remembered the day he patiently explained to me how you go about catching a fish. He was using much the same tone of voice now.

"Now lemme see if'n I got this right. You know some li'l ole gal name of Erda Mae. First place—I don't know of any li'l ole gal by that name so she bound to be a white gal. Then, you done got all het up about somethin' she done or said and you got so upset you done tuck it out on me!" He looked at me carefully. "That's about the best way I can figure it. Is that about the truth of it?"

That was about the truth of it; he had taken my confused thoughts and made them seem clear and childlike—all this in spite of the fact that he knew nothing of what had happened at the church service.

"Yeah," I mumbled, feeling like a punctured balloon. "You've just about got it right."

"What that li'l ole gal done to you?" He was halfway smirking as he spoke. "She got you upset for sho'! What she done, huh?"

So I told him about Erda Mae sitting next to me at the church service, how she had acted and how it had affected me.

"Then her mother came up to the house this morning," I continued, "wanting to know why I had hit Erda Mae's hand so hard. And I didn't know what to say—I didn't know how to tell what happened."

"Just tell her she was feelin' 'tween your legs and it tickled like hell."

"But I couldn't say that to Mrs. Jones."

"And then ask Erda Mae if'n she wanna do it again!"

With that, Leroy began slapping his leg and squealing with laughter, doubling over almost as if he were in pain. When he found breath to speak again, he was giggling slyly. "Bet that li'l ole gal would like that." He grinned at me knowingly. "Look to me like you done got yourself a sweetheart whether you like it or not."

"Sweetheart?" I stood up, outraged.

Leroy pushed me off the stile and took out his knife. "Get out the way, Buster. I gonna change this here letter on the seat."

I didn't realize what he meant until he began looking at his initials on the stile. Then he started talking slowly to himself, ignoring me. "Lemme see now. All I gotta do is whittle out two more straight lines to change this here L to an E." He scratched his head. "But how is I gonna change this R to an M?" He looked up, grinning at me. "She do spell it with a M, don't she?"

"Don't you dare!" I grabbed his arm so hard the knife fell to the ground, and then we were both rolling in the sand at the foot of the stile. At first I was angry, but as Leroy kept laughing and holding my arms, all the pent-up tension began to ease and I was laughing as hard as he. Erda Mae and Mrs. Jones and the church service were forgotten in the joy of being with Leroy; he made the whole episode seem ridiculous and funny.

We both sat in the sandy warmth at the foot of the stile, breathing heavily. Leroy finally picked up his knife, wiped it off, and began whittling on the wooden doll again. I watched him for a time; then he leaned over to look at his work. "Is it gonna be a boy doll or a girl doll?" I asked.

He thrust a piece of carving up in front of my face and grinned. "You don't see no peter on it, does you?" Then he slowly continued his work. "Naw. It's gonna be a li'l gal doll. I get Mamma to fix some kind of dress for it when I get back to the house." He held the doll away from him, examining it carefully.

"Yeah, I think Emmie Lou gonna like it."

I suddenly remembered the fireworks and grabbed his shoulder. "Leroy—we're going to set off a lot of fireworks as soon as it's good dark. Why don't you come over and watch 'em with us this evening?"

He shook his head slowly as he kept whittling on the foot of the doll. "Mamma like me to be around the house on Christmas Eve. I can see 'em from the front door anyway—if'n you got sky rockets and Roman candles." He folded up his knife and stood up. "I better be gettin' back home. It's gettin' late."

I stood up, too, and dusted off my pants. I climbed over the stile and started up the lane to Riverside when I heard Leroy call to me. I turned and yelled, "What? What'd you say?"

He was standing by the railroad tracks, smiling broadly. "Be sure you wish that li'l ole gal a Merry Christmas when you sees her!" And he disappeared down the tracks.

The sun went down in a great burst of fire that evening. Kiddo and Bubba wolfed down their supper so fast that Allie began to laugh as she watched them. "None of those fireworks are gonna explode before you all get out there." She looked all around the table. "I declare, it's a waste of time cooking good food for you children at Christmas. You don't even know what you're eating anyway. Well, come on, Mamma. Let's clear the table so these kids can get started."

We all let out a whoop and made a dash for the front door. Mammy yelled after us. "Put on your sweaters, it's chilly out there!"

Sissy and Billy and I sat huddled together on the front steps. Kiddo and Bubba were dragging a box of fireworks down to the middle of the front lawn. David Wallace was dancing along by the side of them.

"Sissy," Bubba called out. "Come and get David and keep him with you all so he won't get hurt."

She ran down the lawn and grabbed up David, who kept protesting, "I wanna help, I wanna help."

Kiddo came running up with a handful of sparklers. "You all can start with these while we're settin' up the skyrockets. Here." He thrust them into Sissy's hand.

"Now you be careful with those, Mary Evelyn." Allie was standing behind us with the blue shawl around her. "Remember what happened to Buster's neck." I guess maybe I did remember for I held the sparkler as far away from my face as I could once Sissy had lighted it for me. Then we went slowly down the steps into the yard, making circles and zigzag patterns in the dark. Once David's sparkler was lit and shooting out little stars, he dropped it and ran up the steps clutching uncertainly at Allie's skirt. Billy picked it up, still sputtering, and with one in each hand began to make big circles that looked like wagon wheels. Still holding on to Allie, David said, "Billy makes it do pretty."

"You all ready for the skyrocket?" Bubba yelled up to us.

"Cally? Mamma, Papa, come on out for the fireworks."

"You all get ready. Here she goes now!"

There was a sizzling sound, a swish, and a trail of white smoke shot into the air. Nothing happened for a second; then there was a loud explosion, little red and green lights filled the sky like tiny bubbles that floated slowly down to earth and blinked out one by one before they hit the lawn. Everyone let their breath out in a long sigh. There was another explosion followed by a burst of white light far up the lane toward the Jennings place. Their skyrocket burst into silver and gold before it died out behind the bare trees to the north.

"We're gonna set off all the Roman candles at once if we can," Bubba called from the lawn. "Now you all watch this."

I could just make out Kiddo and Bubba in the dark. They were sticking Roman candles in the wet, soft ground, making a circle in the center of the front lawn.

"Daddy? Is Daddy out there?"

"Right here, Kiddo," Cally called back from the porch.

"Bring some more matches and help us light 'em."

Cally disappeared down the yard. Then I could see the three of them by the flare of the matches, Cally and Kiddo and Bubba, running quickly from one Roman candle to another—there must have been ten or twelve—lighting the fuses. They ran to the porch to watch. First one, then a second and a third candle began to shoot up their fiery red trails of light. By the time all of them were sending out streams of fire, the whole sky seemed to be filled with color, cascading up, over, and down on the lawn like a waterfall. Sissy and I stood there watching, clutching each other. She poked me and pointed to her side. David Wallace had come up behind us and slipped his hand into hers, holding on tightly. His eyes were stretched wide, and his mouth hung open as he watched the fountain of trailing fire. Sissy picked him up and held him as he stared at the last of the exploding Roman candles. I patted his arm and was surprised to feel him shaking with excitement. He turned to me and smiled, pointing to the dying fireworks, but he didn't say a word.

"Sissy, you and Buster bring David on in now." Allie was calling from the porch. "Where's Billy? You children come on in now. It's getting too chilly out here." As we came up the steps, Sissy was still carrying David. Billy was standing in the front hall with two burnt-out sparklers in his hands. Allie kissed David and looked at all of us.

"I know two little boys who should be in bed; it's past your bedtime, especially tonight." She gathered us into the hallway. "We've all got to get to sleep pretty quick now 'cause—"

"Santa Claus is comin'!" Billy shouted.

"I just bet he will—as soon as we're all sound asleep." Her eyes were shining. "Now run along to bed, Billy, and remember, don't try to stay awake." She bent over to kiss him, but he was already flying to the back room. Allie laughed. "Good night, Davey Boy. Sissy will undress you and tuck you in." She kissed him, and we walked into the parlor. An Aladdin lamp was standing on the piano, and firelight flickered across the ceiling. The Christmas tree shimmered in the soft light. Allie reached the middle of the room and stopped short. She put her hands on her hips, shook her head, and giggled like a schoolgirl.

"My stars, Bus, I must be gettin' old. Here it is Christmas Eve, and I forgot to light the candles on the tree." She sat down in the rocker by the fire. "I just don't know," she sighed. "Maybe it was the fireworks—weren't they pretty though?—or maybe it was seeing Emma Jones getting so upset about Erda Mae—" She stopped when I looked at her guiltily.

"Are you mad at me about that, Auntee?" I asked. She stopped rocking and held out her hand to me. "Come on over here, Bus. Sit down by me in front of the fire."

I came over and squatted in front of her. "It really wasn't all my fault, Auntee. I was just sitting there singing the carols, and Erda Mae squeezed herself in by me and then she started to—"

She put her hand gently over my mouth and kissed me on the forehead. "Kiddo told me about it. And I'm sure she did exactly what you say she did, so you mustn't feel bad about it. It wasn't your fault, and I'm sure you didn't mean to hurt her at all. You were just confused over it all." She was silent a moment, stroking my hair. "You're probably growing up a little faster than you realize."

She put her hand under my chin and raised my face to hers. "I wouldn't blame you for anything like that because I trust you. You've never given me any reason not to. I trust all of my children." She smiled. "And sometimes like right now I feel like you're one of mine." She leaned back in the rocker gazing into the fire. "I'm not sure, but I think that's one of the reasons Erda Mae acts the way she does. Her mother doesn't trust her, or maybe she's afraid to trust her, I just don't know." She sighed deeply. "I feel awfully sorry for Emma Jones, and, well, I guess I feel sorry for Erda Mae, too."

She sat forward a little in the chair. "You never did know Erda Mae's sister, did you, Bus? Betty Lou?" I shook my head. "She works at a restaurant up in Meridian. She's a waitress, I think. She's about a year older than Kiddo, must be eighteen or nineteen by now. She got into some kind of trouble with a boy." I must have looked startled because she quickly added, "That was several years ago—I don't even know what really happened. But Mr. Jones wouldn't let Betty Lou inside the house anymore, told her not to come back as long as she was alive." Allie's face was lost in painful memories. "Poor Emma, she goes up to Meridian—whenever she can get a ride—to see Betty Lou. Not very often though. She's afraid Mr. Jones will find out and stop her." She looked at me; her eyes were smiling sadly. "That's why she's so afraid—why she can't trust Erda Mae. Oh, she wants to, but she's afraid. I'm sure she knew Erda Mae wasn't telling the truth about what happened in church. But she came down here this morning hoping she was. I don't know what the poor soul would do if anything like that happened to Erda Mae. I just don't believe she could stand it." Allie looked as though she were about to cry.

I touched her knee. "I'm sorry, Auntee." She turned away from her memories quickly and came back to me with a bright look on her face. "I know you are, but what's the matter with us! We can't sit here feeling sorry on Christmas Eve." She stood up and whispered excitedly, "Now you tiptoe back there and see if Billy is asleep yet, and I'll go get Sissy. We've got an awful lot of Santa Claus to get done before morning."

It was pitch dark; someone was shaking me on the shoulder. As I came awake, I realized it was Billy in bed with me. He was raised up on one elbow, whispering in my ear, "Do you s'pose Santa Claus has come yet?" I grinned in the dark and was suddenly wide awake. I strained to listen and thought I could hear low voices coming from the parlor.

"You stay right here," I whispered back. "I'll go see." I found my bathrobe and tiptoed to the door. I opened it and sped through the hall, my bare feet shocked by the cold. There was a flickering light coming from the parlor door, and I stopped on the threshold. Cally was stoking a blazing fire; Allie stood with her back to it in a blue wrapper. Kiddo and Bubba were tightening the handlebars of a tricycle, Mammy and Pappy were sitting on the wooden settee pulled close to the fire, and Sissy was sitting almost under the tree, her knees pulled up under her chin, rocking happily back and forth.

"Billy's awake!" I whispered. "He wants to know if Santa has come yet."

Allie walked over to Kiddo and Bubba. "Have you got it fixed yet?"

"It's all ready, Mother." Kiddo stood up.

"Then, Bus, you go get Billy and bring him around and carry him to the door." We started out. "Wait a minute, wait, wait!" She turned to Cally anxiously. "You and the boys light the candles on the tree. I want 'em to see everything all at once."

I hurried back through the hall so excited I forgot about the cold. I opened the back bedroom door, held out my hand toward the bed, and, still whispering, called out, "Come on, Billy. I think Santa Claus has already been here. Come on, let's go see."

He took my hand and we ran up the hall. Sissy was standing there with David in her arms, still half asleep, and we all went into the parlor together. The tree was ablaze with little white candles that seemed to light up every ornament on either side of it, making sure nothing caught fire on the trees. David raised his sleepy head to look, smiled, pointed, and said, "Fireworks!"

That was the last clear memory I had of Christmas morning. Everything after that became a jumble of laughter, of shrieks, of rattling paper, of "thank you—I love it—it's just what I want," until I found myself sitting quietly by the fire looking at the paper and toys strewn about the room, feeling very content with my own happiness. And that happiness lasted all through dinner, except for two clouds that developed during the day, one much larger than the other.

I was stuffing myself with turkey and cornbread dressing

when the first cloud appeared. I noticed that Allie wasn't sitting in her place at the dinner table. "Where's Auntee?" I mumbled, my mouth full of dressing. "Has she finished already? She hasn't even had any Lady Baltimore cake yet."

"She got a little tired before dinner, Bus." Cally was carving more turkey. "She's taking a little rest. She'll eat something later. I expect she's just tried to do too much for Christmas."

"You want me to take a plate of food in to her, Uncle Cally?"

"No, not now, son. She just wants a little rest." By the time I had finished my second Lady Baltimore cake I was as stuffed as the poor old turkey had been when we sat down to eat. I was licking the last of the icing off my fingers when Mammy called out from the kitchen. "Buster, Leroy is waiting at the back stoop. He wants to see you."

I ran through the kitchen and stuck my head out of the back door—straight into the second cloud of trouble! "Hi, Leroy, come on in."

"I'se gotta talk with you right now. Cain't wait." He looked so distressed I knew something was badly wrong.

"What's the matter, Leroy? What is it?"

"Hush up! Don't be yellin' all over the place." He hopped up on the stoop. "Close the door. Close the door." He was so agitated that I almost slammed the door in my haste to please him. "You just gotta come over to my place. You gotta talk to Mamma. She say she ain't gonna lemme keep the knife!"

"Won't let you keep the—why not?"

"She say it ain't fittin'. She say to me, 'You done stole that knife, Leroy.' And even when I told her you done give it to me you know what she say to me? She look at me and say, 'You done broke my heart 'cause you ain't nothin' but a lyin' li'l nigger!'" He was almost in tears. "She grab that knife and hid it, and she won't lemme have it. Mamma say she comin' over here tomorrow to find out the truth. Buster, you gotta come over to my place and tell her you give it to me."

His face was so troubled I couldn't say a word. I opened the back door; Mammy was stacking dishes by the stove.

"Mammy, can I go over to Leroy's for a while this afternoon?" I hesitated trying to find an excuse. "I haven't seen him but once since I've been here. I'd really like to if it's all right with you."

"Well, I guess so. You can walk off some of that turkey dressing at least." She turned from the stove. "But be sure you wear your coat and cap, and don't stay over there so long that I start to worry."

"I won't," I said, and I ran to get my Mackinaw.

When I let myself out the back door Leroy was waiting by the stoop. We went out the back gate, but neither of us spoke until we had reached the back pasture. When we came to the spot where we had sat down to catch our breath—when we thought the old tramp was chasing us—Leroy came to a sudden halt. He started speaking, but he didn't look at me.

"'Member the time we sat down here, when you was mad about that funny plate your Mammy broke, and you was tryin' to run away?" I nodded my head, but he didn't see me; he was looking at the ground.

"If'n Mamma don't lemme have the knife back, I'm sho' enough gonna steal it—and I'm gonna run away, too, far's I can go, and ain't never comin' back. Never!"

"Leroy." He wouldn't look at me when I called his name. I hesitated, then started again. "Leroy, what happened? Didn't you show your knife to Mattie when I gave it to you?"

He kicked at one of the wagon ruts before he answered. "Didn't see no need to. It was my knife—none of hers." He swallowed hard and took a big breath. "And then last night I showed her the li'l doll I done finish for Emmie Lou, and she ask me how I made it so good. Then I tuck the knife outta my pocket and showed it to her."

He started talking again; he was almost shaking now. "She look at it and look at it, and even she look at me and say, 'Where you get this here knife?' And when I tole her you give it to me for Christmas, that's when she call me a lyin' li'l nigger, and she tuck that li'l stick doll and break it right in two."

He still wouldn't look up. He stood there a moment longer, then he suddenly dropped to his knees, and began pounding the earth with such anger and hatred that I was frightened of him. I was frightened for him.

"Shit on 'em," he began. "I say shit on 'em! Shit on ever' damn one of 'em, and I ain't never comin' back, I tell ya. Never!"

I wanted to touch him; I wanted to be with him, but I knew I mustn't. Not now. I didn't know who "they" were, and I don't think Leroy knew, but I hated them, too, whoever they were, for what they had done to Leroy. I hated anything or anyone that could hurt Leroy this deeply, could make him feel such bitter outrage.

He got up as quickly as he had dropped. He gave me a sidelong glance and said, "Come on. This ain't no good," and we walked rapidly through the pasture to the cabin.

There was a thin curl of smoke coming from the chimney, but no one was in sight. Leroy walked straight up the steps, through the dogtrot, and pushed open the kitchen door. I followed right behind him. Mattie Riley was sitting at the kitchen table, wiping little Emmie Lou's mouth with a cloth. She looked up.

"I done ask Buster to come tell you," Leroy announced and crossed to the woodbox and sat down without another word.

"Hi, Mattie." I stood there, uneasily. "Merry Christmas."

"Merry Christmas, son." She turned to Emmie Lou and lifted her down from the chair. "Now you go along, honey, play with your new dolly that Santy done brung you for Christmas. That's my sweet chile!"

Emmie Lou ran into the front room, and Mattie turned her big eyes on me. She said nothing, but she made me feel guilty, and I didn't understand why. I finally walked over to the table.

"I really did give the knife to Leroy, Mattie, the very first day I got here." She still said nothing; she just stared at me. "It was supposed to be for his birthday, and Christmas, too," I added.

She folded her big hands across the tabletop. "How come you got so much money you can buy a li'l colored boy a 'spensive knife like that?"

"My daddy bought it for me in Cincinnati." I went on hastily. "I'm going to pay him back for it out of my allowance."

"He done bought it for you?" Her eyes got hard.

"Oh, no, Mattie, no! I mean he bought it so I could give it to Leroy for a present. He knew all about it. I just didn't have enough money saved out of my allowance to buy it myself. But he knew I was going to give it to Leroy. Honest he did, Mattie."

Her eyes softened a little, but then she reached in her apron pocket and pulled out the little white card that had been tied to the knife. She pushed it slowly across the table to me. "What do this here Mister Leroy stuff mean?"

I looked down at the printing on the card, "Happy Birthday to Mister Leroy," and saw where I had signed my name. I glanced at Leroy on the woodbox. He was sitting there with his head between his knees. He offered no help at all.

"I guess I'll have to tell you just like I told my daddy about it." And I explained again about how Daddy bought the knife and had the card printed for me because I thought Leroy was one of my best friends. "I guess I started calling him Mister Leroy sorta like a joke, but I didn't want the knife to be a joke. I wanted it to be the best knife I could get him." Then I rushed ahead; not caring what I said. "And I don't see what difference it makes anyway 'cause he is my best friend, and I love him, and if you don't let him keep the knife, then, then, you'll have to give it back to me because I bought it, and then I'll just give it right back to him again!"

I stopped because I was out of breath and very close to tears and afraid I had said more than I should. I looked at Leroy. He was staring at me as if he had never seen me before. I turned to Mattie to apologize. Her eyes were closed; she was rocking her big body back and forth, and speaking in a low soft chant, almost to herself.

"Dear Lawd, Dear Lawd, Dear Lawd!" A great sob shook her breast. "Outta the mouths of all the li'l chillun come the truth, come the truth! You done told us and told us over and over in the Good Book, and we's too scared to listen."

She looked up at me suddenly with big tears rolling down her cheeks. She pushed the chair firmly back from the table, raised her big body in one movement, and walked over to the little shelf above the stove. She fumbled for a moment—fingers searching—finally found the knife, brought it over, and handed it to me. "Here, Mister Buster!" I looked up in shocked surprise. "Give your knife back to Leroy."

"Oh, Mattie, I was just joking. I didn't mean—"

"I ain't jokin'."

"You give it to him, Mattie."

"Ain't fittin'. Didn't have no faith. Didn't believe my own flesh and blood. Called him a thief and a nig—" She stopped and stood like a woman turned to stone. Then she jerked her head, pain showing in every movement of her great body, and walked slowly out of the room.

I looked at Leroy, not knowing what to do. He sat with his hands clinched tightly together in his lap. His eyes were great round bulging circles but seeing nothing. I picked up the knife from the table, walked over to Leroy, and held it out to him; he didn't look at it; he didn't move except for a trembling in his body. I put the knife down carefully in his lap; then he spoke for the first time since he had entered the kitchen.

"I reckon you means it."

"Mean what, Leroy?"

"What you done say to Mamma." He looked at me, and then, "You told her that I'se your best friend." He dropped his eyes. "Ain't never had no best friend—white or colored."

"What do you mean?" I sat down on the woodbox, feeling hurt. "You mean that you're not my best friend? That you don't want—"

"Naw, naw, that ain't what I said. You just mixin' me up—that's all." He jumped up and walked angrily across the room and back. "I cain't talk so good, I knows that's the truth. Think I cain't hear the way you talks and tells about things and got sense enough to know that it sound good?"

He sat down on the woodbox again, frowning, thinking hard. He began to speak slowly, not looking at me, searching his mind carefully for every thought and word he spoke.

"Don't know how it be in them places where you live. But down here a li'l—" He paused, then turned to me. "Down here, a colored boy just don't have no white friends. Maybe they likes us, and some of 'em real good, but they don't like us—like friends." He looked up, begging for me to understand. "Sometime it looks like it's gonna work, but then they change, they grows up and gets older and you know they're different 'cause they acts different to you. And that's just the way it is." He stopped suddenly and turned his black eyes full on my face. "I 'most felt the same way about you, just till this here Christmastime."

I must have looked very surprised because he leaned toward me. "'Member that day on the stile and you give me the knife? Lawd God! Ain't never see nothin' like that. Never felt that way before. And then just like a li'l ole bee buzzin' round and round my head, I thought you was gonna take it back. I knowed you wasn't; I just know for sho' you wasn't, but I was scared you was. And then today when you done told my Mamma that I'se your best friend—" He spoke so softly I could barely hear him. "And then you said, 'I love him.'" He tightened his hand on the knife and said, "I reckon we gonna be friends now till the day we die."

He looked at me and smiled; it wasn't his nasty, teasing smile. I had seen that one many times. This one was different, open and filled with trust. I knew I had found my best friend, and I hoped he had, too.

Then I remembered Mattie. I could still see her pain-ridden face as she left the kitchen. "Leroy," I began uncertainly. "Hadn't you better go see if Mattie—if your mother's all right? She looked so tired when—when she went out."

He was slowly nodding his head up and down.

"That's right. She was hurtin' bad." He looked up at me. "But she gon' be fine now. She know I didn't steal this here knife, and she didn't mean to call me no nigger. She just tryin' to be shore that I—" He thought for a moment, then drew a deep breath. "She just keep on tryin', that's all—just keep on tryin' all the time. She gon' be fine now."

It was very quiet in the little kitchen; there was no sound from Mattie or Emmie Lou in the next room, and Leroy was silent, lost in his own little dreams.

I got up from the woodbox and crossed to the door. "Well, it's getting late, Leroy. I'd better get on back to the house. I don't want Mammy to start worrying about me." I opened the door and turned, thinking maybe Leroy would walk part of the way home with me. He was still sitting on the woodbox, staring with a kind of sad wonder at the knife in his hand. I closed the door softly and walked back to Riverside alone.

When I came in the back door, Mammy was cutting a piece of white meat from the turkey breast. She looked up. "Did you have a good time at Leroy's?" Before I could think what to say, she went on, "Did they have a nice Christmas? How was Mattie? Did you see her?"

I edged over to the stove watching her cut the turkey and lay it on a plate. "I don't think Mattie was feeling so good. She was in the other room most of the time, lying down I guess."

"Is she sick?" She looked up, concerned.

"I don't think so, Mammy. Leroy says he thinks she's going to be fine." At least that part was the truth.

She was putting some warmed-over rolls on the plate and pouring a glass of milk from the pitcher.

"You fixing to eat supper?" I asked.

"No, honey. I'm just taking some food in to Allie. She had a nice long nap this afternoon, and I'm so glad. She needs it. She just overdid things and wore herself out getting ready for Christmas." She put the plate of food and milk on a tray and held it out to me. "Here. Why don't you take it in to her. She'd like that."

I took the tray from her and crept slowly into the front bedroom, one step at a time so as not to spill any milk.

Allie was propped up on pillows, her head turned away from me. I thought at first she was asleep.

"Auntee?" I whispered; then she raised her head to look. She was smiling. "I thought maybe you were asleep."

She laughed. "No, Bus, I've been a lazybones all afternoon. I'm just been lying here watching the fire, seeing all kinds of pretty pictures."

"Mammy sent this in to you." I held out the tray.

"Oh, now. Mamma shouldn't have done that. It's high time I was up and stirring, 'specially on Christmas Day." But she made no effort to get up, other than to raise herself higher on the pillows and take the tray from me. "My, this does look good, doesn't it?" She sipped some milk, looked at her plate and then at me. "Pull that little chair over by the bed and sit and talk to me while I eat."

I didn't do much talking at first, just sat and watched her, and would smile when she happened to look my way. She wasn't really eating; she was playing with her food. That's what Mother called it. "Buster, don't play with your food," she would say. "Clean up your plate."

After she had finished her milk, Allie set the tray aside on the bed and turned toward me. "Bus, I've been lying here this afternoon doing some thinking, and I got to thinking about you and Polly." She put her hand under her head to rest it there. "Your mother and daddy are pretty fine people; I guess you must know that by now. I don't have to tell you that. And Polly is the dearest sister anybody could hope to have. But sometimes—" She looked into the fire for a moment, frowning a little. "Sometimes she worries too much about—things. Things that usually take care of themselves anyway—whether we worry about them or not." She looked at me and laughed. "I bet she'd be in a stew right now if she knew I'd spent most of Christmas Day in bed, don't you?"

I had a fleeting picture of Mother in a stew, and I giggled. "Yeah, I guess that's right, Auntee."

"So I've been thinking that it might be a good idea not to tell her I've been so lazy—just to keep her from worrying about it." She paused and then went on quickly. "And maybe you'd better not say anything when you get back home about—Erda Mae either."

I looked up quickly. "Do you think she'd get mad and think maybe it was my fault?"

Allie grabbed my hand and patted it. "I don't think she'd get mad at all," she smiled. "Except maybe at Erda Mae. But she'd probably start worrying about something that's over and done with, and no real harm done." She raised herself up on one elbow and leaned close to me. "Why don't we just keep it a secret—just between the two of us. That way Polly won't even waste her time fretting over it."

She had said the magic word—a secret!—and she probably knew it.

"Secret?" she asked, grinning at me.

"Secret!" I grinned right back.

I think it was the word secret that made me think of Leroy and Mattie and the knife.

"Auntee, can I tell you something that's sort of a secret, too?" She raised her eyebrows, wondering what I meant. I hurried on. "It's really not a secret because Daddy already knows about it."

"Then tell it to me right now. Wallace is good at keeping secrets, and so am I."

I hesitated, not knowing exactly how to begin. "Well, you see, I bought a knife for Leroy for a Christmas present. I mean Daddy bought it for me really, but I didn't tell Mother. We just kept it a secret between us." Allie was watching me closely. "And then when Leroy came running over here after dinner and told me that Mattie wasn't going to let him keep it—he was awful upset, Auntee, and I felt terrible about it—" And then in little disconnected bits and pieces I repeated the whole story of Leroy and the knife. When I was telling her that Mattie had accused Leroy of stealing the knife and had called him a lying little nigger, Allie flinched as if in some deep pain, but she never once interrupted or took her eyes off of my face. When I finally finished I looked up and said, "You know, Auntee, the only reason I got the knife for Leroy was to make him happy. And he was. I know he was when I gave it to him that afternoon on the stile. But when I went over there to tell Mattie about it this afternoon, I don't know, I almost felt like I'd done something wrong." I lowered my eyes. "Do you think I did?"

When I finally looked up at her face, Allie was crying. She wasn't making a sound, but she was crying just the same. She turned to the fire. "Out of the mouths of babes," she whispered.

"Mattie said almost the same thing this afternoon." I looked at her in surprise.

"Mattie Riley is a good woman, Bus. She may not have much

education, but she loves her family, and she's got a heart as big as all outdoors." She took my face in her hands and kissed me. "I'm glad you gave Leroy that knife. And don't you ever feel bad about it—never again—and don't feel bad about Mattie either." She looked at me; her eyes were shining. "You may not know it, but you gave her a wonderful present, too. You gave her son back to her."

I didn't see Leroy again that Christmas; he didn't come to the house, and I didn't go over to the cabin. Allie was in bed most of the time for two days after Christmas. Mammy insisted all she needed was rest, so I stayed close to the house to be with the folks. When I caught the train for Cincinnati on Saturday afternoon, Allie had been up all day. Just before it was time for me to leave for the station, she called me to her and whispered in my ear, "Secret?" I hugged her and nodded, not saying a word.

Two days before my thirteenth birthday a tattered package arrived in the mail for me. It was from Mississippi, and when I opened it, a wooden chain, two or three feet long, fell on the floor. I picked it up and examined it carefully; each link had been whittled satin-smooth to the touch. There was a card attached to one of the links that read:

> "Happy Birthday to Mister Buster from Leroy Riley.
> (P.S. Carved out of one big piece of hickory wood.)"

SUMMER—1927

We were planning a trip to Terre Haute that summer to visit the Carmichaels, just as soon as school was out. We had never been back to see them or Mrs. Patton since leaving, and I was looking forward to the trip. I would start junior high in the fall, and I wondered if I would recognize any of my old classmates from training school in Terre Haute. Mother laughed at me, saying, "My, but you already sound like an old man at the ripe age of thirteen."

I was finishing my last year at the First District School, and in September I would leave that gray brick building with its circular sliding fire escape forever. One morning, about two weeks before school was out for the summer vacation, the principal sent for me to come to his office. A summons from Mr. Denton didn't frighten me any longer. I liked him. I had carried messages for him to the various classroom teachers many times during the past year, and I was beginning to feel my importance. I was right. He handed me a folded note to be delivered to the fourth-, fifth-, and sixth-grade teachers. As I was turning to leave, Mr. Denton stopped me. "You'll be going to our new junior high school this fall, won't you, Wallace?"

"Yes, sir." I replied.

"I understand from a colleague of mine in the teaching profession that there may be a friend of yours teaching there this fall." He was smiling broadly.

"A friend of mine?"

"I believe so." He sat down behind his desk. "You do remember Miss McArthur, don't you? She taught the fourth grade here about—"

"Miss Lucille McArthur?" I didn't realize I was shouting until Mr. Denton started laughing and held up his hands to quiet me.

"Yes, I see you do remember her all right."

"What will she be teaching, do you know?" I asked excitedly.

"No, I don't, Wallace. My friend tells me she's been working on her master's degree ever since she left here. I know that she has applied at the new school, but I don't know if she's been hired or not.

"Oh, I hope so!" Then, feeling my importance again, I decided it might help if I put in a good word for Miss McArthur. "I think she's a very fine teacher, Mr. Denton."

"Yes, I'm sure she is." He was trying hard to cover a smile. "Now if you don't mind, Wallace, I'd appreciate having that note delivered before we break for lunch today."

"Oh, yes, sir," and I started on my rounds of classrooms.

Miss Lucille McArthur! I couldn't wait to get home at noon to tell Mother the news. I knew she would be pleased at the possibility of Miss McArthur coming back to teach in Kentucky again.

I flung open the front door when I got home, shouting, "Mother, Mother, I've got some good news—wait'll you hear it." I ran through the living room into the kitchen and stopped dead. Mother was sitting at the kitchen table, her head bent low, a handkerchief to her eyes, sobbing pitifully. Even more shocking was seeing Daddy, seated across from her, looking miserable and helpless.

"What's the matter?" I cried. "What has happened?"

"Mother just got a letter from home, son." Daddy's voice was very gentle. "I'm afraid Pug is—your Auntee is awfully sick."

"What's wrong with her?"

Mother raised her head, wiping her eyes and nose. "She's had another baby, and it's just about killed her this time. Dr. Harper told her that she—"

"Now, Polly, honey—"

"Well, it's true, Wallace, and you know it. That's why I've told you over and over—" She stopped suddenly, bit her lip, and looked at me. I'm sure she had forgotten for the moment that I was standing there. She picked up a letter lying on the table and looked at it. "The baby is three weeks old now—John—what did they name him?" She searched through a page. "Yes, here it is. John Curtis Gunn. And Allie hasn't been able to take a step since then. She's been in bed with her leg elevated. She has a blood clot, milk leg they call it, and Dr. Harper has warned her that she mustn't—she mustn't—and if she—" She broke into sobs again and put her head down on the table.

Daddy jumped up, knelt down, and put his arm around her, murmuring over and over, "Now, Polly, now, honey."

I stood there feeling lost and lonely and afraid.

"Come on in the living room, honey, and let's sit down and talk this over." Daddy was leading her out of the kitchen. "Anyway, maybe it's not as bad as you think it is." He sat down with her on the sofa. "But I'll tell you what we're going to do. You sit right down and write Effie Carmichael that we won't be able to come; just tell her why, and then we'll just hop on the train and go down to Riverside, and you can see how things are for yourself." He tilted her chin up. "Now, Muddie, wouldn't that make you feel better?" I hadn't heard him use that term of endearment in years. She had been crying so hard that Daddy was speaking to her like a little girl.

She raised her head from her shoulder. "Would you be able to get off and come with me?"

He smiled at her, wiping some tear streaks away. "I'm sure I could, honey; in fact, I was planning on it."

Mother looked up and saw me standing in the doorway. "Oh, but I forgot." She looked distressed again. "Bus won't be out of school for another week or ten days. We won't be able to—"

"Now don't worry about Bus. We'll take care of that." He glanced at me. "Won't be any problem for you to get out a few days early, will it, Bus? When you explain to 'em what it's about?"

"I'm sure it won't." I went over and sat down on the sofa next to Mother. "I'll tell Miss Rawlings what's happened, and she can maybe give me my tests early or something. I'll talk to her about it right after school this afternoon." I looked over at Daddy. "When do you think we could leave? So I can be sure to tell Miss Rawlings?"

"Let's see now." He took out his little pocket calendar. "Today is Monday. I think I could get things cleared up at the post office by Friday." He turned to Mother. "If I can get train reservations for Friday or Saturday night, think you could be ready by then?"

"I'll be ready whenever you are. Thank you, Wallace." She leaned over and kissed him hard on the mouth, then looked at him steadily for a moment before she spoke again. "And I promise you—I'll make it up to you." She put her head on his shoulder again and rested it there like a child.

At school, Miss Rawlings said not to worry, my grades were good enough, and under the circumstances, four or five days wouldn't matter. "And I do hope you find your aunt much better when you get there."

We left for Riverside on Saturday night that same week, but when Kiddo met us at the station, he didn't give us much hope that Allie was any better.

"How is your mother, Kiddo?" were the first words Mother spoke as soon as she stepped off the train. All that afternoon during the trip I had noticed the closer we came to Enterprise the more silent Mother became. She would stare out the window for long periods of time, saying nothing, almost as if she were seeing nothing. Daddy made several feeble attempts at conversation, but he soon gave up and turned to watch the passing scenery.

Kiddo and Daddy were busy loading our bags into the backseat of a Chevrolet sedan, and apparently he didn't hear her, or maybe he hadn't wanted to hear. When we settled in the car, Mother touched his arm and asked him again, "How is Allie?" There was urgency in her voice now.

"She's just about the same, Aunt Polly," he said as he started driving the Chevrolet down the rough road to Riverside. I wondered vaguely when they had bought the car, but with Kiddo's next words I forgot about it.

"She hasn't been out of bed yet. Dr. Harper says she mustn't move her leg until that blood clot has completely disappeared."

He stopped talking until he had forded the Jennings' branch. When we were past it, he turned to look briefly at Mother again. "Aunt Polly, it really is awful looking, all swollen and—just awful looking. But the thing that scares me most about it—" He was silent for a moment, then when he spoke again there was a strained, choked sound in his voice. "Mother hasn't complained about it—not once. About being in bed, I mean. Most of the time she just lies there, looking out the window, not saying anything." He turned the car into the lane leading to Riverside. "I don't know whether Mammy wrote you or not, but she hasn't been able to feed the baby since he was born. Mammy put him on a bottle the very next day, and he seems to be doing fine. But every time Mammy brings him in and lays him down next to Mother, she just—" There was a sudden quiver in Kiddo's voice. "All she does is just stroke the baby's cheek and says, 'Poor little Jackie Boy. Poor little baby.'"

We were passing the Jennings place, and one of the children waved. No one else noticed, but I waved back. Everyone was silent again until we had driven up in the front yard.

Then Daddy turned to Kiddo and asked quietly, "How is Mammy holding up?"

"She's tired, Uncle Wallace. I've never seen her look so tired. But, of course, she never complains."

He stopped the car by the front steps and cut the motor. Mother jumped out and ran up the steps into the house. I started to follow, but Daddy grabbed my arm and held on to it.

"No, Buster!" He spoke quietly but firmly. "Not now, son. Leave your mother alone for a few minutes. She needs to see Pug by herself, just at first anyway." He turned back to Kiddo. "How is Cally doing?"

"Pretty good I think, Uncle Wallace. When Dr. Harper came by last week I heard him tell Daddy he might as well go back to work. That's the main reason we bought the car this spring. Daddy drives Mr. Jennings up to the creosote plant one week, and then Mr. Jennings drives his car the next." Kiddo opened the car door and climbed out. "We can be getting your bags out. You and Aunt Polly and Bus are gonna sleep in the back bedroom." He grinned at me. "We set a cot up in there for you, so you won't sleep so late every morning. Come on, Yankee Boy."

We got the bags and went in the house. As we walked past the front bedroom I looked in. There was no one there. I looked up at Kiddo, wondering. He pointed to the closed door of the parlor.

"Mammy and Daddy moved her bed in there, so it would be quiet and she could rest more at night." It wasn't until then that I noticed how still the whole house was; it held a nighttime, tiptoeing feeling, and I found myself whispering for the rest of the day.

After I had put my bag under the cot, I walked through the dining room and looked in the hall; the parlor door was still closed. I hadn't seen any of the folks except Kiddo since our arrival. I turned and wandered back to the kitchen. Sissy was standing over the stove watching over a kettle of boiling water.

"Hi, Sissy."

She turned and looked at me. Then without saying a word she ran over and threw her arms around me, hugging me tight for the longest time. When she broke away I could see little beads of sweat standing out on the bridge of her nose. She looked tired, and when she finally spoke she sounded tired.

"Oh, I'm so glad you all have come. Mother's been awfully sick, but I think she's a little better now. Where's Aunt Polly and Uncle Wallace?"

"Mother's in there talking to Auntee."

"Oh, good. I'm glad. Mother's been asking over and over when you all would get here. This'll make her feel better, you'll see." Sissy went back to the stove to look at the water. "Mother's got something on her mind, something that worries her; I don't know what it is. But I heard her say to Mammy yesterday, 'I want to see Polly the minute she gets here—you bring her right in here to me.' And she made Mammy promise."

"When can I see her, Sissy?"

"Probably sometime tomorrow, after she's had her bath and all." She turned to the kettle once more. "I think these bottles are sterilized by now."

"What are those for?" I asked as she began lifting glass bottles out of the boiling water with a big long fork, setting them upright in a dishpan on the table.

"Baby bottles for Jackie Boy. Mammy's going to fix his formula this afternoon."

"Where is the new baby?"

"He's in the front bedroom, asleep I think. He's a beautiful baby. I'll take you in to see him soon as I get all these bottles out."

After she'd finished, she set the kettle on the back of the stove, wiped her hands on a towel, and then took my hand. "Come on," she said and led the way into the front bedroom.

At first I could see nothing in the crib. There appeared to be a rumpled sheet across the top of the bed, but when Sissy pulled it slowly back I saw a little auburn head appear. The baby was lying on his stomach, with one hand plastered against his cheek.

"He's beautiful," I whispered, and as I looked, his mouth began to make sucking noises. Then suddenly his little face became beet red, and I heard Sissy say, "Oh-oh! I bet he's gonna need changin' right away." Almost as soon as she said it, there came a soft mewing sound from the crib, and the baby's hands began moving aimlessly.

"He's waking up," she said. "I'll change his diapers, and then call Mammy so she can fix his formula."

I had never seen a baby that small. As Sissy lifted him from the crib, he seemed to weigh no more than a few pounds, but apparently I was wrong for she carefully laid him down on the big featherbed and exclaimed, "My but you're getting to be an armful, you know that, li'l ole Jackie Boy?"

The baby's eyes wandered around as if searching for sight or sound, and then he let out a wail that was startling. I couldn't believe that so much noise could possibly come from so small a body. It grew in volume as Sissy removed his diaper, and almost immediately it seemed the bedroom was filled with people. Cally and Mammy rushed in first, wanting to know what was wrong with the baby; Mammy immediately took charge, cooing and soothing the outraged infant, and Cally sat down on the foot of the bed, gently stroking the baby's head.

"Is this little Jackie Boy?" I heard someone say. I looked up; Mother and Daddy had suddenly appeared and were standing on the far side of the bed.

"Can I hold him, Sissy?" I heard Mother say.

"Just as soon as I get him changed, Aunt Polly." Sissy went on cleaning up the baby's bottom. In the midst of it, she looked up. "That new formula of Dr. Harper's must be agreeing with him, Mammy. He doesn't seem to be constipated anymore. See?" She thrust the soiled diaper toward her.

"Well, that's a blessing," Mammy said, taking the diaper and examining its contents carefully before wadding it up. "Maybe he'll sleep longer at night, now that he's getting regulated."

Sissy had finished pinning the fresh diaper around the kicking legs; she picked up the baby, held him carefully over her shoulder, and, whispering gently in his ear, she said, "Come on now, Jackie Boy. Let's go over here and see your Aunt Polly."

Mother sat down in a rocking chair, and Sissy deposited the baby in her arms, took the soiled diaper from Mammy, and left the room. I started to follow her, but Mother called to me, "Come here, Bus, and look."

I crossed the room slowly and stood by her side. The baby was nestled in her arm, still making little sucking noises and mewing faintly, but he was no longer crying. Mother looked up at me smiling, but I knew she had been crying before she came in the room.

"Isn't he the prettiest little baby you ever saw?" She turned again to the bundle in her arms and stroked his chin.

I was beginning to feel afraid of something, something I couldn't quite grasp. I stared at the baby and said nothing. Mother looked up at me as if waiting for an answer.

"He sure is the littlest baby I ever saw." I knew from the expression on her face that wasn't what she expected me to say. She looked down and began stroking the baby's hair gently, first one way and then another.

"Just feel how soft his hair is, Bus," she said. "Soft as down. But be careful of the little soft spot on his head."

"I'd better not touch him." I drew back. "I might hurt him."

"Oh, you won't at all. Not if you're careful. See?" And she continued to stroke the baby's head.

I backed away. I suddenly felt alone and lost. The room seemed too small; there were too many people smiling and watching. I didn't know what they wanted me to do or say. I knew I wanted to get out of the room, get away from the baby that my Mother was holding and stroking so gently. I was searching for any excuse at all to be alone.

"I—I think I'd better change my clothes and see if I can help Sissy," I said, and I fled to the back bedroom.

I lay down on the little cot under the window and was surprised to feel my heart beating so rapidly. I took a deep breath and tried to relax, but there was a tight hard knot in my stomach. I raised up to look out the window. The big oak in the back yard was spreading its leafy shade in the long late afternoon shadows. I watched idly as a mother hen, closely followed by five or six of her biddies, scratched around the foot of the tree searching out food for the chicks. Then I suddenly saw Sissy again, standing over the hot kitchen stove boiling baby bottles, and I heard Mother saying, "Isn't he the prettiest little baby boy you ever saw?"

I swung my legs over the edge of the cot, unlaced my shoes, and took them off. I don't remember how long I had been sitting there, staring at nothing, before I noticed that the door between the parlor and the back bedroom was open. I couldn't see into the room at all; the door was only slightly ajar, but I suddenly felt a desperate need to see Allie right away. I stood up and was walking softly across the room when I heard the voices. Allie was talking to someone.

"I'm glad you think so," I heard her say. "But I also think you are a wonderful liar."

"I mean it, Pug. You look fine to me."

When I heard Daddy's voice coming through the crack in the door I grabbed the bedpost and stood perfectly still—holding on to it hard. "You really are feeling better, aren't you, Pug?"

"I guess I am, Wallace." I heard her give a little sigh. "It's just that I'm so weak, just can't seem to get any strength back, none at all. I s'pose one reason—I've been in here so long—in bed like this, not being able to move or turn or—" Her voice became so faint I couldn't hear it at all. Then Daddy spoke up. "Well, you mustn't tire yourself, now."

"I'm not really tired, Wallace. I'm just tired of me."

Daddy said something I couldn't hear. Then there was silence for a long while. When Allie finally spoke again, she sounded stronger. "Mamma's gonna be comin' in here any minute complaining I'm talking too much. So please, Wallace, let me say what I want to say, and don't shush me like Mamma does every time I try to talk about it." Allie seemed to take a deep breath and start all over again.

"I've never felt like this after any of my babies were born. I just seem to sort of float. Sometimes I'm here, and then sometimes I feel like I'm very far away. It doesn't frighten me, it just makes me wonder if—" There wasn't a sound for a moment, and then I heard Allie say, "I've already talked to Polly about this, but I told her I had to see you first before she said anything to you. Wallace, if anything should happen to me—NO! please, Wallace, let me finish." She caught her breath and started again. "If it should, would you and Polly take my little baby and raise him for me? I know it's asking an awful lot, but I'd feel so much better if I knew that you and Polly—the two of you were—any little baby needs both parents, and Mamma is getting too old, has worked so hard all her life, and somehow I just don't feel that it would be right for them to—to have to—I think—" Her voice stopped, but I wasn't sure because I couldn't hear anyway; my ears were ringing so hard that I eased down on the bed and sat there not moving, scarcely breathing. When I could hear again, Daddy was talking.

"—and nothing will happen. But if it does, Pug, I promise you, we'll raise him and love him just as if he were ours. I promise you faithfully, Pug."

I thought I heard Allie whisper thank you. Then I heard a faint stirring, and the door to the front hall opened and closed, and Daddy left the room.

I don't know how long I sat there. I wanted to get up and close that door, to close it and lock it, to shut out something so close that I couldn't see it or hear it. But I couldn't move; I tried to get up, but my legs felt so weak I was afraid I would stumble or fall and disturb Allie.

Somewhere, from very far away, someone was calling my name. I heard footsteps cross the dining room and go into the kitchen. I heard some dishes rattling, and then I heard Sissy's voice clearly as she came back into the dining room. "We're just having some leftovers tonight, Aunt Polly. There hasn't been much time for cooking around here."

I got up from the bed and went over to the cot and stretched out on it with my face to the window. I heard Mother ask, "Did Buster ever change his clothes? Is he still in there?" and Sissy said, "I don't know. I haven't seen him, Aunt Polly."

I heard Mother come in from the dining room. I pretended to be asleep. She crossed to the cot, and I could hear her breathing softly. "You asleep, Bus?" she whispered. When I didn't answer, she tiptoed across the room and closed the door quietly behind her.

I was asleep when Mother and Daddy came into the bedroom later that night, but I must have waked up while they were undressing in the dark. After they were in bed I heard them whispering to each other, softly, carefully, so as not to disturb me.

"Wallace?"

"Hm-m-m?"

"Did Allie—did she say anything to you in there tonight? I mean—" Mother was groping. "Anything about the baby? If anything should happen—"

"Sh-h-h." Daddy turned over in the bed. "Allie's gonna be all right, honey. You mustn't worry like this."

Mother was silent for so long I thought she had gone to sleep. But suddenly she was whispering my name. "What about Buster?" She paused. "Do you think we should say anything to him about—"

"Polly, honey, no, of course not. Nothing's going to happen. You'd just be upsetting him for nothing. Now try to get some sleep."

"Oh, Wallace. I'm so afraid."

"Sh-h-h." There was a faint movement in the dark. He must have held her in his arms and kissed her, because I could hear nothing more except the frightening silence of the room and the quickened beating of my own heart.

Cally went back to work at the creosote plant the next morning. From the porch I saw him go into the parlor to tell Allie goodbye. When he came out the front door to get in the Chevrolet, Mammy was following him. "Isn't this Mr. Jennings' week to drive to the plant?" she asked.

"Yep, sure is, Mammy, but he's got the runs and can't get very far away from the pot." As he was opening the car door, he called to Mammy. "In case you need anything in a hurry, just have Kiddo or Bubba run up there. He'll be glad to let 'em borrow his car." He started the motor and drove off down the lane. She watched the dust rise up after the car until it was out of sight; then she turned and saw me. "Well, Bus, you just sitting out here this morning all by yourself?"

"Yeah, I guess so." I looked up as she crossed to me. "Everybody seems to have so much to do around here, I just thought I'd try to keep out of the way." I turned to ask, "Where's Billy and David? I haven't seen 'em this morning at all."

Mammy must have realized how lonely and left out I felt. She put her arm around my shoulders and said, "They go down to Mrs. Jennings every morning to spend the day, so they won't be making a lot of noise when Allie's asleep." I nodded dismally.

"Tell you what," she said suddenly, and I felt her arm tighten around me. "After I give Allie her bath and get her all fixed for the day, why don't you take her breakfast in to her, hmm? I think she'd like that."

"Sure, all right." I got up and followed her into the hall. She went into the parlor, and I heard her say, "Good morning, honey. Did you spend a good night?" As she closed the door, I wandered into the dining room; the rest of the folks were still sitting around the table drinking coffee. Sissy was giving the baby his bottle, and he was sucking at the nipple lustily. I sat down by Mother. "Mammy says I can give Auntee her breakfast this morning."

"Oh, good, Bus." Sissy was smiling as she looked up at me. "She's been wantin' to see you." She turned to Mother. "Aunt Polly, would you see if Daddy remembered to crush some ice this morning before he left?"

"I'll do it, Sis." Daddy got up and went to the kitchen. It seemed strange for Sissy to be giving orders to the grown-ups, but then, everything seemed strange at Riverside now: Mammy spent the better part of each day in the parlor with Allie, and we seldom saw her from morning till late afternoon; Sissy had seemed to take over the general care and feeding of the baby; and here it was past the middle of June already, and no one had even mentioned any plans for the Fourth of July.

I heard Daddy pounding away in the kitchen, and I went out there. He had a little piece of ice tied up in a piece of sugar sacking and was crushing it with a hammer. Mammy came bustling into the room; she fixed a cup of hot tea; then she pulled a piece of dry toast from the warming oven and put it all on a tray.

"Wallace, fill me a glass about half full of crushed ice." When he did, she poured a very little bit of grape juice over it, set it down on the tray, and turned to me. "There now. I guess that about does it." She held the tray out to me. "Do you think you can carry this in to your Auntee, or had I better do it?"

"Oh, I can carry it just fine, Mammy." She walked ahead of me and opened the parlor door. There was a little table and chair by the bed between the windows; I headed for it to put the tray down so I wouldn't spill anything. Then I looked up.

I don't know what I expected to see, but Allie looked fine to me. She was half propped up with several pillows under her shoulders, and she was wearing a pretty white nightgown; her hair was brushed back and fell shining over the pillow, and she was smiling, both arms held out to me.

"Oh, Bussie, Bussie, am I glad to see you!" I leaned over carefully to kiss her, but her arms went around me and pulled me down until I was sitting on the edge of the bed with my head half on her pillow. Then she whispered in my ear, "I guess we kept our secret pretty well, didn't we?"

I wasn't sure which one she meant, but I raised up and

nodded my head. Her gray eyes were gazing at me as warmly as always, but there were deep shadowy circles under them, and they looked tired.

"Mammy let me bring in your breakfast." I got up from the bed and picked up the tray. "So you'd better eat it while it's hot and before the ice melts."

"All right, Bus. Put it down here on the bed and hand me that towel, so I won't dribble it all over my nightgown."

I got the towel and smoothed it under her chin, and turned to leave. "Oh, for heaven sakes." She had picked up the toast. "Stay and talk with me for a minute. The way Mammy keeps people out of here you'd think I had something catching."

I sat down in the little chair and watched her slowly sip her tea. She broke off a piece of toast, then looked up at me. "My, Bus, how you have grown since last Christmas. We sure had a good time then, didn't we?"

"We sure did, the best Christmas I think I ever had." I began to relax a little.

She was spooning up some of the grape-flavored crushed ice to suck it. She looked at me, her mouth filled with it, and giggled softly. Then she began to mumble through the ice. "Remember the story about the little boy? When his mother told him if he'd be real good, she'd bring him something nice?"

I didn't remember, but I nodded my head and said, "Uh-huh."

"That's just the way I feel," she went on. "I've tried to be so good and do everything they tell me to and look what they bring me for something nice!" She held up another spoonful of crushed ice. "This is a poor excuse for Mammy's homemade ice cream."

I was about to say maybe she could have some in a few days, but she suddenly dropped the spoon, and the melting ice ran down on the towel.

I picked up the spoon. "Here you are, Auntee," I said. "Don't worry, it didn't get on your nightgown." She didn't reach for the spoon; her hands were lying limp on the bed. She was breathing very queerly, and small beads of perspiration stood on her forehead.

"Call Mammy." Her voice was just a whisper between breaths. "Call Mammy, please, quick!" Her eyelids were fluttering, and then again faintly—"Please hurry!"

I ran into the dining room yelling, "Mammy, Mammy, somebody come quick! Something's wrong with Auntee!"

Daddy and Mammy came running in from the kitchen; Mother jumped up from the table, upsetting her chair, and Sissy pulled the nipple out of the baby's mouth and stood up. "What is it, Bus?" Her eyes were wide with fright.

"I don't know, she just said—" By that time, Mammy and Mother and Daddy were in the parlor; the door was wide open. I heard Mammy saying, "Allie! Allie, what is it, honey?" Then Mother went flying back to the kitchen. I looked in through the door and saw Daddy and Mammy lifting Allie higher on the pillows. Daddy was leaning over her saying, "Pug, Pug, can you hear me, Pug?" Mother came running back from the kitchen, calling on the way, "Mamma, there isn't any spirits of ammonia. I can't find any—"

"Run up to the Jennings' and see!"

Mother started out the front door, turned, and saw me standing by the stairs. "Buster, run to the Jennings' as fast as you can. Ask if they've got any spirits of ammonia."

I stood there looking at her dumbly, not moving.

"Hurry, Buster, for God's sake, hurry!" Mother pushed me toward the door, almost screaming at me. I took off down the lane through the lower gate, up the lane, never stopping until I was almost in sight of the gnarled tree root when I fell. I got up, and limped on until I saw the little yellow house. I ran into the front yard yelling, "Mrs. Jennings, Mrs. Jennings!" I banged on the front screen door. "Mrs. Jennings!"

"Now just hold on there whoever it is, what in the world is—" She cut herself short when she saw me and opened the screen. "Why, Buster, what is it? Come on in."

"I can't, Mrs. Jennings." My chest was hurting for air. I

couldn't seem to get enough. "Have you got any spirits of ammonia? It's Auntee! She needs it bad."

She didn't say another word, but she seemed to understand. She ran into the kitchen and hurried back with a little bottle in her hand. "Here," she said. "Now go! Run!"

I ran out to the front gate, but she called after me. "Tell your Mammy not to worry about Billy and David. I'll keep 'em here until—until somebody—"

I didn't hear the rest because I was already flying down the lane to Riverside. I was about halfway home when I saw Bubba racing to meet me. He was breathing hard and wet with sweat. "Did they have any?" He looked and sounded wild.

"Yes," I gasped, and he grabbed the bottle and went running back toward the house. I was glad. I couldn't run anymore. I didn't have enough breath left. I began to walk as fast as I could. When I reached the little rise in the lane, where you could see all of Riverside at a glance, I saw Mother standing by the gate waiting for Bubba. He rushed past her without a word, and he ran past Daddy, too, who was walking slowly down to meet Mother. When I finally reached the gate, Daddy was holding her in his arms, and saying "I'm sorry, Polly, I'm so sorry, honey, but she's gone." And the last clear memory I have of that dreadful morning was of my mother. She pushed my daddy away from her, shaking her head and saying, "Oh no, oh no!" and started to run pitifully up the path to the house, as if she could stop what was happening inside.

I sensed right away there was nothing more that I could do. I sank down helplessly on a stump and realized that my right leg was hurting terribly. I sat there rubbing it, until my Daddy came over and sat down by me and asked, "Are you all right, Bus?"

I looked up into his face. I saw real concern there, concern for me, the first that I had noticed since we arrived at Riverside. "Yeah, I think I'm okay." I looked at him and then asked, "Is Auntee—is she—"

"She's dead, son! And there isn't a damn thing that any of 'em up there can do about it." He sat there by my side, looking out over all the Jennings' pasture. There was a cow standing near the barbed wire fence; she looked up at Daddy and bawled mournfully. "That's right, Bossy," he said, "not a diddly-damn thing!" Finally he got up, slowly dusted off his pants, held out his hand, and said, "Come on, Bus. Let's get up to the house."

I remember the next days only as a dream; isolated moments were quite clear; others were indistinct and wavered in my mind. I remember Sissy sobbing mournfully on the front porch; I remember Cally sitting by the bed in the parlor stroking Allie's cheek and saying, pitifully—almost smiling—"She looks just like she's asleep." I remember two men drawing up in a hearse and going into the parlor, but I never saw them again. Life at Riverside changed; it was no longer quiet and secure in itself. People I had never seen came and went, bringing country flowers, fresh-cut zinnias, petunias, bleeding hearts, and potted ferns, and food was forever filling the house to overflowing.

Ordinarily it would have been better than any Fourth of July feast; platters of fried chicken, bowl after bowl of green beans, two Lady Baltimore cakes, and enough pies to choose from to last for a week. Billy and David stuffed themselves endlessly; they sensed that something was wrong, but they could see no reason for letting good food go to waste. And so they ate, everything and anything that caught their fancy. As for the grown-ups—even me and Sissy—they were always tasting but never really eating.

Late in the afternoon, the day after Allie's death, as I was sitting quietly alone on the front steps, I watched a horse and buggy coming up the lane. Then I recognized Mr. and Mrs. Jones, with Erda Mae sitting between them. I had said hello to so many strangers that I felt numb. Well, I wouldn't be here to greet these people. Erda Mae was the one person I would not talk to today. I got up, in full view of the new arrivals, and walked deliberately into the house and out the back door. I had seen enough of grown-ups with their sad eyes and quivering lips, and I knew I couldn't cope with Erda Mae. I wanted to be alone. I walked back of the barn, wandered through the pecan grove, and finally came out into the lane. Without any thought of direction, I headed for the stile down by the railroad tracks, pulled there as always.

I must have had some vague idea of finding Leroy, and when I came to the stile, there he sat, hunched over in his usual position, whittling away on a piece of pine wood.

I didn't speak, and neither did Leroy; he merely scooted over onto his side of the stile. I climbed up and sat down by him. He kept on whittling for some time; then finally he blew away some shavings and said very casually, "She daid, ain't she?"

He made it sound so natural, so normal, that I looked at him for the first time. And I found myself answering, almost as casually, "Yes, she's dead!"

He said nothing more for a while; he whittled away aimlessly for a moment, then closed his knife carefully, putting it in his pocket. "I was comin' over to see you yestiddy mornin', but Mamma told me it wasn't no time to be gettin' in your Mammy's way—with Miss Allie sick and all." He fumbled uncertainly for a minute. "And then about dinnertime Mr. Kiddo come runnin' over to ask Mamma if'n she would help out, an' that's when he done told us about—" He stopped suddenly and looked up toward the tracks; there was almost a smile on his face as he remembered something. "Miz Allie was a good lady."

"Yes, she was."

He gave me a quick sidelong look; then, feeling satisfied that I was all right, he said, "I'se sorry, Buster. I'se really sorry." He looked up toward the Chunky River bridge. "But you all don't hafta worry about her no more; she done found her place."

I looked at him, not understanding. "Where—what do you mean?"

I could hear that cowbell tinkling from somewhere across the tracks. Leroy seemed to hear it, too, or perhaps he was listening for a train. He was silent for a long time, and when he finally spoke again he was almost whispering.

"Miz Allie was always good to me—never treated me like I was—" He stopped and then giggled softly as he continued, "'Cepting one time she heared me sassin' Mamma in the kitchen, and God a'mighty she come flyin' out there mad as a wet hen—I thought for sho' she gonna hit me." He smiled to himself. "But I ain't never sass Mamma again—that's for sho'!"

I shifted uneasily on the stile.

"What did you mean, Leroy—when you said Auntee had found her place?"

"She done gone straight to heaven!"

"How do you know?"

"'Cause Mamma done told me all about it one time last winter."

He looked up at the tracks as if listening for the train. Then he went on slowly. "There was a preacher man come here sometime last year to Enterprise; he was a colored man. I didn't go to hear him. I was settin' Emmie Lou. But Mamma went for two nights in a row, and she thought he was real good." He smiled, suddenly remembering something. "I 'member she come home one night tellin' me about how you gets to heaven. Told me I'd hafta change my ways if I was ever gonna get there!" He chuckled to himself again, then looked up at me solemnly. "That preacher man say there's only two kinds a people knows for sho' they goin' to the good place. One of them's a soldier that dies in battle fightin' for his country, and the other one's a mamma that dies after her li'l baby's been born."

He was quiet for a long time; then he looked at me matter-of-factly and summed it all up. "So I reckon Miz Allie ain't frettin' none today."

We sat there for a little while longer, feeling comfortable, secure in our own tight little world. Then I remembered, for the first time that summer. "Leroy, that was a beautiful chain you carved for my birthday. I keep it hanging right over my bed."

"Yeah! That work out real good, didn't it?" Again we were silent. There seemed to be nothing more to say. I could sense Leroy was getting restless, an uneasiness to be gone, to be doing something, to be away from me. And then it came to me; he was afraid, too. This death wasn't part of him. Oh, he was sorry about it, but he couldn't or didn't want to share in it. Finally he stood up, stretched himself lazily, and jumped off the stile.

"I'se gon' do me a li'l fishin' 'fore dark. That's when they

bitin' the best." He took a few steps, then turned to me one last time. "I see you sometime 'fore you leave." He ran up the bank of the roadbed, waved to me once, and disappeared down the tracks, walking the crossties down to the Chunky River bridge.

I sat there for a little longer. The air was very still, but it wasn't hot. A bird flew over my head and perched on one of the shining rails, pecking away at something I couldn't see. I watched him for a while, delaying the trip back to the house, but I knew it was getting late and I had to go back soon. As I got up and was stepping over the stile, my eyes caught the carved initials on the top step. I bent over and traced them with my finger. B.B.—L.R. I wondered how long they would last, if anyone would ever know whose initials they were. There was a tightness growing in my throat. I kept tracing Leroy's initials over and over until the letters became so blurred I couldn't see them. Then I began crying. For the only time that day or the next, I put my head down on the stile and wept, sobbing until my body felt dry.

Just before dark I got up and walked slowly down the lane to Riverside; I never came back to the stile again that summer.

When I reached the house, Mattie Riley was in the front hall, cleaning lamp chimneys and trimming the wicks. She looked up as I came in. "Where you been? Your mamma done been worried sick about you! This ain't no time to be addin' to the trouble. Where you been all this time?"

"I was just sitting on the stile talking to Leroy, that's all."

"Settin' on the stile, just talkin' to Leroy!" She looked up suspiciously. "Where he at now? Gone fishin'?"

"I don't know where he is, and I don't care." I was tired of questions; I was tired of being polite to people. "Just leave me alone."

She must have sensed what I felt. Her eyes looked at me gently, and her voice grew soft. "Supper laid out on the table in there. Go on and fix you somethin' to eat and you feel better."

"I don't want anything to eat. I'm not hungry!" I stormed out of the hall to the back bedroom and lay down on the cot.

I turned my face to the window. The last lingering daylight was falling on the back pasture. I saw Bubba herding a stray calf or two up to the barn for the night; I guessed he and Kiddo would be milking the cows before they came in to eat something, or maybe they wouldn't; the daily routine of the farm was too uncertain these days. As I watched from the window, one of the calves ran ahead for a short distance, disturbing a flock of late-feeding birds who flew up and slowly circled the sky. I watched as some of them settled in the big oak tree; others flew on over the house searching out another night roost. When I looked for Bubba again he was gone from view, and the pasture was now all shadowed over. I heard a katydid begin its quarreling game—katy-did, she-didn't, she-did, she-didn't—and for the first time in my life it had a lonely sound. I felt lonely and lost, too.

I twisted over on my back; it was dark in the room now, and I knew that Mother would come looking for me any minute. And I knew that she would ask me the same question she had been asking yesterday and today, ever since the undertakers had left: "Honey, don't you want to go in to see Allie?" And I would answer, as I had for the past two days, "No, Mother, I don't think so, not yet anyway." I had never seen a dead person before, and I wasn't sure that I wanted to see one now—even if it was Allie. I remembered when Mrs. Patton's son died in Terre Haute, she had wanted me to see his flowers, but I told her I didn't want to see Claude. So everyone in the room had stood in front of Claude's casket so that it was hidden from view. That was as close as I'd ever been to a dead person.

I saw the door to the parlor opening, and Mother stood there, silhouetted in the lamplight, peering into the bedroom. She whispered a question in the darkness. "Bus?"

"Here I am, Mother, on the cot."

She fumbled her way through the dark and sat down beside me. "I was worried about you, Bus. Where've you been, honey?"

"I was just walking around for a while."

Her hand searched for my face and patted it. "Are you all right?" she asked quietly.

"Sure, I guess so."

She cleared her throat; I could feel the question coming before she asked it. "Have you been—"

"No! Not yet."

The word "corpse" made it worse. I held myself rigid, waiting out her silence. She sighed again deeply, and I felt the tension pass. She wouldn't ask me anymore.

"Have you had anything to eat, honey?"

"No, not yet, Mother. I'm really not hungry."

"Well, you'd better get something from the table. I've never seen so much food; it's just going to waste in there." The cot creaked as she stood up. "Daddy and I are going to sit up with Allie tonight. Mamma and Pappa have got to get some rest before the funer—before tomorrow. We'll be right in the next room if you want us for anything." She started out and then stopped. "Oh, and did I tell you? Uncle Will is coming. He'll get here on that early morning train. Poor Billy! It must have been a lonely trip for him, all the way from New York." She crossed the room and stood by the door uncertainly. Finally she said, "Get a good rest tonight, Bus," and she walked into the parlor and softly closed the door.

I did sleep, the early part of the night, and I must have slept soundly, for when something—someone—awakened me in the early hours of the morning, I felt lost as I tried to find my way back from sleep. Then I became aware that the parlor door to my bedroom was open; someone was in the room, and I turned icy with fear. I wanted to call out, but my tongue wouldn't move. Then a shadowy figure walked quietly back into the parlor, and I saw with relief it was Daddy. I raised up to be sure, and then Mother crossed into view and kissed him.

"I'll be back just as soon as I can," Daddy said. "Shouldn't be too long if the train is on time." I guessed he was going to meet Uncle Will at the station.

I was about to lie down again when I heard Mattie Riley's voice coming from the parlor. It surprised me so that I sat up on the cot, very still, listening to her.

"Miss Polly, why don't you go along with Mister Wallace to the station. Your brother gon' be so glad to see your face when he climb off'n that train after that long trip. You go on along now. I'll set here with Miss Allie."

"Oh, Mattie, I won't want to leave you here all alone." Mother hesitated for a moment. "I wouldn't want Allie left—"

"Now, Miss Polly, you know I ain't one of them scary, sup'stitious niggers." Mattie's voice sounded a little hurt. "Ain't plannin' on leavin' Miss Allie for a minute, not a single sol'tary minute. Now you just go right along. I be settin' right here when you gets back."

Mother disappeared from my view, but she must have been crying softly because her voice was shaking when she said, "Oh, Mattie, you dear, dear soul."

A few minutes later I heard a car drive away, and a deep stillness took over the house again.

There is always a stillness, a country stillness in the early morning hours in a place like Riverside. Night isn't over, and sunup is still an hour or two away. It is a waiting time when people and animals—even birds and breezes—seem to be holding their breaths. Maybe I might have noticed it before, once or twice, when I was very small and woke up in the dark and had to go to the toilet. Then Daddy would take me by the hand, lead me to the back stoop, and let me pee in the sandy loam; the path to the privy was too uneven to walk in the quiet dark. But if I remembered anything, it was the stillness, the unearthly stillness of the early country morning. The stars would seem bright enough for the picking, the sky quiet and undisturbed, and all of the countryside carefully waiting, waiting.

A floorboard creaked heavily in the parlor and brought a shiver to my spine. Consumed with fear, but finally overcome by curiosity, I got up from the cot and tiptoed quietly to the parlor door, almost afraid to look into the room. Mattie Riley had dragged her chair across the floor—that had caused the noise. She had placed the chair by the side of the coffin, and with a big sigh, she sat down. She bowed her head, her hands folded tightly in her lap. Then I could feel the hairs on my neck; now she was peering into the depths of the casket and talking quietly—talking to Allie! I held my breath to listen.

"Oh, Miss Allie, Miss Allie. I sho' didn't know you was so pretty." She slowly sank into the chair, resting her hand on the side of the coffin, patting it. Then she began talking, simple, childlike words. "Don't you fret none, now chile. Ole Mattie Riley right here with you. Ain't gon' leave you for a single sol'tary minute."

She was quiet for a while; then she edged up closer to the casket, as if she were soothing a frightened child. "Ain't gon' be long 'fore mornin'. And then the good Lawd, He gon' reach out His hand and carry you up on a big ole fleecie white cloud. Be just like floatin' down on Chunky River—only softer. And then He gon' blow that horn, but it'll sound so soft you won't even have to stop up your ears." Tears were rolling down her cheeks now, as she looked into Allie's face.

"Oh, Miss Allie, Miss Allie, I sho' didn't know you was so pretty." Her great body began to shake with true religious fervor; back and forth it bent in slow perfect rhythm; there was a soft humming at first that I didn't recognize, but halfway through, I remembered; I had heard it many times before.

"Comin' for to carry me home.
I looked over Jordan, and what did I see?
Comin' for to carry me home.
A band of angels comin' after me—"

She suddenly stopped in the middle of her singing and raised her eyes to the ceiling. There was a great wonder and joy and pity on her face. She was seeing something far beyond the ceiling, something that only her faithful heart and eyes could see. Finally she spoke to Him, "Has you got her, Lawd?"

He must have answered because she nodded and gave her Lord a piece of advice; tenderly pleading, she whispered, "Receive her easy. Ain't she pretty?"

She was still sitting there transfixed as I walked slowly over to the casket. I looked down on Allie's face with no fear at all. She was resting, filled with peace, and so was I.

"She's beautiful, isn't she, Mattie?" I whispered.

"Course she is, chile. She done see the face of the Lawd!"

Slowly, gradually, after the funeral, things and people returned to normal. I wasn't aware of it happening until I heard Mammy laughing in the kitchen one day. She was almost cackling as she said, "I declare, David, you do take the cake. Now get out of here!" I heard her give him a sound smack on the bottom, but when he ran into the dining room he was laughing, too. It was the real first laughter I had heard at Riverside that entire summer.

Then I began to notice another difference. Sissy was gone from the house for long stretches at a time, sometimes for an entire afternoon, and it was Mother who was taking over the care of Allie's baby. She would feed him his morning bottle, then give him his bath in a big washtub on the kitchen table, and then carry him out to the front porch and rock him to sleep. It seemed to me she spent most of her days either feeding him or rocking him to sleep; even Mammy no longer interfered with Mother's routine where the baby was concerned.

But the day finally came when I began to help. I was

stretched out on the cot in the back bedroom; Mother had put Jackie down on her bed and was changing his diaper. After she had finished, she picked him up, nestled him to her breast, and whispered happily in his ear. "Now then, I just bet you feel better, don't you, little Jackie Boy!"

I watched her idly for a moment as she cooed gently to the baby. Suddenly she exclaimed, "Oh, my stars! I forgot all about sterilizing those bottles." She started toward the dining room, then turned rather flustered to put the baby down on the bed.

"Here, Mother, I'll hold him while you do that." I got up and crossed to her. She looked at me, surprised and a little uncertain; I had never held the baby before, had never offered to, and I suppose she thought that I might not know how. She hesitated and then crossed to a little rocker. "All right, Bus. Here. Sit down here, and I'll hand him to you. Be careful of his little head now." She put him in my arms and watched carefully to see that I was holding him right. When she was satisfied, she smiled at me and said, "I'll be back just as soon as I've sterilized his bottles."

I sat there rather stiffly, somewhat afraid at first. The baby felt as warm as a piece of toast right out of the oven and smelled just as fresh. I bent over slightly to look in his face; he was staring at me steadily, his eyes big and unblinking. I was so surprised for a moment all I could do was stare back. He kept on staring, his gaze never wavering, until finally I laughed and said, "What you lookin' at me for like that, Jackie Boy? You don't know who this is, do you?" I must have been laughing or speaking too loud; his mouth turned down and a tiny frown came over his face. I was afraid he was going to cry. I lowered my voice almost to a whisper. "Oh, now, let's don't cry about it. It's gonna be all right. Nothin's gonna hurt you, don't you know that?" I kept smiling as I talked and put my finger up to stroke his chin as I'd seen Mother do so often. Suddenly his wandering hand caught my finger accidentally, and his fist closed tightly around mine. "What do you think you've got there, Jackie Boy?" I whispered, and then slowly his face broke into a smile. I leaned over and kissed him gently on the forehead.

I was rocking him slowly back and forth, singing "Go tell

Aunt Rhodie the old gray goose is dead" when I looked up and saw Mother standing in the doorway. I don't know how long she had been there, but there were tears in her eyes.

"Hi," I said, a little embarrassed. "I was rocking him to sleep. Is that all right?"

"Of course it is, Bus." She came over and sat on the edge of the bed. "Where did you learn that song?"

"Oh, I heard Auntee singing it lots of times, when she was getting Billy or David to take a nap." I looked surprised. "Why, haven't you ever heard it?"

She nodded her head slowly. "Oh, yes, Bus, many times. I was just thinking—" Then she stopped and looked out the window. The room was very quiet except for the creaking of my rocker. I kept humming softly to the baby, and when I looked down again, his eyes were slowly closing. I continued rocking slowly back and forth; Jackie's hand gradually released and fell from my finger. He sighed once and was asleep.

I looked up at Mother. "When are we gonna take him home with us?" I asked.

She turned from the window so quickly I was startled and had to ease the baby closer into my arms.

"What did you say?" She was staring at me, open-mouthed.

"I said when are we leaving? When are we going to take Jackie Boy home with us?"

"I didn't know that you—" She kept looking at me, unbelievingly. "Who told that we—" She was almost stammering. "Did Daddy say anything to you before he left? What did he tell you?"

"He didn't tell me anything, Mother."

"Then how—"

"I heard Auntee talking to Daddy about it."

All the air seemed to leave her body; she just sat there, looking small and lost. "When—" She caught her breath. "When did you—"

"Remember that first day we got here?" She nodded dumbly. "And we were all in the front bedroom looking at Jackie Boy? And you were holding him, and you asked me if I didn't want to feel his head?" Mother was watching me closely now. I grinned at her sheepishly. "I didn't want to because—well—I'd never seen you hold another little baby just like that, and I—well, I guess I was just a little bit jealous." I looked down at the baby asleep in the crook of my arm. "But when you rock 'em to sleep like this, and they—" I looked up quickly and said, "You didn't see him grab hold of my finger, did you, Mother?"

She shook her head mutely, reached for a handkerchief in her apron pocket, and held it to her nose for a moment. When she took it away, her face was composed, and she asked calmly, "Go on, Bus. You were telling me about Allie talking to Daddy. What did she say to him? Do you remember?"

"Sure I remember," I said. "And it scared me at first, because I didn't know exactly what she meant. I couldn't see either one of 'em. That door right there, it was just open a crack, but I could hear 'em all right." And as best I could I told Mother what Allie had said to him that night, and especially about the last promise that Daddy had made to her. "I promise you, Pug. We'll raise him and love him as if he were ours. I promise you faithfully, Pug!"

After I had finished, I looked up at Mother once more. "So when are we going home with Jackie?" I asked. "I sure bet Daddy'll be glad to see us."

She was regarding me strangely, leaning toward me, still a little uncertain, as if she couldn't quite be sure of what she had heard. "You're sure that—" She hesitated only a second. "I mean—you won't mind having a little baby around the house?" She smiled. "He won't be quiet like this all the time, you know."

"Oh, sure, I know. Like Billy or David when they were little. He'll cry when he's hungry or if his diapers need changing or if he's scared maybe. But we can take care of him okay, and I can help after I'm out of school in the afternoon. And—" I got very excited and leaned toward Mother, forgetting the baby in my lap. "What'll we call him? Jack Gunn Briggs? Or just keep it like it is, and add the Briggs. When are we gonna adopt him? How long does it take, Mother?"

She was silent for a long time, picking aimlessly at the cover on the bed, not looking at me. "Cally wants us to raise this little baby just as if he were our own and do everything we can for him, just as Allie wanted—just like we'd do for you. He says he knows that's what Allie would want. But he asked us please not to adopt him, legally. He said he just couldn't stand to give up one of his own children as if he didn't even want him." Then she raised her eyes to mine. "So I guess we won't adopt him legally."

I looked down at the sleeping baby I was holding and then raised my head quickly, a little worried. "But we're gonna keep him anyway, aren't we?" I asked.

"We certainly are!" she smiled.

"Well, then everything is all right with us." I felt relieved. Then I looked up and giggled. "Maybe this boy will adopt us when he grows up."

Mother stood up, walked slowly over to the rocker where I was seated, and knelt by my side. I felt her arms around me, heedless of the sleeping baby, and turning my face toward hers she said quite clearly, "I'll never love you more or feel as proud of you as I do right now."

Jack was a little over two months old when we left for Kentucky. And for some reason, for the first time in my life, I was happy to be going back. I had always hated the first days of August; it always meant that we would soon be leaving Riverside. But this summer it was different. For one thing, I saw very little of Sissy. She was always going somewhere with Jack Del Buno, who was leaving for college that fall, going to their favorite swimming hole they called "The Falls," going to his aunt's over in Old Enterprise for an ice cream social, or just taking a walk up the lane, talking and joking by themselves. I loved her still, and I knew that she loved me, but it was different somehow.

I don't suppose I ever once stopped to think that we were growing up and not apart. And she seemed to grow up quicker than I, especially that summer after Allie's death. When I thought about it, if I did, I suppose that was the only reason we were no longer inseparable.

Kiddo and Bubba were never at home. One evening after supper we were sitting on the front porch, waiting out the heat of the day, when Mammy suddenly turned to Cally and asked, "What'd you say that girl's name was, Cally? The one Bubba's been dating so much? Easter what?"

"Thornton. Easter Thornton, Mammy."

She was silent for a moment, rocking and fanning. "You don't think he's really serious, do you?"

Cally laughed in the early darkness. "Good Lord, I hope not, at least not yet. Why he's still got two more years of high school, and I surely do want him to finish."

"Yes, I know. That's what Allie would sure want too. But—" She stopped, and the unspoken sorrow hung over the porch like the heat.

Cally's rocker creaked as he stood up. "Well, time enough to think about that in a couple of years." He stretched his body and yawned. "Right now it's time for me to think about bed. I'm ridin' with Mr. Jennings to the plant this week, and he always leaves right on the dot. Good night, everybody."

No one ever told me and I never asked, but I think that Kiddo was really serious about Margaret Harper that summer. He was always finding some reason to drive to Stonewall in the evenings, and I know he couldn't be going that often to the picture show; it was open only on Friday and Saturday nights. Besides, he had taken Mother aside one afternoon and asked her if she thought it would be all right if he brought Margaret over to the house some evening.

"Why, Kiddo, I don't see why not."

"I mean, you don't think it's too soon after—"

"Of course I don't." Mother put her hand on his shoulder. "Why, Dr. Harper was here every week, sometimes twice when your mother was so sick, and she thought Margaret was lovely." She smiled up at him. "If you'll just let us know ahead of time, we'll fix some chicken salad and have cookies and ice tea. We'll just have a quiet little family party. It'll do us all good."

Margaret came and played the piano for us while Kiddo stood like a statue in his good white suit and held the lamp for her to see. And we had the cookies and ice tea, too. Except Margaret was the only one who drank the ice tea. The rest of us only sipped it, trying not to gag over it, hoping desperately that Margaret wouldn't ask for more. Mammy had forgotten that she was out of sugar, so she emptied what was left in the sugar bowl into Margaret's glass and called us one by one into the kitchen, issuing dire warnings not to make faces over the bitter tea. Bubba, who had just finished reading *The Virginian*, leered at Sissy and Cally and me and said, "Smile when you drink that, partner," and I exploded into laughter.

That was about the only time I saw Kiddo for more than a few minutes for the rest of the summer.

Of course, Billy and David were always there; playing down by the well, begging to go to the branch or to the river for a swim, asking Mammy every other day to make some homemade ice cream, "plain panilla" Billy called it. They were much less aware of the changes taking place at Riverside.

I didn't realize how little or perhaps how much Allie's death had affected them until one afternoon as I watched them playing together on the porch. Several boards had rotted away near the end of the porch, and Cally had pulled them up, meaning to replace them as soon as possible. The two children were standing over the opening, lowering a heavy length of wood down to the ground below.

I looked at them, as Billy gave several directions to his younger brother. "What are you all doing?" I felt uneasy even as I asked.

"Playing funeral at the graveyard." David was so intent upon the game he didn't even look up.

"You all stop that right now, you hear?" I looked in the front hall and was thankful that neither Mammy nor Mother was in sight. "Don't play that game anymore." I took the board and threw it into the side yard.

Billy stuck his tongue between his teeth. "What'd you do that for? Why not? Why can't we?"

"Because I said so, that's why!"

I couldn't, I didn't know how to explain.

Something was coming to an end. I didn't know it. I could only sense it. The last week we were at Riverside I was restless and uncertain. I wanted to stay near Sissy constantly but very often she wasn't there. Whenever I could I found excuses to go over to Mattie Riley's place to visit Leroy, and when I got there I suddenly wanted to be back at the house again and wondered why I had come. One morning after breakfast I kept sitting at the table long after Mother and Mammy and Sissy had started their daily chores. No one had asked me to help, and I hadn't offered. When Mammy had finished the dishes she came bustling through the dining room and saw me still sitting there staring at nothing. She folded her hands across her apron and eyed me closely. "Something the matter, Bus? You feel all right?"

"Yeah, I guess so." Then I hurried on. "Yeah, I'm fine, Mammy."

I went out the front door, down the lawn, and sat on the well trough. There were a couple of watermelons weighted down in the well that Pappy planned to cut late that afternoon. I slid my fingers along their shiny green veins; the water felt icy cold, and I shivered. I jumped up quickly and started down the lane, going nowhere, anywhere. I had almost reached the stile before I knew it. When I saw it, I stopped. Another hundred feet or so I could climb up on it and wait for a passing train. I listened; there wasn't a sound, not even of a passing bird. I looked up; long white mares' tails were stretched across the sky, making the sun look weak and watery. And from a distance I could hear Allie's voice again as she stood on the front porch looking anxiously at the clouds. "Sure is a gray washday. Hope it'll give the clothes time enough to dry."

I shivered again, turned, and walked slowly back to the well. I leaned over the spout and let the cold water trickle down my throat. It felt good; it felt reassuring; it was as cold as ever. I wiped my mouth dry with my hand and walked on toward the house. Halfway up the lane I saw her; she was sitting in the hickory rocker on the front porch, stringing a lap full of beans, and she was watching me closely, half smiling. For a moment I wondered why she was wearing her blue shawl. The sun wasn't really hot, but it wasn't cool enough for—

"Bus, where've you been, honey?" Her smile seemed a little

worried now. "Mammy thought maybe you weren't feeling too good."

The blue shawl disappeared when she spoke, but Mother was still there and she was still stringing beans.

"Oh, I'm okay, Mother. I just went down to the well to get a cold drink." And I walked up on the porch, sat down by her side, and helped her finish stringing the beans.

The day before we left to go back to Covington, Mattie Riley came to the house to do some hand washing for Mother and the baby. Leroy came with her. Mother had lots of last-minute jobs to do that day: getting Jackie Boy's clothes ready, preparing plenty of formula for the trip back, packing her things and mine for the next day. She asked if I would take care of the baby, so Leroy and I rolled him out under the big oak tree in the back yard and put the mosquito netting over the buggy. We took turns rolling him back and forth, and he was soon fast asleep. Leroy and I stretched out under the tree, not talking much, just trying to be comfortable, trying to be relaxed in each other's company. But somehow it didn't seem to be working today. Leroy would ask a question, and I might grunt out an answer. Time seemed to hang heavy between us. Once he asked, "You all gonna ride on that sleepin' car again?" And I mumbled, "Uh-huh. I guess so. Sure." After that we were both quiet for a long time. An old Rhode Island Red hen came slowly clucking and pecking away for food near the base of the tree. She cocked her head at us and let out a low lazy squawk and scratched the dirt around her.

Leroy twisted his head at her and called, "Chicken shit on you—you ole chicken!"

She ruffled up her feathers and ran squawking off toward the orchard in search of a June bug she had spotted.

"Watch her now!" Leroy turned to follow the hen with his eyes. "She gonna near about wear herself out trying to catch that ole June bug. Just watch her now!"

I didn't even turn around. I kept looking up through the tree branches and finally sighed, "Aw, who cares. Like you said—chicken shit!"

Leroy looked at me and was silent. He took out his knife,

pulled out the big blade, and began playing mumbly peg in the soft earth. I watched him halfheartedly until he said, "You wanna play it?" and held the knife out to me.

I shook my head, turned over on my stomach, and started pulling aimlessly at the grass. He scooted over and leaned down, looking at me closely. "What's the matter, Buster?"

I looked up into his face. His big eyes were almost spilling over with concern.

"Oh, I don't know, Leroy." And once I had said it, I realized I really didn't know. At least I didn't know how to express what I felt. "It's just that everything seems so different now." I pulled at a blade of grass. "Kiddo and Bubba and Sissy seem so grown-up all of a sudden, and I've got a new little baby brother—at least he seems like a brother." I stopped and then tried again. "Everything seems to have stopped at Riverside since—I mean, nobody seems to make any plans for anything anymore. It's just as if—" I stopped. I couldn't think of anything further to say.

"Ain't no fire in the fireplace no more."

"What?" I looked up so startled that Leroy hastened to explain.

"Last week when Mamma come home from over here, she was feelin' so bad." He looked up through the leaves as if remembering what Mattie had said. "We was sittin' at the supper table and Pappa asked Mamma, 'What's the matter with you?' and she say, 'They doin' the best they can over at the Neals', but the fire done gone out of the fireplace since Miz Allie died. They ain't got nobody to build it up again now.'"

I looked at him for the longest time, and he kept watching me with a kind of misery in his eyes. He didn't say another word, and I couldn't for several minutes. Leroy had said it better than I ever could.

"Yes." I finally managed. "That's just about the way it is."

Mother came out on the back stoop and called to us. "Bus, will you bring the baby in now? It's time for his bottle."

I started wheeling the buggy up to the back stoop. Leroy followed me to the steps; then he turned and walked to the back gate.

"See you next summer, Mister Leroy!" I yelled as I pulled the buggy up the steps.

He looked up at me, grinning with that nasty smirk on his face, bowed to me a couple of times and said, "Yassir, Mister Buster, yassir!" and trotted down the path toward home. As he reached the pasture gate, he turned and waved one last time. I didn't know whether I wanted to laugh or cry.

We caught the afternoon train for Covington the next day. Cally said goodbye to us early in the morning. He went to the back room where Jackie was sleeping and was gone a long while. When he came out he looked at no one; he walked stone-faced through the door and down the lane to the Jennings' place to catch his ride.

When it was time for Bubba to drive us to the station, Mammy kissed and hugged us both, took the baby in her arms, whispered something in his ear, and handed him back to Mother.

Her face was gray, but she was not crying, only trembling slightly.

"Go, now! Please! And God go with you." She walked into the kitchen and closed the door.

Mother stood there uncertainly, looking after her until Bubba called, "Come on, Aunt Polly! We don't want to miss the train."

We got into the car—Bubba, Mother, and the baby in front, Pappy, Sissy, and I in the back along with the bags. The car started, and as we drove down the front lawn, I looked back; I could see no one—nothing moving at Riverside.

When the train had screeched to a stop, the porter helped Mother up the steps with the baby, and I followed quickly. We were already settled in our seats before the train started, and when it did, I was not aware of its moving. The folks were waving to us as we passed the station platform, and I pressed my face against the window, waiting for Riverside. I craned my neck, looking for the first landmark, and suddenly there it was! And there he was, standing on the top of the stile, waving wildly. I waved back and tried to smile, but it was a poor attempt, for my eyes were beginning to blur. Mother touched my shoulder and was pointing out her window. Then I saw the white towel—or was it a sheet?—being flung up and down from the back stoop of the house. We both sat there waving frantically, watching until we could see it no more. Then we turned away from the windows, not daring to look at each other.

I picked up the baby who was lying on the seat by me and began bouncing him up and down on my knee. Then suddenly, unbelievably, for the first time in his life he cackled; Jackie Boy laughed out loud! I looked at Mother; both of us were so startled we could not speak. I bounced him again, and he laughed for joy. Then Mother and I were laughing with him, laughing and crying, the three of us together.

Far up ahead, the engineer blew the whistle for the Chunky River bridge, and the train picked up speed. With every turn of the wheels it was taking us farther and farther from Riverside and closer and closer to home.

EPILOGUE
CHRISTMAS—1976

I went back to Riverside again on Christmas Eve. The sun was brilliant in a cloudless sky as my wife and I drove down Interstate 59 from Meridian that morning. I had seen the old homeplace only twice before in the intervening years; in 1966 when Daddy died and we buried him in the little country graveyard close-by, and again in 1968 when Cally joined him and the others—Allie, young David Wallace, Pappy, and Mammy—in the same quiet spot. Mother was the only one of her immediate family still living and had recently moved from Arkansas to Mississippi to be near her living relatives and, as she said, "closer to Daddy."

Just before Christmas we had heard from Bubba's son, David, that Riverside was being resold, and I knew that I could not leave Mississippi without seeing the old place again. Sissy wanted so much to go with us that morning, but she was expecting fourteen for a family brunch on Christmas. As we were leaving she said, "This food won't cook by itself, so you all see it and tell me how it looks when you get back."

We took the North Enterprise exit from the interstate and turned left toward Enterprise. I began searching the woods for some remembered landmark. I couldn't find the old Carpenter place, but suddenly on my left I saw the Clark house, and cornered across the road from it stood the Jennings place, painted white now with an enclosed porch. I stopped the car at the crossroad and looked up toward Riverside. The two white columns were the first things I saw standing straight and tall and luminous, and finally I realized that the whole house had been freshly painted.

I drove slowly down the lane through a mud puddle at the foot of the front lawn and followed a gravel and grass-grown circular drive to the front porch. I cut the motor and sat still, looking out over the west pasture that once was Pappy's cornfield. Olive was opening her door.

"Aren't you going to get out?" She was watching me closely and spoke very quietly.

"Yeah—yeah, I sure am."

I opened my door and closed it with such a loud bang that on the far side of the Jennings' pasture a cow started bawling loudly. And suddenly I could hear again my Daddy's voice that faraway summer telling me and the cow that Allie was dead.

"That's right, Bossie, they can't do a diddly-damn thing about it."

I didn't realize that I had spoken aloud until Olive asked, "What did you say?"

"Nothing, honey." I took several steps from my car and turned to look.

The outlines of the house were exactly the same. The double front door and the fanlights above it still had the original wavy glass I remembered as a child. As I was looking, drinking in its beauty, I became aware of many changes. The front porch no longer ran the entire length of the house, the small side columns were gone, and the steps were now gray-painted concrete. There was a new gray roof, and both tall chimneys had been carefully remortared. And the whole house was a blindingly beautiful white.

I walked up the solid concrete steps to the front door. It was locked. I peered through the hall window. The bannister rail was intact, the curving stairway was carpeted in green, the walls papered in a soft yellow and green. I stepped to the parlor window; the room was paneled and one small corner was enclosed—a bathroom? a closet? The old stoop was now a covered back porch, and more concrete steps led up to sliding glass doors opening into the dining area. The kitchen and dining rooms were now one big room with a countertop dividing them. A country kitchen? I laughed to myself. Yes, a country kitchen of the 1976 variety.

We walked slowly around to the front, and I saw that the artesian well was gone, but I found a low, muddy depression where it used to be. Pappy's pecan grove was still there, but the trees were so big you couldn't see the railroad tracks anymore. The lane leading down to the tracks was grown up in pine trees and fenced in. I wondered for a moment if I could find the stile—

Leroy's and mine—and smiled halfheartedly at my own sentimentality. Could that have been more than fifty years ago? Surely not! For I could still hear Kiddo's voice as he knelt by me, surveying the ruined sand castle he and Bubba had built for us and then destroyed in mock battle.

"We all had fun playing with it while it lasted, Bus—but like Mammy always says, nothing lasts forever."

"You about ready, honey?" Olive was even then at the car door. "It's getting chilly out here."

"Coming—right away."

I turned for one last look at the old house with its newly acquired lease on life, and suddenly I sensed that I wasn't saying goodbye to anything. Riverside isn't a house. It is a place in the heart.

www.ingramcontent.com/pod-product-compliance
Lightning Source LLC
Chambersburg PA
CBHW030358310726
48979CB00001B/361

* 9 7 8 0 8 1 3 1 1 8 0 7 9 *